TREY: SON OF TALLAV

SONS OF TALLAV #4

CAILIN BRISTE

Hot Sauce
PUBLISHING

For Ian, who continues to grow daily into the man I've always known he could be.

ACKNOWLEDGMENT

To DC who encourages me more than she probable ever knows. Trey is for you.

To Lea Scafer for always expressing in the kindest terms possible where logic and consistency fail me. And for dealing with the damn commas.

To Mitch Workman for polishing the final manuscript.

To my readers who share my love for the Sons of Tallav.

Especially to my husband who makes life bearable while living in an RV in the blast furnace that is the Arizona desert in July. He's still the finest looking man at the swimming pool.

PART I

EDUCATED BY THE MASTER

1

I t hadn't occurred to Trey that LS *Quantum* and Beta Tau were two sides of the same coin. Sure, LS *Quantum* was a spaceship, and Beta Tau was a planet. But he'd read the LS *Quantum's* brochures, and in every other respect they were the same large, climate-controlled settings designed to provide trendsetting pleasure venues to paying customers and entertainment for all ages and palates, including his own kinky tastes.

The insight came when a middle-aged woman eased alongside him, brushing her shoulder against his and asking if he was headed to the LS *Quantum* and if so, where his cabin was located on the ship. Her skimpy halter, skintight slacks, and the bright pink hair she was sporting did nothing to enhance her appeal. This was Beta Tau all over. The glare he aimed at her didn't force her to step back. *Good gods! I'd be at* Quantum's *shuttle service gate if Patsy O'Shaughnessy hadn't insisted on meeting me here.* He scanned the customers of the bland space station lounge. *No. Still on my own.*

An expert at fending off tourists on Beta Tau, he'd offer to take them to the club, tie them up, and use a bullwhip on them. Most scurried away. He handed anyone who accepted his proposition over to staff at the club. Bondage was part of his personal kink, but he preferred to use a flogger.

The whip was the specialty of the Whip Hand's owner, Randolph Meryon, Trey's boss.

The neon-haired tourist ran a finger down his upper arm. "Maybe we could get together on board? I've heard bald men are really good in bed."

When he dropped his gaze to where she'd touched him, the woman tittered. Eyes narrowed, he leveled his full focus on her. "Sure. If you're into knife play, I might be able accommodate you. I'd have to ask my girl-friend. She's the one who does the cutting." He followed his words with a feral grin.

The tourist turned pale. "No thanks." She scuttled back to her friends who'd been watching the exchange. Wide-eyed, they left the lounge, several looking back over their shoulders to get another glance at him.

With a grimace, he settled in to wait. This wasn't a vacation, and he wasn't a tourist. Nor was he on his way to *Quantum*, away from his normal haunts on Beta Tau, to indulge in BDSM. No, he had undertaken this two-week-long trek in his capacity as the Whip Hand's private club manager. Rand had hired a young woman to open and run a new venue on Beta Tau based on the Cosmic Cabaret, one of the famous attractions on LS *Quantum*. After getting firsthand experience of the cabaret's shows, Trey was to provide his BDSM expertise to tailor O'Shaughnessy's plans.

Crazy idea. At least I didn't have to travel economy class and spend my nights in a sleep tube. Rand had paid for a cabin that, although small, had allowed Trey to escape most human interaction for the two weeks he'd been aboard the space liner, sleeping, reading, meditating, and sleeping some more. Perhaps his reintroduction into the hum and clatter of humanity after his break had him on edge.

No perhaps about it. He was ready to bellow at the entire spaceport to shut up. Life would be so much better if half the population were fitted with ball gags.

Here he was, per Ms. O'Shaughnessy's request, and she was not to be found. He eyeballed the entrance, considering whether he should head over to the gate to wait for his shuttle, when a shock of color came flying into the lounge. The slender woman, dressed in a bright, grass-green sleeveless blouse and short skirt, skidded to a halt. Splashed across her face was a wide grin as brilliant as the lime green that tipped the ends of her copper hair. She was looking straight at him. This must be Patsy O'Shaughnessy. With a wave she headed for him.

"Hi. Sorry I'm late. Ya wouldn't believe the crush of folks leavin' *Quantum* today. I'm Patsy. Trey Johansson. Right? Mr. Meryon sent your picture, so I recognized ya. Although I don't expect there's many men that look quite like ya."

When she paused for a breath, Trey inserted a few words into her verbal onslaught. "Yes. I am."

"I'm excited to meet ya. And to work with ya. I have so many plans I can't wait to share. Our shuttle back to *Q*—that's LS *Quantum* for short— boards in about fifteen minutes. We have time for a quick drink if ya'd like, or we could head to the gate. I could use a drink. Dashin' around." She waved her hand in the air. "I'm so thirsty now. I'm gettin' an orange fizzy. What would ya like?"

Pleasant expression on her face, Patsy waited for a response.

"Oh, uh. Sure, I'll have what you're having."

"Be right back." She twirled and headed toward the bar.

Wow. That accent sounded Irish. And not Tallavan faux Irish. Light complexion, freckles, copper hair, wearing green…stereotype, sure, but damn, if she wasn't Irish, he'd eat a whole pan of fried blood pudding. Something he hadn't tasted in a long time. Fried eggs, tomatoes, white-and-black pudding. A full Irish breakfast like his mother made better than any other cook on Tallav. He missed his folks and his mother's cooking, but Tallav would never be his home. Even if he'd been a member of the aristocracy, he would have left the Tallavan matriarchy in the dust as he had the moment he was of age.

"Here ya go." Patsy handed him a large disposable cup and took a long drink from her own. "Ah. That was what I needed. I had cobwebs in my throat."

Trey tipped his cup back and swallowed three gulps of the sweet orange liquid and remembered why he never drank fizzies. The carbonation bubbled up his nose. He pinched his nostrils, squinched his eyes shut, and waited for the burn to abate.

"Got fizz up your nose, did ya? Ya should drink more slowly if ya can't handle the sparkly. I never have a problem. My whole system's plumbed with synthsteel."

Was this slip of a girl offering him advice as though he were some—"My delicate feckin' nose thanks ya for the interest in its well-bein'."

With blue eyes aglow, she leaned toward him. "Think nothin' of it. An féidir leat labhairt le haon Gealic chun dul leis sin blas na hÉireann?"

Sarcasm was lost on Patsy O'Shaughnessy. "It's not an Irish accent. I'm from Tallav, which was infected with a fanatic love of all things from the Emerald Isle when the planet was founded. I never had the time to learn Gaelic, but many Tallavans do."

"Standard it is then. We have somethin' in common. I'm proper Irish. *Erin go Bragh.* 'Tis a pity ya don't speak Gaelic. I don't get to speak it this far from home. Oh, goodness. We need to head over to the gate. Our shuttle will be boardin' soon."

On the way out of the lounge, Trey dumped his fizzy in the trash receptacle. Patsy was ahead of him by a couple of strides, so he had a full view of the subtle twitch her ass made while she walked. *Nice.* From her employment records he had gleaned that she was thirty years old, although she looked younger. That fell within his range, five years either side of his own age, for women he would date. But Patsy O'Shaughnessy was off-limits despite her engaging effervescence. This was a business relationship. For the next two-and-a-half weeks, they'd be working together. Besides, whether she'd kissed the Blarney Stone or not, the woman could talk. By the end of a day spent with her, he'd need to escape to his own room. Plus he didn't do vanilla. Patsy wasn't bland, but neither did she scream kinky despite her association with Cosmic Cabaret and now Randolph and the Whip Hand.

Still, he could look. He'd never been drawn to big-busted women, but a tight bottom was a delight to behold. And touch. Squeeze. Slap. He heaved a sigh. Too bad. He'd already plastered a don't-touch sign across her miniskirted bum.

TREY JOHANSSON WAS every bit as good-looking and well-built as Patsy expected. But she hadn't been prepared for the sheer size of the man. He towered over her. And muscles! Her fingers wouldn't reach around his biceps.

She'd researched Randolph Meryon's home planet, Tallav, to prepare for her job interview. It was a surprise to learn that Trey, or Master Trey as he was called at the Whip Hand, was also from Tallav. He was a BDSM master. A tingle flittered the length of her spine. He'd been sent to gain firsthand knowledge of the Cosmic Cabaret to help her with reinterpreting it for a BDSM venue.

The name hadn't been chosen yet. Her preference was to include *cabaret*. Beyond that she hadn't come up with anything catchy if Rand asked for her advice. Trey's other task ought to assist with that. He was to teach her about BDSM. How he would approach that was the big question. Would he want to initiate her into the BDSM lifestyle or only explain the different aspects of kink and fetish? How far should she let him go if he wanted to make his lessons more real?

A quick glance over her shoulder assured her every inch of the giant with piercing deep brown eyes was following her to the shuttle gate. *Oh my gosh, he's checking out my ass.* Her cheeks heated. Why oh why did she have to have pale skin that showed even the slightest blush? Why couldn't she have been born with dark amber skin like the delectable man behind her? *Pull it together, girl. It's a guy thing. Their eyes are naturally drawn to tits and ass.*

An announcement stated boarding for their shuttle flight would commence in five minutes. Inside the gate seating area, Patsy turned to face Trey. "We have a few more minutes. Shall we sit, and ya can double-check that your bags have been loaded."

Trey pulled a hand-comm from his pants pocket, held it to his ear, and made the call to the automated baggage handling system. After assuring the comm was off, he put it away.

"Ya use a hand-comm? Ya don't see many people that do. I'd probably lose one, so my internal comm is a true blessin'. I don't know how people lived in the past without an EBC. All my data is there at the tip of my thoughts. I was told everyone received nanite injections to build their internal server when they were infants."

"I'm not a fan of tech. I like to keep things simple."

Trey Johansson was even more intriguing than she'd imagined. "So, ya don't have an EBC. Where do ya store information? How do ya know when someone is tryin' to contact ya? Goodness. How do ya exist without bein' able to connect with governmental systems? Bankin' systems? Will there be a problem boardin'?" *Why hadn't he or Mr. Meryon told her this?*

"Stop." Trey narrowed his eyes and raised his hand. "Stop. Let me answer one question at a time." In the pause that followed, Trey raised an eyebrow.

Oh, he wants me to acknowledge him. "Yes. Understood."

A flush of pleasure went through her when he smiled. "Good girl. I have an EBC. Every child on Tallav receives one. I use it when necessary. My work-related data is kept on servers like most of yours is. You access it through your EBC. I use a vidscreen." He patted his pocket. "My hand-comm signals me when I have a message. It tracks callers, just like your internal comm. I don't like cluttering my mind. It destroys inner peace."

He dropped his chin and looked at her as though he were expecting her to say something. But, for a change, she kept quiet. Her thoughts were bustling with everything she had learned about this man. That *good girl* was patronizing but so very BDSM master–like, especially coming from a hunk of handsome with a voice like smooth dark chocolate. She'd liked it. File that away for future reference on female reactions to Doms.

Into the lapse in conversation Trey said, "My luggage is loaded."

"Oh, good. We're all set then."

Silence dropped between them again. Patsy was relieved when the gate announcer gave them the go-ahead to board. Behind her, Trey placed his palm on her lower back, guiding her through the other passengers who were standing and collecting their carry-on bags. The instant his hand spanned her back, its warmth and size made the hairs on her arms rise. *Please let the feckin' man offer me hands-on BDSM lessons.* She'd kill to see him naked, but it had to be his idea, his suggestion. This job was the break she'd been waiting on, and she wouldn't botch it by coming on to a fellow employee.

On board, they found their seats and were settling in when a group of ladies, one with neon-pink hair, passed them. Each one stared at Trey and then Patsy as they hugged the far side of the aisle as closely as possible and scooted by. The woman in back nudged her companion to hurry when Patsy smiled at them.

Trey grunted. Patsy turned to look at him. He had a smirk on his face.

"Do ya know them? They looked like they'd seen a ghost and were runnin' for water."

"No."

He continued to grin, but Patsy didn't see what was funny. His next statement didn't clear things up.

"They must not favor green."

"Afraid of green. That's not after bein' a real phobia."

"It is. Prasinophobia. Fear of the color green."

"That's a funny thing to know. You're not afraid of green, are ya?"

"Would I be sitting here if I were?" He pointedly trailed his gaze over her. "One of the classes at the Opio Institute where I worked covered the use of fear by sadists. You can make someone fear any color if you condition them to it."

The Opio Institute. That was the sex school where he'd trained dominants and submissives. "Doesn't sound like fun to me."

Trey chuckled. "I didn't figure you for a sadist."

"Er." The man had a way of throwing her off stride.

"It wouldn't be fun for me either. But fear of color can be used by a sexual sadist to get a satisfying response from his play partner."

"Remind me to stay away from sexual sadists."

Another chuckle. "It's going to be difficult avoiding your new boss."

Patsy blushed and furrowed her brow. "I forgot he's one of those."

Trey's expression became enigmatic. "Don't worry. You'd have to play with him to experience that side of his personality."

Sweet mother Mary. I'll not head that direction. "I'll be dead and my ashes scattered before that happens."

Heated intensity bloomed in Trey's gaze. "Good."

Oh Lord, I'm in for it now.

2

The first impression Trey received when peering at LS *Quantum* from the shuttle's window was its massive size. No wonder it didn't dock at space stations. What station would want that behemoth blocking half of its slips?

Once their shuttle docked at the Blue Star Line terminal, Trey stood in the queue with Patsy waiting to present their idents. Vidscreens hung overhead, advertising *Quantum*'s top attractions. A bright swirl of fire introduced the Cosmic Cabaret to newly arrived visitors. Poi dancers. The vid flowed from one act to another, touting trapeze artists, slapstick comedy, juggling waiters, a scantily clad female singer, and musicians on stilts.

Why did Rand send me here? Some cracked notion that I'm the perfect candidate to explain BDSM to Ms. O'Shaughnessy and work with her on the trip back. This is Sylvia's specialty, not mine. Accuracy in the BDSM presented at the new cabaret? How the hell do you make burlesque accurate?

His own venue, the Whip Hand's private club, was the only space Rand owned where true BDSM was practiced. The public club, that Sylvia ran, had started as a place to learn about and watch experienced tops and bottoms play. With the latest renovation, it had been transformed into a theater. Tickets were required for all performances.

A BDSM cabaret fell into the show category. In the private club no one was paid to appear. Rand had given Trey encouragement to make the play space as authentic as possible. Not an easy task considering the constant turnover in participants. The first thing Trey had done was tighten security. Real play meant real risk. He'd also expanded the training required before someone was accepted into membership in the club. Dilettantes could damage the atmosphere of a play space. That should be his focus. Not this new cabaret.

"Don't say you're already tired. Or is the waitin' in line puttin' that surly look on your face?"

Trey shifted his attention to Patsy, who was using her hands to add flourishes to her words.

"I've a full day planned tomorrow. Are ya hungry? If ya are, we can stop and get a bite before headin' to my room. But we don't have to. I can order delivery. Pizza. Noodle bowls. Sushi. Whatever ya like. Or ya can go straight to bed."

"You're up." With a gesture Trey motioned for her to turn and face the security person scanning visitors' idents. When Patsy was passed through, Trey stooped and placed his face into the scanner and his finger on the ident pad. A beep signaled the equipment had completed its task. Trey straightened.

"Trey Johansson. Resident of Beta Tau. How long will you be staying?"

"Five nights."

"Thank you. Please hold out your hand." When Trey did, the man secured an ident bracelet to his wrist. "This is your pass for entry into all complimentary and purchased events and meals. Do not remove it until after you leave LS *Quantum*. You may proceed."

Patsy waited a few steps ahead. Before she could recount his options, he held up a hand. "I'll grab a bite in my room. Pizza is fine. Mr. Meryon booked a suite for me on the Nebula deck, 43131."

"Er." Patsy bit the nail on her little finger. "About that."

Trey didn't need his years of training submissives to apprehend that the king-size bed in suite 43131 no longer awaited him. Patsy O'Shaughnessy's face was as easy to read as a five-year-old's.

"Where am I sleeping?"

"I figured to save Mr. Meryon money by havin' ya sleep at my place.

The office in my staff quarters had a pull-down bed, so ya see, it was perfect. And workin' together would be easier. So I canceled the suite. Your spaceflight had already left Beta Tau, so I had no way of lettin' ya know—"

"Where am I sleeping?"

"I thought they'd allow me to stay in my quarters. Callendra said it wouldn't be a problem. But they booted me and turned my cabin over to the new CC stage manager. She booked me into a tiny cabin, which was a blessin'. It's impossible to get a room on short notice. But I'd already cancelled your suite. And last minute all that was available were single and double sleep tubes with shared lounges."

"We're sharing a cabin?"

Patsy averted her gaze. "Yes."

"Look at me."

When she did, her eyebrows were gathered in a pained expression, her arms dangling limply at her sides.

As he would with a contrite novice submissive, Trey gentled his voice. "*A leanbh*, tell me your plans. I'm sure you've found a solution to the problem."

She lifted her hands so they could rejoin the conversation. "I have. The cabin I was given has enough room for both of us. Bedroom. Bathroom. And a lounge with a kitchenette and table for eatin' and workin'. The sofa is plenty big enough for me to sleep on, so ya can take the bed. Queen-size, not king, so it's goin' to be a bit small"—she looked him over and grinned —"but I expect findin' things to fit ya is a challenge."

"It is."

Patsy tugged his hand. "Let's go. I'll order the pizza while we're walkin'. Plain cheese okay?"

"Sure." With a sigh Trey followed her, listening to the lovely burr of her voice as she answered the auto-comm's questions concerning size, toppings, and delivery location. Despite what she'd said, he'd be sleeping on the sofa. More likely the floor. Early training on Tallav to put women first remained an ingrained habit. That meant she'd be in the bed. It probably wouldn't hurt him to be reminded what it felt like to bed down on the floor, since it was a punishment he often meted out when necessary to club submissives.

Her comm completed, Patsy slowed and looked over her shoulder. "My cabin's on the far side of Q, seven decks higher. I'll take ya up the central lifts. A mini-tram entrance is just over there." She took his hand and pulled him in the direction she pointed.

They waited in a short queue, climbing into a car after it stopped before them.

"Welcome aboard. What exciting LS *Quantum* location do you wish to visit?"

Patsy responded to the car's interface with clear enunciation. "Central lifts. This deck."

"Central lifts. Shuttle deck. Enjoy the trip."

Trey chuckled. Beta Tau's tram system didn't allow for individualized destinations. And no pleasant voice offered polite greetings.

The tram had four seats, but no matter which spot Trey occupied, his size meant he'd be touching Patsy. If she sat across from him, their knees would touch, or beside him, their shoulders would brush. When she took the seat opposite his, it was worse than he'd expected. He'd have to spread his legs. Between his knees, Patsy tried to cross her legs, causing her already short skirt to inch higher and show more of her thighs. She settled for scooting as far back in the seat as possible and pressing her knees tightly together. When she noticed her skirt had ridden up, she tugged the hem down, her face blooming with color.

That was the second blush he'd caught gracing her cheeks. He pretended not to notice to give her time to recover. "Besides the Cosmic Cabaret, what's special on *Quantum*?"

A sparkle appeared in her eyes, and she leaned forward. "You're goin' to love the central lifts. Completely transparent." Her voice went dreamy. "It's like floatin' on a current of air. Risin' up like a golden eagle."

"Is that right?"

Brought back to the tram and Trey, she grinned and tapped his shoulder. "No teasin'. You'll see."

On exiting, Trey looked toward the lifts and drew in a sharp breath. People were floating unsupported by anything he could see.

Patsy giggled. "I told ya. Come on." She pulled him to the line at the standard-looking lift doors. While they waited for their turn to enter, Trey watched as the people who had gone into the lift became visible, floating up the shaft. Finally the doors opened for them. They walked the solid, brick-red path into what seemed like an ordinary lift. A family of four joined them.

"Please take hold now. Once the lift is in operation, handholds will not be visible. What deck?"

"Asteroid, please," Patsy said.

"Corona," said the adult male of the other group. The boys were brothers, made apparent by their looks. The younger one clapped his hands rapidly. "Hold on, boys."

"This is marv, Dad," the older one said. Both complied, grabbing on to the railing that circled the lift.

"Sorry. They're excited."

"Of course they are. I'm excited, and I've been up the lifts before. Goin' down takes a stout heart though." Patsy winked at the boys.

"We are lifting."

Around them the walls, floor, everything faded to nothing, and they rose. Trey's instant reaction was to brace himself and to put an arm around Patsy's waist. But the floor was as solid as it had been before it disappeared, and the railing was sturdy under his hand.

Patsy tipped her head back to look at him. "Takes gettin' used to."

"It does. But I see what you mean about feeling like a bird."

The boys were stomping their feet and chortling. They at least hadn't had a problem adjusting to the lack of visual support. But their mother was turning green and clutching her husband.

Their upward journey stopped, and the lift reappeared around them.

"Asteroid deck."

The path from the opening lift doors was navy blue this time. Tension eased from Trey's body as they stepped out. His hand was still anchored to Patsy's waist. He pulled it away, feigning casual ease, and stuck both hands into his pockets.

Patsy grinned broadly. "That was fun."

She meant the lift ride, but holding on to her had been enjoyable in a different way. One he wanted to pursue. Maybe when they were back on Beta Tau when he was no longer responsible for her. What were

Randolph's exact words? Something about taking care of her as only you can. What had the man meant?

His attention was drawn back to the present when Patsy claimed his hand and pulled him toward another mini-tram entrance. "We'll have to take another tram unless you're up for walkin' a fair distance."

Crammed into the tram, they arranged themselves as before, her legs between his. The car swooped into a tunnel that ran between decks. "I should probably warn ya—"

What now? Without speaking a word, he narrowed his eyes and waited for her to continue.

In quick succession she winced, bit her lip, and rapidly spilled the bad news. "I had to clear out my storage area and my wardrobe space, so the cabin's a tiny bit crowded with all my stuff." She held her hands up. "But don't worry. I've hired a cratin' company to come pack what I don't take in my luggage into a cargo container and get it to the spaceport. It'll be out of our way tomorrow."

"I see. That shouldn't be a problem."

She released a long sigh. "Good. I was a little worried. What if ya were claustrophobic. You're not a klutz? Because if ya are, it might be tricky."

He laughed at her expression, a cross between concern and wariness. "Thankfully for you, I'm not."

The tram arrived, and they disembarked with Patsy once again taking his hand to quicken his pace. "We need to hurry. The delivery bot won't wait if there's no answer when it arrives at the cabin." She pulled him left along a corridor lined with doors. "This way. Oh goodness. The bot's almost to my door." She dropped Trey's hand and pelted along the hall.

Trey didn't speed his own pace, enjoying the scene as Patsy engaged the bot in conversation with the requisite hand motions she used while talking to people. When he reached her cabin, the bot was zooming away, and Patsy was grinning at him, pizza box in hand.

"Mmm. Can ya smell it? There's nothin' like pizza in the whole wide universe." With a nod of her head at the cabin's interior, she said, "Go on in."

The cabin was much smaller than Trey had imagined. Patsy's belongings were piled in towering stacks of bins. "Where?"

"Left and then right. I promise there's a path through to the kitchenette and table."

Following her instructions, Trey wound his way to the table. It, at least, was empty.

"Have a seat." Patsy deposited the pizza. "I'll get plates and napkins. What would ya like to drink? I'm after runnin' out of fizzies, which ya probably won't mind. I've plenty of Q water. It's bottled on the ship."

"Water's fine."

After taking a bite of pizza, Trey waved his slice in an arc at the crowded room. "Where did you keep all this stuff?"

"Mmpf." When Patsy finished swallowing, she responded. "Some went into my staff storage locker. But the rest I kept in my cabin. It wasn't much bigger than this, but at least I had a space to myself and didn't have to share a dorm room like the performers do. I lined my walls with racks and shelves wherever I could and binned things by category. The gray bins are my set tools. Blue is for costumes. Green is my personal bits and pieces. Red is my dancin' gear. Yellow is my magic kit."

Trey brought his gaze back to Patsy. "You perform?"

"I tried." She flashed him a half smile. "I started as a magician's helper." She gave a flourish with her hand and grinned. "I'm not really built for that role, but Harry the Magnificent was desperate, and I came cheap."

"You're built fine from where I'm sitting." Trey enjoyed the flush that brightened her cheeks.

She covered her reaction in a rush of words. "Then I did a stint as an Irish step dancer. Performed in a big stage show. Eventually I found my callin' behind the scenes. Done a bit of everythin'. Costumes, set, props, and a dreadful six months as a director's assistant. I moved up to stage manager here at the CC."

"You should get rid of some of this stuff rather than cart it with you. Randolph will give you the funds to replace whatever equipment you need. You're not being hired to make costumes or sets."

After a feint at crossing her arms, she shrugged. "I'm a tryer, not a chancer. Sure as I left somethin' behind, I'd be needin' it."

"Things can always be replaced."

She turned her face and looked to the side. "Some things can't."

Her statement sat between them, a cold lump of truth, until she briskly slapped her palms to the tabletop. With a tip of her head toward the bedroom, she said, "Your bed's waitin' for ya. The toilet's a cubby inside. I laid out extra towels for ya. I'll do the cleanin' up and settle in on the sofa."

Trey rose from the table as she did and gathered the disposables. "You'll take the bed."

"I'll take the sofa." The plates clattered as Patsy inserted them into the dish fresher.

"Don't be stubborn."

The fresher snapped closed with a bang. "Ya don't fit on the sofa. I do."

"You and all the stuff you've piled on it?"

Hands on her hips, she turned to face him. "I'll move it."

"And block the only way out of this fire trap?"

"I'll not be sharin' a bed with a man I've just met."

"I didn't ask you to."

"Sure and there's only the one bed. Where did ya plan on sleepin'?"

"I'll take the floor."

She glanced around, flicked her hand in the direction of the only clear space, and cocked an eyebrow at him. "And block the only way out of this fire trap?"

Stabbing a finger toward the bedroom, Trey asked, "Have you filled that room too?"

Lips pressed together, she glared at him. "No."

"Then I sleep on the floor in there."

"Oh, you're so manly. And me a wee girl in need of pamperin'. I've slept on the floor before."

Trey scowled at her. "I'm Tallavan. A man doesn't let a woman sleep on the floor."

"You're a stubborn son is what ya are."

When he made no response, staring at her with an implacability reminiscent of an ancient tree, she threw up her hands. "Fine. Ya can sleep on the floor. Since ya find it necessary to put yourself last, I'll use the toilet first too."

The sight of her flouncing away made Trey grin. Teaching that pert woman to submit to him would be entertaining. Randolph's instructions could be construed to include initiating her into a Dominant/submissive relationship. Maybe. Something to consider.

He waited until she popped her head out of the door and said, "Your turn."

The sleeping space wasn't large, but there was enough room for him to stretch out fully. Patsy was burrowed into the covers, facing the wall. Inside the bathroom, he stared at himself in the mirror. Damn. His luggage with his toiletries had never arrived. He borrowed a swig from Patsy's nanite-laden mouth rinse and swished it around before spitting it out. Anything else could wait. After removing his shirt and slacks, he folded them and walked back into the bedroom.

"Is there a spare pillow?"

Without turning to look at him, Patsy reached behind her head for the second pillow and threw it at him. He snatched it from the edge of the bed, holding it front of himself.

"And a blanket?"

She rolled over, and her eyes went wide. "Ya sleep in the nude!"

"No." He pulled the pillow away to reveal his briefs.

"As good as." Back turned to him again, she said, "Top shelf of the closet."

"Thank you."

"Think nothin' of it."

"I won't."

A snort muffled by the covers was her only response. He chuckled. She was cute with her Irish feathers ruffled.

FECKIN' MAN! WHY did someone so exasperatin' have to be built like a god? Standin' there in his underpants. All his glory on display except for his private bits, which weren't exactly hidden by that layer of cloth.

The closet door slid shut with a *thunk*. A snap sounded when he whipped the blanket out. It was impossible to ignore the rustling noises he made fluffing the pillow and settling himself.

"Lights off." The room went dark. "Good night."

Sure and he's nothin' but courtesy. She snapped back her response. "Night."

Another of his chuckles grated across her nerves.

How am I supposed to sleep with him in the same room? The irritatin' man is too damn hot. Stubborn idjit. He can have the floor and welcome to it. She readjusted the pillow, released a sigh, and determined to stop thinking about him.

I don't have that much stuff. It just looks like a lot crammed in here. Sure and he's got himself a fine lot of toys for dominatin' women. Would he leave it all behind when he moved? What does he know about all the scrimpin' and savin' I've done to pay for every single thing I own? He was born on a wealthy planet. I earned more in sore feet and muscles than I did credits as a dancer, so I keep what's important. Thank you, Master Trey, for noticin'. Lucky for him to be born big and dominatin' and able to earn his keep at it. I need my stuff. Who knows if I'll keep this job.

The *bing bong* of the entry chime sounded. *What the...?*

Trey sat up at the same time she did.

"Who could that...?"

"It's my luggage. Lights on."

"Oh."

He peeled back the blanket and stood.

"You're not answerin' the door in your underpants."

"It's probably a bot."

His momentary hesitation gave her the chance to move the covers aside and get between him and the door. "I'll answer it."

"I suppose fuzzy jammies with bears and pink hearts is better."

"It is." She threaded her way to the cabin's entrance, greeted the bot, and accepted the luggage. After the door closed, she turned to push the suitcase.

"I'll take that."

With a shriek she jumped. "Feckin' man! Ya near scared the red out of my hair."

The glare she aimed at him was met by an expression of regret from Trey that didn't quite hide his amusement. "Sorry. I didn't want you to have to negotiate the maze with that thing."

Patsy felt her checks heat. Once again she had a full view of Trey in all his magnificence. This time, because he was closer, every fine detail of his washboard abs covered in smooth, taut skin and the line of dark hair that disappeared into his briefs was distinct. Her girlie bits lit with flaming desire. She jerked her gaze to the luggage. "Get on with it then."

The sight of his wide palms and long fingers sent another ache of longing through her. Every part of him was like an erotic overture calling her to immerse herself in decadence. He maneuvered the suitcase so he could push it along, and Patsy's knees went weak. His bum was within easy reach, and it was begging to be stroked. She balled her fists and plodded after him.

When he reached the kitchenette, he picked up the bag and stood aside so she could move by him. "Ladies first."

Without a word she slid past him, working hard to give the impression that nearness to his nearly naked body didn't affect her in the least. She scrambled onto the bed and under the covers, sitting, watching him.

"Where should I put this?" His gaze traveled over the tiny room. "There's no room in the closet with all the shoes."

"It's not that many shoes. The closet's small."

Trey threw his palms out to the side. "So?" He glanced toward the corner of the room where there was space between the head of the bed and wall.

Oh hell! If he puts it there, he'll be loomin' over me every time he wants somethin' out of it. She scanned the room, came up empty, and pointed at the corner. "You'll have to put it there."

He strode around the bed and deposited the suitcase. All attempts to keep her gaze from straying to his briefs were for naught.

"My cock is getting uncomfortable with you staring. If you don't want me getting ideas, you should stop lusting after it."

Patsy huffed out a breath. "I'm not lustin' after it. It's just...abnormally large." *And growing bigger from the look of things.*

"I like to think of it as just right."

"I'm sure ya do." She slumped into the bed and covered her head with the blanket. "Good night."

A thump sounded. "Ouch. Just my toe. Nothing to worry about." The room grew quiet. "Good night, *a leanbh.*"

She ignored him and lay still, listening, unable to sleep. When he began to snore softly, she whipped the blanket down and took a deep breath.

Patsy O'Shaughnessy, you've got to get ahold of yourself. You're playin' with fire. The man's a Dom. If you start in with him, you'll soon be doin' everythin' his way. If he was here to help her understand dominance in a D/s relationship, he was off to a fine start, although the descriptions she'd read hadn't included stubborn or pigheaded. Or full of himself. Canceling his suite had been a big mistake. Even if they'd been in her larger cabin, the proximity to him would still have been much too close. All because she wanted to save some money. Not even her own credits.

Shut your eyes and go to sleep. You can figure this out tomorrow.

3

Trey woke early, sat, and stretched to work out the stiffness in his back. Patsy was lying on her side facing him, her countenance smooth with no hint of the varied expressions that broadcast her emotions when she wasn't asleep. He wanted to tweak her nose to see the glare that would follow. Instead he stood and inched his way to his suitcase, slowly picking it up to carry it where he had been sleeping, the only floor space large enough for him to rummage in the bag. When he reached the foot of the bed, she rolled over, opened her eyes, and sat with a look of panic.

"It's just me. I'm getting my luggage and going to take a shower. Go back to sleep."

Without a word she flopped back down and shut her eyes.

The shower tube was attractive, but its amenities were the bare bones allowed to economy guests. At home he could stand under pulsating hot water for as long as he desired. Here he was limited to a sixty-second rinse, followed by a mist of biocleanser and another brief sluice of water. It would have to do.

Wearing fresh clothes, he stepped back into the bedroom and pocketed his comm. Patsy was flat on her back. The noise he'd made, including knocking his elbow against the edge of the sink, hadn't roused her.

The bed sank beneath him when he eased onto it next to her. Relaxed and splayed out, she was tempting. He could slide the covers off and peel her out of those awful pajamas to reveal her long legs and pert breasts. His cock hardened, but it wasn't in control.

He needed to be careful, to a certain extent because he worried about mishandling this assignment from Randolph, but also because he liked her. Most women reacted to him in one of two ways. They wanted to sleep with the dangerous-looking Dom, or they were afraid of him. Patsy hadn't acted either way. This was her future, and he didn't want to wreck things for her.

With his finger barely touching her, he drew a line down her cheek. "Ms. O'Shaughnessy. It's your wake-up call."

No response.

"Ms. O'Shaughnessy. Time to get up." He smoothed his knuckle over her cheek.

Her face crumpled, and she opened her eyes. Her brows knit together. "I don't remember invitin' ya to join me on the bed."

Went to bed snippy. Woke snippy. With a finger tap to her nose, he said, "You didn't. Time to start the busy day you have planned for me." He stood, stepped to the door, and looked back at her. "Stop wasting time. Breakfast's on me, and I'm starving."

Seated at the table, he pulled out his comm. He needed to clarify things with Randolph. "Rand, I've met your Ms. O'Shaughnessy, and she's a dynamo. Beyond what she's read, she doesn't have a clue about dominance and submission. You said I was to take care of her as only I can. Am I correct in assuming that means I can engage in some hands-on training, because that's where this is headed unless you tell me otherwise. Comm me back ASAP."

When she appeared fifteen minutes later dressed in another sleeveless shirt and short skirt set, this time in a colorful floral fabric, he was surprised at how quick she'd been. Her green-tipped hair had led him to believe she was a primper, but apparently not. She didn't need to be. Everything about her was fresh, pretty, vibrant, and somehow, freckles and all, far more attractive than the sultry types he usually went for.

A smile wreathed her face. "I hope ya slept well. I know I did. But then I wasn't on the floor." She winked at him. "Shall we go? You're not the only one who's starvin'. And breakfast is on the Cosmic Cabaret's owner.

Callendra comped me the room, which includes meals in the assigned dinin' room."

"I'll eat twice as much then. You're in a good mood. New day, fresh beginning?"

"Yes. I was…a little peeved at ya last night, but I realize now ya were just tryin' to be helpful. Ya didn't know ya were treadin' on hazardous ground. Come on."

Being dragged around by the hand by Patsy was becoming a habit. For now he'd allow it, but if he trained her in submission, it would stop. She rushed around entirely too much. He didn't.

The cabin door auto locked behind them. "The dinin' room for this section is down the corridor and to the left."

Trey followed Patsy through the buffet line, piling food on two plates. They sat at a table for two in the corner.

She eyed his breakfast. "Ya can always go back for seconds."

"Mmph." He swallowed the bite of French toast. "I will. This is good." He noticed that she didn't talk as much while she was eating. Probably couldn't, not because her mouth was full but because her hands were busy with her eating utensils.

"I have a question, and I know it's intrusive, but I think if I get to know you better, I might avoid the hazardous ground you mentioned."

Her face grew wary. "Okay. But I don't promise anythin'."

"Why are your things so important to you? I mean, I understand mementos and keepsakes, but tools are tools."

Lips pressed together, Patsy didn't respond immediately, then after a quick nod of her head, she said, "I didn't leave Ireland because I wanted to. It was that or remain a stage gofer for two decades before I was gifted—and I do mean gifted—with a rise in position to assistant to the head gofer. Prop master was a lofty job beyond my pull. And I didn't want to be prop master. I wanted to be, at minimum, a stage manager."

"Why couldn't you become a stage manager?"

After a long sigh she said, "Let me explain Earth to you. It's not like any other planet in the universe. Everyone wants to visit their historic homeland. It's become a giant tourist attraction. Everythin' revolves around keepin' guests happy and satisfyin' their expectations of an authentic Earth experience. The guilds rigidly control who is allowed into the different professions. Even with an advanced degree in specialty entertainment, I was slotted into the prop position because I was reachin' outside my family's tradition. I was lucky to be able to switch guilds at all."

"So you applied for jobs off planet?"

"I did, but no one cared about my education credentials. They wanted experience workin' in a big show. Movin' props around for a medieval reenactment dinner show in an old castle didn't count for much. I hired on as housekeepin' on a space liner. That's where I met Harry the Magnificent. He was an entertainer on board. His helper left him for a wealthy billionaire. When we arrived in the Alpha Centauri system, he hired someone better suited, and I joined an Irish dance troupe.

"It all worked out. But I've never had more than what I can take with me. And I've never known when a job will end and I'll be scramblin' to make ends meet again. So I keep my stuff. My reputation has been built on bein' able to fix any problem that arises durin' a show. Sets. Costumes. Props. I've even stepped in to perform a minor part for a clown troupe. I can do it all. But not without my bits and pieces."

"You became a stage manager, and now you'll be creative director of Randolph's cabaret. Looks like you've made it. Fulfilled your dreams. Maybe you can let go a little."

"I didn't get this far by bein' optimistic. 'Prepare for the worst' is my motto."

"That's a depressing way to live."

"No, it isn't. I cover my ass, but I don't worry. Livin' foolish will result in a far more depressin' mess."

"The show must go on."

"Yep." She twirled her fork in the air. "I need to catch up on my eatin'. You've nearly finished your first helpin'. It's your turn. How does someone become a professional Dom?"

Trey grunted. "I stumbled into it really. Like you, there was nothing for me on my home planet. My parents were in service on Tallav to one of the first families. That didn't appeal to me, so I saved and took transport to another planet in the sector. I was young, worked at manual labor, and partied on my off time. An acquaintance invited me to visit his club. Turned out to be a BDSM club. Things clicked. An older Dom mentored me. Eventually I made it to Beta Tau and the Opio Institute, where I trained professional dominants and submissives. Last year Randolph asked me to take over managing the private area of the Whip Hand."

"So you're good at makin' women do what you say."

"No." He waved a finger in the air. "It's not about one person bossing the other person around."

"No?"

"No. It's a dynamic between two people, one who is dominant and the other submissive." There was no way he could explain this without demonstrating what he meant. BDSM was often subtle. The nuances could take a lifetime to learn. Yet he had to instill some kind of understanding in her before they arrived at Beta Tau.

"It's clear I have a lot to teach you, but right now I'm getting more breakfast."

PATSY BIT HER lip as she watched Trey walk away. The man was so damn sexy. He'd said teach, not train. But if training landed her in his bed, she could handle a little submission. He was built like a love machine, broad back sloping down to narrow hips and an ass that would fill a woman's hands while he was thrusting inside her. If he demanded she fall to her knees and suck his cock, she'd hit the ground in an instant. If he made the first move, she was all in. But that didn't mean she was submissive. Just hungry to indulge in playing the flute of a man who made women do triple takes. She enjoyed giving pleasure to a man, but she liked receiving it too, a give-and-take of equals.

Sauntering back over, munching on a pastry, Trey was oblivious to the people scampering out of his way. It wasn't so much that he was menacing but that he had a presence that others deferred to, like an ancient warrior king. He'd look damn fine in a loincloth with an enormous sword sheathed in a scabbard strapped to his back. A dagger at his hip and a blood ruby hanging from a wire pierced through his earlobe. Long shaggy hair...no, keep his head shaved as it was.

"Did I spill something on myself?" Trey examined the front of his shirt before placing his plate on the table and thrusting the last bit of the pastry into his mouth.

"Er. No. You're fine." *Great. Now he's goin' to think I'm lustin' after him again.*

"I wondered. You were staring at me."

"Was I? I didn't realize. I was considerin' my plans for today."

"Which are?"

"First, we're goin' to visit the venue itself, go backstage, and maybe up on the catwalk. I thought it might be helpful to see how the magic"—she lifted her fingers and made air quotes—"happens."

Trey licked his lip to catch a drop of syrup. "Sure."

Patsy sat mesmerized for a moment.

"Anything else?"

"Huh? Er. Yeah. I want to introduce ya to the CC's creative director. And I invited some of the cast to lunch with us. This afternoon the cratin' company is comin' to pack my things. Ya can explore Q while I deal with that."

"Sounds good." He swabbed the syrup from his plate with his last bite of French toast. "I'm done."

They bussed their dishes, and Patsy led Trey out the door and toward a mini-tram station. "It's faster to take the mini-tram on this level rather than the Cabaret's. Helps avoid the tourists and long lines."

Once again Patsy found her legs trapped between Trey's in the mini-tram. She'd looked forward to it. "Tell me about Beta Tau. What's it like?"

"Quite a bit like LS *Quantum*."

"But it's a planet. That's a big difference."

"Yeah. But it's all under climate-controlled domes, and because it's a pleasure planet, there are tourists everywhere."

"So are there water restrictions like on Q?"

"No rationing. It is all desert, but they have water production facilities on planet. There's plenty of room for the containment fields needed, plus the facilities are all well removed from populated areas."

"We're here. The closest lift is to the right."

Patsy took his hand, tugging him. When he pulled away, she turned to look at him. He stood with his hands on his hips, glaring at her. "I'm not a little boy that needs to hold your hand and be dragged along."

"Er. Sorry. I usually walk fast, and I didn't want to leave ya behind."

"There's another solution." He watched her. When she didn't respond, he frowned at her. "Slow down!"

"Ya don't have to growl at me. If ya can't keep up to my pace, ya should have said so before. O' course I'll slow down." *Feckin' bossy man!*

In the lift they stood side by side, both with their arms crossed over their chests. Trey stopped and looked around when they reached the Xventure Entertaiment deck where the cabaret was located. "Very nice."

Patsy bounced on her heels and smiled. "It is, isn't it? Q is a classy ship. None of that rococo frilliness, gold leaf, and giant plasti statues of ancient gods."

"Ah. The Vegas dome on Beta Tau. That's the perfect description of it. I like this though. It's almost like you're outside taking a stroll through the theater district of a metropolitan city."

"But clean and without rain or snow," she agreed. "Come on." She reached for his hand but snapped it back before touching him. Instead she pointed. "This way."

Trey had no problem keeping pace with her. His strides were longer than hers. There really had been no need for her to haul him around like she had. "Ya were right. Ya have no trouble keepin' up with me."

"Thank you." He looked down at her, no smile, just the same intent expression that seemed to be his default.

"Now if I take your hand"—she slipped her fingers against his palm —"it'll be me bein' friendly."

He tightened his grip and grinned. "I like that better."

For a moment Patsy became light-headed. When they reached the unobtrusive door that opened onto the corridor that led backstage, she used the action of keying in the pass code to refocus her mind. The hallway sloped to a junction of three doors. Patsy opened the one on the left.

"This is the side entrance to the theater. There's a matchin' door on the other side that the food service uses." She made a broad sweep with her hand. "The layout is typical. Let's go up onstage; ya can see better from there." Sets of three steps were spaced evenly around the circular stage.

Patsy took the closest set. When they reached the middle, she flung her arms wide. "Here it is. The Cosmic Cabaret."

"Nice."

"It's meant to mimic an old-Earth spiegeltent. They were wooden tents that could be moved from place to place. The CC is as authentic as possible. The wood is real mahogany. The beveled mirrors, leaded stained glass, and the velvet and brocade fabrics replicate the originals built in the early twentieth century on Earth."

She pointed to the ceiling, which was covered in a cluster of objects. "When the show's live, a hologram of radiatin' stripes made to look like the peak of a circus tent covers all that up. Real canvas would interfere with set changes."

Hands on her hips, she skimmed her gaze over the venue. "Do ya have any questions?"

Trey pursed his lips, shook his head, and said, "No."

"Most of the apparatus the cirque uses is brought down from the ceilin'. Sound and lights are controlled from the booth at the back. The set master's controls are up there, too. A good set master can change backdrops and major set pieces very quickly usin' gravity fields. The small stuff is handled by stagehands. The stage itself is retractable, sinks into the floor and slides into its bay, and another stage moves out and up to take its place." She turned and strode to the center and pointed to the set pieces dangling above. "All the big props are in the fly. There's also a catwalk we use sometimes. Glamourine always opened her act by comin' down reclinin' on a chaise lounge. What do ya think?"

"Nice."

Nice. Is that all he has to say? Patsy sighed. "Would ya like to see the shops or the dressin' rooms?"

"I expect they're standard."

"They are." She put her hands on her hips. "This didn't take as much time as I expected. Are ya sure ya don't have any questions?"

"No. It's pretty much what I imagined."

"Okay. Well, we might as well see if Jason is in his office." She moved toward the center steps but halted, jumping and trying to snatch a dangling bright red streamer. "The cleanin' crew missed this." She jumped again, but the ribbon was well beyond her reach, caught on one foot of a hat rack used in the clown act.

"Let me get it." Even jumping, Trey couldn't reach it.

"I'll boost you."

Before Patsy could agree, he'd wrapped his massive hands around her waist and lifted her high. *Sweet Lord! The man's face is in my crotch.* Warmth flooded through her.

"Can you catch hold of it?"

"Er. I think so." She stretched and yanked. The streamer fell to the ground. "Okay. I got it."

"You did?"

"Yes. Ya can put me down."

He let her slide gradually until they were face-to-face, her feet still off the floor, and her hands atop his shoulders. Her nipples peaked into hard buds, an ache building between her legs. She glanced from his eyes to his lips. Was he going to kiss her? Her heart thudded in her chest. He inched closer. She returned her gaze to his.

"Thank you for the tour."

"You're welcome."

Then he let her slide until the soles of her shoes thumped against the floor, and he released her. When she wobbled, he steadied her, but he didn't wrap his hands around her again, something her whole body screamed for him to do. She wanted to plaster herself to him and grind against the hard length she'd felt in his pants. *Feckin' man is too damn hot.*

"Er. Thanks." She gestured to the streamer and stooped to pick it up. Did he groan? Wadding it, she plastered a smile on her face and in a purposefully bright voice said, "Let's go find Jason. He said he wanted to meet you."

Trey cleared his throat. "He's the cabaret's creative director?"

"Yes. Follow me."

TREY TOOK another swallow of the frothy fruit shake he'd chosen at one of the snack shops that could be found around every corner of *Quantum*. He was relaxing on a bench in a quiet oasis of a shopping area where he could watch passersby. An elderly gentleman was napping, chin to chest, on another. Behind some large potted plants a middle-aged couple were doing what he was, resting from an hour or more of walking. They'd spent theirs shopping, as the bags clustered at their feet attested to. He'd used LS *Quantum*'s guide, accessible via his EBC—he wasn't a dinosaur, after all— to check out several of the ship's amenities.

The crating company was scheduled this afternoon to pack Patsy's things, so he'd left her to oversee them and set out to explore and think. Lunch earlier had turned out to be a good-bye celebration for Patsy. She'd planned on eating with a few friends, but the staff and performers of the Cosmic Cabaret surprised her with a huge going-away. From the number of people that offered Patsy gratitude for specific moments when she had done them a kindness, it was obvious these people regarded her highly. She'd covered for them, stitched a split seam, found a missing prop…made them look good. Randolph was lucky to get her.

The behind-the-scenes tour hadn't changed his opinion of a BDSM cabaret. He should wait until after this evening's dinner show, but what he'd gleaned from *Quantum*'s guide lined up with what he'd expected. Patsy could recreate the CC on Beta Tau, but slanting it to reflect every-thing that BDSM encompassed? It didn't seem possible. Bondage, disci-pline, dominance, submission, sadism, and masochism were the major elements. He hadn't a clue how Patsy might maintain a modicum of the truth of what was often a ritualized, rule-laden lifestyle. That there were rules baffled a subsection of the tourists that visited the Whip Hand to view what to them amounted to an exotic animal show. Randolph recog-nized the problem with perpetuating misunderstandings about BDSM. But a BDSM cabaret wasn't the ideal place to promulgate facts. Even though Patsy filled her head with details, they wouldn't help her determine with a gut sense of rightness when an idea or act was a corruption of the lifestyle.

His comm vibrated in his pocket. The screen showed a message from Randolph.

Trey, I trust your judgment. I believed introducing Ms. O'Shaughnessy to a D/s relationship would be useful, but I couldn't determine if it was feasible or whether Ms. O'Shaughnessy would be open to the possibility. That's why I sent you. I didn't give you a heads-up, because I wanted you to come to your own conclusions. Your work at the Opio is ample proof you can work with all types of people, and that you'll use proper precautions. Be careful. I don't want to lose her.

With a scowl Trey pocketed the comm. That settled that. He would initiate Patsy O'Shaughnessy into a D/s relationship. Ideas about where to start filled his mind. Patsy wasn't his personal sub. The situation resembled the mentor/student bond he'd employed at the Opio. With one difference: he'd never been as attracted to one of his students as he was to Patsy.

It was baffling. He liked women who were small and firm, physically pert. That was Patsy. Pert bottom. Pert breasts. But he'd always avoided talkative, sassy women, which was the other definition of pert. She was lively, full of energy instead of the quiet, self-effacing submissives he'd typically claimed as his own. Not that he'd had many. His work kept him too busy to take care of a sub properly.

Patsy was a short-term project. He had the next four days on *Quantum* and the two weeks of the trip back to Beta Tau to instill in her a solid foundation in true BDSM. To do so would require a unique approach. One that would help him control his desire to strap her to a bed and leisurely plunder every inch of her body while helping her distinguish the lines of power running between a Dom and sub.

He rose to his feet and stretched. Time to head back and dress for the Cosmic Cabaret dinner show. After letting himself inside, he scanned the cabin. Without Patsy's bins and piles it seemed spacious, which would make the plan unfolding in his mind easier to implement.

"You're back." Patsy's voice sounded from the bedroom. When she stepped through the door, Trey froze in place. She was stunning, dressed in a dark blue frothy gown that made her breasts appear ready to burst free. A long slit revealed close to the full length of one shapely leg. His fingers itched to slide up her thigh and discover what lay hidden beneath. He scowled. There was no relief in sight for the chub he was sporting.

Patsy widened her stance and placed her hands on her waist, elbows extended. "Ya need to get dressed. I don't want to miss even a second of tonight."

Pretending to tip his hat to her, Trey said, "Yes, ma'am. At your service." It would be fun to teach this woman to guard her tongue. He strode to the bedroom, pulled out the dinner suit he'd brought with him, washed, and changed.

From the sounds coming from the main room, it was apparent Patsy was talking to herself. When he stepped through the door, silence fell. He looked up from shooting his cuffs. She was a vision, her face aglow with a rosy flush. With a smirk he said, "I'm ready."

Lips pressed tight and brows knit, Patsy glowered at him. She huffed. "So ya are. Let's go."

4

The Cosmic Cabaret had been Patsy's life for the last three years. This was the final time she'd witness what she had helped create. If she returned, it would all be different. When she'd seen her first performance from the audience instead of backstage, she'd been enthralled. It had been the cirque full of brilliantly costumed acrobats whose every movement was carefully choreographed into an effortless kaleidoscopic scene. The mood-enhancing scent that was added to the air filtration system in the cabaret wafted around her, bringing the same tingle of excitement. It was an aroma she had come to associate with the CC and the frisson of anticipation for the enchantment to follow. The burlesque and musicales had been entertaining, but the cirque would always be her favorite.

The maître d' was resplendent in red and white striped pants. Patsy followed her to a table on the lower level closest to the action. Tonight, the dinner show would be burlesque with its mix of comedy, singing, dancing, and striptease acts. Trey insisted she needed to learn about BDSM, but it was equally true that he needed an understanding of what a cabaret show encompassed if he was going to help her figure out the kinds of performances that fit a BDSM cabaret. Burlesque by nature was bawdy and irreverent. It mocked the serious-minded. Trey didn't seem like a person who would enjoy his lifestyle being the butt of jokes.

A glance at him as they were seated gave her no clue to what he was thinking. He wasn't frowning, but neither was his expression pleasant. On him, staid was intimidating because he was such a big muscle-bound behemoth of a man. Many of the show's players interacted with the guests. He would make the perfect foil for their antics. Whether that spelled trouble was yet to be determined.

Trey looked at her from the touch-pad menu he'd been perusing. "The food looks good."

"Chef is amazin'. Even the vegetarian option is five-star magnificent. But I'd advise ya to try the Bayou because it includes Chef's famous blue-crab gumbo. Ya haven't lived until you've tasted it."

"Menu one it is, then. The blackened ribeye sounds good, too."

"Enter your choice on your menu. It's linked to your seat."

After entering their selections, they set the menus aside and looked at one another. Patsy's gift for conversation failed her, perhaps because of the intensity of his gaze. It was as though he were consuming her with his eyes. The silence between them took on a life of its own, expanding until it surrounded them in a bubble that excluded the other sounds inside the cabaret. He seemed unfazed by it, but Patsy urgently wanted to cross her arms and tuck her hands behind her elbows.

When he at last spoke, she leaped on the opening. "I'm looking forward to the entertainment too."

"Ya are?" Her cheeks warmed. "O' course ya are. I guess I was a little uncertain. Ya haven't said much today. I don't know what you're thinkin'. Whether ya believe I can create the proper atmosphere for a BDSM cabaret."

Now he scowled, upping his intimidation factor by ten. "I'm sorry. I didn't mean to make you feel as though you were on trial here. Randolph hired you because he thought you were the right person for the position. He's seldom, if ever, wrong about people. I'm trying to absorb as much as I can about the Cosmic Cabaret to give us a point of shared reference. It's all new to me. I've been to strip clubs before, but that's not the same thing."

Patsy sat straighter. "No. Absolutely not. The stripteases aren't about getting naked. They're meant to tantalize, promisin' somethin' but with-holdin' it, and when the big reveal comes, the audience gets a brief glimpse, and the performer exits the stage."

"Sounds like orgasm denial. Maybe burlesque and BDSM can find some common ground."

Her chest lightened as though a helium bubble had burst inside her, brightening her mood. "I knew we could." She grinned broadly. "There's a new comedy act tonight that I helped hire, Charles and Sadie Camp. They play off one another brilliantly. Charles is the straight man, and Sadie is a hoot. I can imagine an act like them at the new cabaret."

The server arrived with their first course, a bourbon champagne cocktail. Trey raised his glass. "To you and your new adventure on Beta Tau."

Taking a sip of her drink, Patsy eyed him over her glass, awaiting his response.

"Mmm. That's quite good."

"I was worried for your delicate feckin' nose after the orange fizzy did ya in."

Trey laughed. "Aren't champagne bubbles supposed to tickle, not burn?"

"Yer right. Did they tickle you?"

"I'm not ticklish."

"Oh my, am I ever. The bottoms of my feet are the worst. Touch them and you're likely to get kicked."

The intensity of his gaze ratcheted up. "I'll remember to restrain you if I decide you need tickling."

With eyes narrowed, Pasty said, "Trey Johansson, I was after believin' ya were a Dom, not a sadist."

"It's not an either/or. Sometimes it's both. I'll admit to a narrow streak of sadism, but that's not unusual in most people. It's what you do with it that counts."

The conversation was interrupted by the room darkening. Ethereal music played while large metallic balls of gold, silver, bronze, and copper floated from the ceiling toward open spots on the floor throughout the cabaret. When they touched, they burst with an explosion of glitter. Showgirls dressed in a minimum of spangles and feathers stood and strutted, hands on their hips, smiles wide, to positions facing the diners in the circle that cut a swathe between the tables on the cabaret's lowest level and the stage.

Patsy wasn't surprised that Trey's gaze was riveted on the dancer closest to their table. The woman was statuesque, athletic, and had a chest three times the size of Patsy's own. Dancers shimmied, swayed, and kicked their legs high in unison, finally working their way onto the stage where they were joined by more scantily clad entertainers with huge feathered headdresses. When the troupe finished their choreographed routine and promenaded offstage and out an exit, Patsy's eyes prickled with tears. The show must go on. It was going on without her, and the players weren't affected by the loss. *That's the way it should be. I left things so the next stage manager could take over without a hitch. It's all good.*

Their gumbo arrived. After his first bite Trey said, "This is good. Shrimp and"—he stirred the soup with his spoon—"what's this kind of sausage?"

"Andouille."

"I like it. Too bad it's such a small bowl." His concentration remained fixed on the gumbo until he'd eaten it all.

Patsy ate hers quickly, wanting to ask him his opinion of the show so far. "Did ya like the bubble dancers?"

He tapped his spoon on the table. "They were fine. That must be hard on their knees. Do they dose with speedheal after every performance?"

"Some probably do. Any other observations?"

"Not really. Good-looking women barely dressed in feathers and rhinestones. Most men go for that kind of thing."

"But ya don't?"

"No. I mean, they're nice to look at, but I'm not much into watching entertainers."

Patsy wasn't sure if that was a good thing or bad.

The servers removed their dishes while the master of ceremonies introduced Charles and Sadie Camp.

Charles, dapper in a flashy evening suit, clapped his hands together and said, "Looks like a lovely crowd tonight. Say hello, Sadie."

Sadie rocked back on her heels, the fringe on her flapper-style dress swaying. "Hello. Oh look, Charles. I think I know that man." She pointed straight at Trey.

The focus of the audience narrowed on Trey.

Peering at Trey, Charles asked, "Who? The big fellow with the pretty girl?"

Sadie nodded. "Mmhmm. I think I sat on him before."

Charles's eyebrows shot up. "Sat on him?"

"Yeah." She squinted at Trey. "No. I'm wrong. It was another guy. Just as big and stern."

"And you sat on him?"

"Yeah. Oh, not him." She flicked her hand at Trey.

"The other big guy."

"Yeah, the other one." With a soft giggle she peered at Charles.

"Sadie, are you going to tell me why you sat on him?"

"Oh sure. I thought he was a chair."

The audience laughed, and Sadie beamed at them.

"A chair."

"Yeah," she said, nodding her head.

"I'll bite," Charles said to the audience, then to Sadie, "Why did you think he was a chair?"

"He didn't move. Just like him." She waved at Trey.

Patsy bit back the giggle that was close to bubbling out of her. Trey sat with the same noncommittal expression.

"I assume he was sitting on a chair."

"Well of course he was sitting on a chair. Otherwise I couldn't have sat on him. Really, Charles, sometimes you're very silly."

This garnered another burst of amusement from the diners.

Charles looked at them and raised his eyes to the ceiling. "Mmm."

With a smile Sadie said, "Yeah."

"What did this man who you thought was a chair sitting on a chair do when you sat on him? Did he jump up in surprise?"

"Oh no." She looked at the floor where she was rubbing the toe of her shoe. "He put his arms around me."

"He what?" Charles put his hands on his hips.

"Yeah. I'll show you." Sadie bustled down the stage steps and headed straight to their table. Patsy bit her thumb. Every eye was once again on Trey.

He stiffened when Sadie plopped herself into his lap. She tapped his arm and said, "Put your arms around me."

Patsy covered her mouth to hide her laugh when Trey obeyed and encircled Sadie's waist. He glanced at her with a look of pained acceptance.

Sadie patted his arm. "Just like this."

From the stage Charles asked, "Then what happened?"

"We sat. Me on him on the chair."

"You on him on the chair. Sat. How long did this go on?"

"Oh not long. Just when we were getting comfortable, his girlfriend came along."

"I'll bet she had words to say."

Murmurs from the audience suggested they agreed with Charles.

Sadie nodded her head. "Oh sure. She told me to get up. It was her turn to sit on him."

The laughter Patsy had been trying to contain burst from her. Trey's expression became a tinge more aggrieved.

"Her turn?" Charles asked.

"Yeah. He was really good at putting his arms around a girl sitting on his lap."

"Was he?"

"Yeah. So I got up and let her sit down." She patted Trey's hand. "You can let me go now, big fella."

When Trey released her, she stood up and said to him, "It was very nice to sit on you."

"You're welcome." His deep voice and staid expression added to the humor of the moment, making Patsy laugh out loud again.

Sadie turned to Patsy and said, "You should try it out. He's very good too."

To which Patsy snorted and slapped a hand to her thigh. Trey gave her the stink eye and then smiled.

Through the rest of the seven-course meal, Patsy kept her focus on Trey. He'd been a good sport with Sadie and was enjoying himself if the occasional smile and nod of the head was proof. The food was a definite hit. With sweet mascarpone cheesecake and amaretto biscotti on the menu for dessert, she decided to save space and not eat the sixth course, scallop cakes served with a cilantro lime aioli and pan-seared green beans. Trey ate both hers and his.

A pair of servers they hadn't seen before started around their circle of tables. One man gathered plates and stacked them in the other's hands. They both appeared to be ham-handed, dropping plates or letting them slide from the pile. Each time, they recovered by using their feet, slipping a dish back in place with a toe or popping one in the air with a heel to grab in the nick of time. When the stack looked particularly precarious, rather than take them away and return for more, they continued stacking, and the pile grew taller. The server carrying the dishes veered left and right trying to keep the wobbling stack from falling. When the pair had collected the dishes from the last table, the pile was well over the second server's head. He staggered about, and just when he got the entire pile balanced, he tripped and the stack fell like a column heading toward the floor to shatter. The audience gasped. The other server dashed and caught the top, tucked it under his arm, smiled, and saluted the spectators. The server who had tripped did the same on his end, and the pair carried the dishes sideways out the serving entrance.

Showgirls, dressed this time in miniscule thongs and under-bust corsets that exposed their breasts, returned for another medley of tunes, dancing, shimmying, and bouncing. Dessert was served, and while Trey and Patsy ate their cheesecake and biscotti, Marie Cantable, the CC-renowned torch singer, ended the evening with captivating renditions of old-Earth rhythm and blues songs.

5

Several times during the evening, Trey had noticed Patsy's eyes misting over, especially when Marie Cantable closed her set and the show with a song about needing help from friends. She sang it straight to Patsy. These people had developed an affection for Patsy. Whether that was common among the show business crowd, he didn't know. It spoke to Patsy's generosity of spirit.

When the performance ended, Patsy clutched his hand. "Let's go down to the dressin' rooms."

"Sure."

Tears fell as she said her final good-byes to the players who remained. Marie Cantable swallowed her in a fierce hug, placed kisses on both Patsy's cheeks, and said, "Gonna miss you, sweet girl. Maybe I'll come and check out your new cabaret." She glanced over her shoulder at Trey. "If they grow all the men in that backwater as big and good-looking as this one, it's a place I need to explore." Her voice was a mellifluous purr. "But I'll leave him to you." She returned her gaze to Patsy, pulled her into another tight hug, and said, "I wish you could stay, but I know you gotta go."

Released from her arms, Patsy took Marie's hand and choked out a response. "Already miss you. Keep the others in line."

"Will do, baby girl. Now head on out to your new life."

Patsy turned and, once again tightly gripping Trey's hand, rushed out to the corridor that would take her away from the Cosmic Cabaret for good.

To allow her time to gain control of her emotions, Trey waited until they'd made their way back to the Xventure Entertainment deck's main walkway to speak. The sinfully exotic scent she was wearing had tantalized him all evening, tempting him to haul her to her cabin and get his fill of her. If this had been a purely personal relationship, he'd have done just that. Instead he asked, "Do you have any other plans for tonight?"

"Er. The Spector Station is right here. We could get a drink. It's a 1920s old-Earth speakeasy. Or there's the Phoenix Stardust, a dance club, but with the clothes we're wearin' we'd want to get naked. Because of the glow paint."

"Unless you really want to, I had something else in mind."

Her pupils dilated. "Er. Why don't we get a drink?"

"Alcohol would interfere with my plans."

"Oh. Er. Okay. Back to the cabin then?"

Trey nodded. He hadn't expected Patsy to get a case of nerves, but the normally expansive hand motions she made while speaking had become fidgety. Perhaps the fact that she was taking the final steps of saying good-bye to the CC was affecting her. He'd like to think it had something to do with being alone with him, but he'd already spent a night sleeping on her bedroom floor without eliciting any demonstrable anxiety. More likely she was worried about his opinion now that he'd taken in a CC show. Understandable, because she wouldn't like what he had to say.

If she was angry with him, it would be easier to keep at bay the thoughts of how he would peel her out of that dress whispering around her body. The soft, sensual swishing of the fabric filled him with a longing to smooth his fingertips over her skin.

Silence weighed between them as they walked along the corridor teeming with people from a variety of Federation worlds, each intent on wringing every bit of fun from their stay aboard LS *Quantum*. At one point a raucous group of young men headed their direction. Trey picked Patsy up at the waist and deposited her on his other side, so he was between her and the rowdies.

"Er. Thanks."

He scowled down at her. Patsy broke eye contact, flicking her gaze left and right as though she was looking for an escape route. How the hell was he supposed to remain the aloof training master when he burned to scoop her into his arms, rush to her cabin, and plunge inside her. His desire for her went beyond anything he'd experienced for years. If it weren't for the task Randolph had set him, he would have already seduced the woman into submitting to his own brand of dominance.

Reel it in, Johansson. You're scaring her. He tucked his hand into hers, and she returned her gaze to him, a tremulous smile flirting at the edges of her lips.

Once inside the main room of her cabin, they stood a moment. "Er."

"Why don't you go change into something more comfortable. Pajamas would be good."

Trey slipped one arm from his jacket.

She didn't follow his suggestion immediately. "What about you?"

"I'll be fine."

"Okay."

He laid his coat over the back of a chair and seated himself on one end of the love seat. Heaving a deep sigh, he relaxed into it. With Patsy already tense, he would have to be careful how he approached their discussion. Her temper was quick to spark, but it flashed hot and brief rather than burning long.

When she reappeared, wearing baby-blue, faux-silk pajamas, she gave him no chance to initiate the conversation, breezing into the room with an air of nonchalance, avoiding direct eye contact. "So, what did ya think?"

"I loved the trapeze act with the monkey on his own rig imitating everything the artists did, but it was a little weird that they were all wearing monkey masks." He kept his gaze riveted on her. *Why the hell couldn't she wear flannel again tonight?*

Opening the cooler and sticking her head in, she said, "Every show has at least a bit of the three main themes of the cabaret: burlesque, musicale, and cirque. Tonight was mostly burlesque, so the cirque act fit into that. Would you like somethin' to drink?"

"No. What themes do you imagine for the cabaret on Beta Tau?"

She closed the cooler without removing anything and looked at him, eyebrows pinched in a pensive expression. "Somethin' similar, but quite a bit more risque. The CC is a time-travel experience. Customers are meant to immerse themselves in the 1920s and '30s of old Earth."

The Patsy Trey had met yesterday would have spilled her plans in his lap. She'd grown cautious, which was his fault. He hadn't been circumspect about his doubts. The bins of stuff she couldn't leave behind attested to her fear that she was always one step away from disaster stealing her security. His intention had been to help her, but it probably didn't feel like that to her. What he had to say now would make things worse.

"Randolph will expect a lot more nudity, not just a striptease and sequined and feathered showgirls."

Her voice hardened. "O' course. We've talked extensively. I know what he requires."

"Do you?"

She squared her shoulders and glared at him. "I believe I do."

"I disagree."

"Can ya be more explicit?"

"Anyone with a ticket to a BDSM cabaret isn't expecting trapeze artists and monkeys."

She pinched her lips together, attempting to control her anger. "The actual acts would be refined. Rather than a scantily clad woman singin' bawdy songs, it would be a Dominatrix singin' about what she likes to do to her subs. She'd be dressed in black leather and carry a flogger that she slaps against her leg or uses interactively with audience members. Or a spankin' act could use a monkey to do the thwackin'."

"That right there is an example of what you don't get about BDSM. Monkeys spanking girls."

Trey could almost see the steam rising when she fisted her hands and said, "Burlesque is a parody, an exaggeration of real life and sometimes grotesque. That's its nature."

Now he was getting ticked. "Nature! You have monkeys spanking girls, and you've just associated BDSM with bestiality. That's a connotation Randolph wants to avoid. These are tourists you're planning to entertain. Most know little about BDSM, and what they do believe is often wrong."

"Aren't ya the one who's supposed to be teachin' me what BDSM means? So instruct me. Reveal these deep dark secrets that I'm unable to plumb without the assistance of a master practitioner."

His lips twitched. She'd taunted him to do what he'd already planned. The tension in his body eased. "I can teach you many things, but I can't make you submissive."

Cheeks pink, she responded, "I don't have to be a true submissive, just assume the role."

"You think playacting will help you discern the truth about BDSM?"

A glint of fire snapped in her eyes. "It's a start."

Warmth spread through Trey's body. He'd have less than three weeks to show her aspects of herself she'd never guess were hidden inside her. He was certain he could put her into a more submissive mind-set in the bedroom, but even with a limited amount of time he had to do this the right way. Tonight, he would hold off on sex. He wanted her mind clear to think about the lesson he intended to teach her. But tomorrow...who knew where he might take things.

"Patsy O'Shaughnessy, from this moment until we reach Beta Tau, you will be my submissive 24-7. You will do as I instruct. You will not speak unless I give you permission or ask you a question."

She stiffened. Trey pursed his lips. That was too strict a rule for her to keep, but tonight he wanted her thinking, not talking.

"We'll both be feeling each other out as we go along, so if you have a question, you will first say, 'May I ask a question?' If something is happening that puts you in distress, you may say the word 'red,' and I will stop and evaluate the situation. You may use the word 'yellow' if you wish me to slow down what I'm doing or need a break. I will determine if that is necessary, unlike with the safe word 'red,' for which I will immediately halt. Do you understand?"

Her eyes had widened, pupils dilated. She pinched the fabric of her pajama pants between her fingers. "Yes. What do ya intend to do to me? Why can't I talk? You're not going to hurt me, are ya?"

"I will do anything I deem necessary to help your understanding of BDSM grow. You chatter entirely too much, rattling off questions as they flit through your head."

She fisted her hands again. "I do not chatter. Or rattle."

Trey mentally sighed. "By remaining silent you will have the opportunity to discover the answers yourself. Don't overuse the right to ask questions. I don't promise to answer them, and I will take the privilege away if you abuse it."

"Fine."

"As to hurting you. It's not my intention to cause you harm or pain of any kind, unless I'm forced to discipline you. Punishment can take many forms and does not have to be physical, but you won't like it."

The angry expression left her face. "Okay."

Without taking his gaze off her, Trey settled onto the sofa. "Sit at my feet."

"What?"

Trey raised an eyebrow at her. "Sit at my feet. Make yourself comfortable. You'll be there for a while."

Patsy moved toward him cautiously, settled on the floor, facing away from him, her shoulder near but not touching his thigh, and sat cross-legged, folding her arms over her chest.

"Hands in your lap." He'd work on teaching her the proper way to kneel and present herself to him later.

He allowed five minutes to pass during which Patsy twisted and released the fabric of her pajama bottoms. She startled when he spoke. His voice sounded gruff even to his own ears. "When a Dom introduces a novice to the lifestyle, both he and his potential submissive spend a good amount of time discussing expectations and boundaries. I won't be doing that with you, but I want you to grasp how important it is for BDSM partners to communicate before they play with one another. Ours will be a brief eighteen-day tutorial that will end once we arrive on Beta Tau.

"Whether you acquire anything useful from this attempt will be up to you. At the Opio Institute, where I worked, the men and women who trained in BDSM skills had already determined their preferences. They weren't complete novices as you are. I realize you've done some reading on BDSM, but I'm going to start fresh, as though you know nothing."

Patsy cocked her head to the side.

"It's important that you have your facts straight. There's a lot of variation in how people approach BDSM, but Randolph will expect you to maintain an atmosphere that is transparent about the risks involved and that kink, as with all types of sexuality, must be consensual.

"You'll be dealing with audience members with varying levels of familiarity with BDSM. Those who are well versed in the lifestyle will call the cabaret out for anything that rings false. But most will be those who prefer vanilla sexual practices. They find sugar kink with its light bondage, spanking, and mild domination titillating. Beyond that the terms 'abnormal' and 'depraved' filter into mainstream descriptions of fetish and kink. My job is to give you the tools to reflect the truth of BDSM in the cabaret's performances, but I honestly can't anticipate if the result will entertain the average sex tourist."

It amazed Trey that Patsy had remained, mostly, quiet and still throughout the longest stretch of words he'd spoken to her since they'd met. Even now, after reiterating his doubt, she'd squirmed and huffed out a breath but hadn't requested permission to ask a question. *"A leanbh,* I will not let that deter me from doing everything possible to help you succeed."

Her spine curved, and her shoulders slumped forward. Trey winced. With the barest of nods she acknowledged his promise. He bent toward her and rubbed her back. When she straightened, he stroked her head. Earlier she'd done something with hairpins that made her look exotic with the green tips sticking out in little tufts. When she'd changed, she'd taken it down. He preferred it this way, soft with nothing in it to interfere with touching it. In an instant he slid his hand up her nape, threaded his fingers through her hair, palmed her skull, and turned her so he could see her eyes.

The smoldering intensity that met his gaze came close to crushing his resolve to keep from turning things sexual. His impulse had been to pull her onto his lap. With the way his cock had just responded, he couldn't do that. But gods, he wanted her there, wrapped in his arms where he could touch and taste. She smelled absolutely delicious and girlie. Rather than femme fatale musky spice, she was refreshing, delicate, floral purity. Not that she was innocent. No one running a burlesque show could claim to be an ingenue.

For now she'd have to remain on the floor. "Turn to face me."

When she settled, he assumed the persona of an instructor, speaking in a didactic tone. "There are different types of submissives. Sexual submissives are probably what you and the public think of when they hear the term. Another type is the service submissive. Sex doesn't have to be a part of that kind of D/s relationship and often isn't."

The heat had gone out of Patsy's gaze. Good. He relaxed. "A service sub has a strong desire to care for her master. That can include cooking, cleaning, managing his finances...anything he asks her to do for him. She may be a powerful businesswoman, but when she is with him, she allows him to tell her what to do. Her satisfaction comes from his appreciation of all she does for him.

"There's an important point here I don't want you to miss. Those in the lifestyle talk about power exchange. And it is an exchange. It's not one-sided, one person giving up his rights to another without getting something in return. Ceding power over your choices to another can always be withdrawn if the dominant doesn't meet his end of the agreement. It's not legally binding, but the contract between a Dom and sub spells out what each party initially wants from the other. As the relationship grows, that can change.

"I want to start by giving you a taste of how a Dom might treat a service submissive. Tonight there will be nothing physical between us except to encourage or discipline."

Patsy's face had scrunched in the adorable expression she made when confused. "May I ask a question?"

"Yes."

"I thought BDSM was all about different kinds of kink. Aren't ya goin' to show me what it feels like to be flogged or suspended in rope? How am I to know what is realistic if ya don't?"

Trey grinned at her wickedly. "I'd enjoy tying you up and dangling you high enough that I could tickle your feet. But two-and-a-half weeks doesn't allow time to demonstrate every fetish or kink to you. I'm sure there are some I've never heard of. Humans are an imaginative species. The private area of the Whip Hand offers a full menu of BDSM practices. You can continue your research there. My goal for the trip to Beta Tau is to provide you with an understanding of the dynamics."

The thought of showing her all the Whip Hand offered and then demonstrating it made his groin ache. He glanced away before returning his gaze to her. "The truth is, I see nothing of the service submissive in you. Whether you are sexually submissive, I have yet to determine, but it's not unusual for sexual submissives to be dominant outside the bedroom.

"I'm deeply attracted to you. You're very much my type, and I would enjoy making you my submissive, but it's important that you understand that a D/s relationship, sexual or otherwise, can be very intense. Sex creates emotional bonds. Our responses to each other can muddy the waters, and might interfere with your grasp of what I'll be teaching you about BDSM. This is something as your Dom, I will be evaluating. Safewords apply to more than just the physical acts we engage in. If you are emotionally or mentally distressed by our interactions, I expect you to use them. Understand?

Her expression was thoughtful. "Yes."

"I meditate regularly. While I do, I want you to face the other way and thoroughly consider everything I've told you."

She nodded.

"When I tell you to do something, your response is 'yes, Sir.' Do you understand?"

"Yes, Sir."

Trey watched as Patsy returned to her original position. He placed his palms on his thighs, closed his eyes, and began the breathing routine he used to start meditation.

During the hour he spent internally focused, her head fell against his leg. She'd fallen asleep. He eased forward and lifted her in his arms. With a mutter she burrowed into his shoulder. Unable to resist, he nuzzled her hair. So damn sweet.

In the bedroom he gently placed her atop the covers. The urge to lie beside her and pull her against him, to experience her body pressed against the erection straining inside his slacks, was powerful. Too powerful. He wouldn't stop with holding her. Once he was in that bed with her, she would be his. He'd tie her hands over her head with his belt and feast on every perky bit of her. That wasn't fair to her. She needed to be awake and alert before they engaged in anything physical. He shook off the desire pulsing through him, taking hold of the comforter on the other side of the bed and dragging it over her.

Tonight he was back on the floor. He'd sleep in her room because he ought to keep track of her. That's what he told himself, but it was a lie. He wanted to look at her as he fell asleep. The air was close and warm, so he stripped, pulled his pillow and blanket from the closet shelf, and settled himself on his side between the bed and the closet on the dense carpet. One more night on the unforgiving surface.

Patsy's hand, no longer punctuating her speech, lay on the edge of the mattress, palm up, fingertips poised in the air as though she were reaching out to him. He supposed she was. She needed Master Trey to help her make a success of her new job. But the physical attraction that was simmering between them was something else. Patsy O'Shaughnessy was special. He'd only met one or two women that had attracted him the way she did.

Her personality offset his own stolid nature. He was turning stodgy. Randolph had told him to have fun on this trip. His two weeks aboard the space liner to get to LS *Quantum* had been pleasant, but he wouldn't characterize them as fun. Not until her exuberant rush into the space station lounge had his trip sparked to life. Hell, he enjoyed Patsy even when they were arguing. Was he screwing up an opportunity for happiness if he limited their relationship to the time needed to travel to Beta Tau? Or by turning it into something longer, would he destroy his orderly, peaceful lifestyle? *Maybe vacation's the perfect time to try something new.*

Her hand begged to be touched, clasped tightly while he fucked her hard and long. Gods. He swiped his palm down his face. What if she wasn't sexually submissive? Vanilla sex hadn't been a part of his life for years. If that's what she liked, to be gently seduced and coddled in bed, he wasn't the right man. Exceptional though she was, attempting to make her something she wasn't would be a mistake. No other conclusion was possible.

The attempt to train her as a sexual submissive could be over by tomorrow. If she wasn't submissive, training her as one was wrong. Dominants were always made to experience the submissive side of the equation, to give them hands-on knowledge of what it felt like to be tied, spanked, or flogged. But that's all it was. They weren't expected to get into the head space of a true submissive.

He shifted to his back. I'll have to figure out another way to help her.

6

Patsy woke feeling rested and stretched, arching her back and luxuriating in the sensual glide of her pajamas. It wasn't until she rolled to her side that she remembered Trey and that she was supposed to be his service sub. He lay on the floor, one arm over his head. His blanket had been pushed low so that it angled across his hips. Every bit of his muscular chest and torso was on full display. The man exemplified the word *built*. If he had his way, she'd never get to explore the tantalizing buffet spread before her.

Such a pity. He said he was attracted to her but had the half-assed notion that becoming sexually involved would muddle her understanding of BDSM. *Feckin' man.* If that were true, why was BDSM defined as kinky sex? He had some other reason for holding her at arm's length. He'd said she was his type, which she took to mean he liked his women slender with small breasts. Or he was a legs man. She wore her skirts short for a reason —distraction from her lack of voluptuous curves. The erection she'd detected sliding down his body on the CC stage hadn't been her imagination. He wanted her, but he was restraining himself.

She'd put real effort into considering what he'd told her about BDSM and service submissives last night, trying to internalize it. The facts were straightforward. Service subs liked to *serve*. Not hyperspace science. But it wasn't her. Sure. She liked to help people, and certainly as stage manager at the CC she'd taken care of problems the players encountered. That wasn't the same thing. It was her job. Outside the CC, she didn't have a burning need to tend to anyone but herself.

The crucial question in her mind was, what next? Trey hadn't given her any directions to follow this morning. She was probably supposed to be preparing his breakfast, readying to serve it to him on her knees with a look of meek contentment on her face. Like she would ever want to do that. Which was why he didn't strip her naked and have his way with her. She really wasn't his type. He was a Dom, a Master. The women he took to his bed would be completely submissive. Not a chance in hell she'd fit that description.

How was she supposed to gain an inner understanding of BDSM if he was training her to be something she was not? How long was this taste of service submission going to last? It was a complete waste of time and effort. She would put a stop to it. But first she would get dressed. No more serious discussions while she was wearing pajamas.

Naturally he's blocking the closet. She slid from the bed and maneuvered her way along him until she reached his feet. His legs were spread wide enough apart for her to step in the puddle of blanket between them. With one foot lifted, she was poised to move when he turned his head and made a snuffling sound. She froze for a moment. Fearing she might lose her balance, she withdrew her foot.

The minute or two she waited to assure herself he was still asleep were interminable. This time when she eased forward, he remained motionless. She paused in the gap to release the breath she'd been holding. From this angle he looked like a Greek god in repose. If she sank to her knees, she could crawl up his body and be at his cock before he could stop her. Move his underwear out of the way, and she'd take her first taste of him. Her girlie bits tingled their approval. While she stood hovering above him, the sheet that covered his groin twitched. Fascinated, she watched it jerk again. The tip of a burgeoning erection slipped out.

Feckin' man is nude. And he's more temptin' than the apple in the garden. Stop starin' and get on with ya. Putting thought into action, she placed one foot between Trey and the closet, standing astride his left leg when he rolled to his right. She lost her footing and attempted to throw herself to the floor beside him. Instead she landed squarely on top of him, her hands planted to either side of his hips and her face in his crotch. Torn between nuzzling him or lifting her head, she pushed to a kneeling position.

Trey sat and stared at her, wide-eyed. A wicked smile flashed at her. "Did you lose something?"

"Ya tripped me."

"Seems to me, *a leanbh*, you should still be in bed. I didn't give you permission to get up."

"Your permission is no longer required. I'm usin' my safe word. Red, red, red, red, red." She glared at him. "The feckin' idea that you're goin' to show me what it means to be a service submissive is addlebrained. I'm no more a service submissive than ya are a unicorn. And stop flickin' your cock at me. I noticed it. It's big and brawny just like you. Satisfied?" Shifting to stand, she continued. "I'm gettin' dressed, so we can carry on this conversation fully clothed. I'll take my clothes in the bathroom, and ya can get—"

Unprepared for Trey to grab her and pull her back on top of him, Patsy shrieked and scrabbled to escape from him. In a move that left her trembling, he flipped her onto her back and covered her with his body. His face hovering above hers, he said, "I agree."

"Ya agree?"

"I agree. I'll explain. Later. Now I'm going to kiss you. Use your safe word and I won't, but the longer we lay here, the harder it will be for me to stop myself from ravishing you."

"By all means, ravish away. I'm happy to submit to that."

His voice roughened. "Are you?" Instead of crashing his mouth to hers, he skimmed her lips with his, gentle as a soft breeze.

"Feckin' man, don't tease me."

"I'll kiss you how I please, and when I'm done, you won't have any complaints."

"Prove it."

Rather than respond with words, he chuckled and returned to his task with greater fervency, delving inside her mouth. She sucked on his tongue, reveling in the taste of sizzling hot man. His kiss may have begun in the shallows, but now he was taking her to depths she'd never experienced.

She was in over her head, but arousal buoyed her, lifting her to float on waves of pure carnality.

When he pulled back, she drew in a breath and gazed into the face of the stern, dominant man who personified the title of Master.

"Nothing to say?"

He waited a beat. "I didn't think so." He rose to his feet and stood over her.

Is that it? Is he going to kiss me like that and then deny me because I'm not submissive enough for him?

With her heart drumming and her lungs refusing to work properly, she allowed him to pull her to stand.

"Take your clothes off."

Every nerve in her body chose that moment to tingle with an extra burst of energy.

"Now, *a leanbh*. I don't like to wait."

She gave him a cheeky grin. "Yes, sir." She toyed with her top button for a few seconds, waiting for a reaction. Even though she wanted to be naked before this man, to have every inch of herself available to him, she intended to ignore his warning and take her time. When he narrowed his eyebrows at her, she unbuttoned her pajama shirt, slipped it off. The faux silk dragged over her hypersensitive nipples, stimulating them to hard peaks. The heat of his gaze burned a trail along her flesh.

"You're trying my patience."

She pushed the pants to her ankles with languorous movements, slid one foot from a bunched-up pajama leg, and flicked the other to send the garment sailing past him. "Am I?"

With a growl he ripped the covers from the bed. An excited shudder coursed through her. His hands clamped around her waist, he lifted her as though she weighed nothing and set her in the center of the mattress. "Stay there."

The decision to comply or not was easy. The man was glorious, both fully aroused and smoldering with irritation. Her curiosity to discover what he would do next won out. She lay still, observing his every action, sitting abruptly when he tore a long strip from the sheet. "What are ya doin'? I'll have to pay for that."

He grunted and glared at her.

"Fine. You're obviously in a state," she said, waving a hand in the air. "Rip the thing to shreds if it pleases ya."

"I intend to."

"Don't let me stop ya."

"I won't."

Patsy flopped back down, muttering to herself. "Can't handle a taste of his own without gettin' bothered and shreddin' the linens."

After knotting several strips, Trey crawled up the foot of the bed and sat astride her.

"Ya didn't wear your underpants last night."

"I got hot." He gripped her arms and brought her hands above her head. It took less than a minute for him to wrap the torn sheet around her wrists and securely tie them together.

"You'll notice I'm complyin'. Lettin' ya have your way with me."

"You're every dominant's dream submissive."

"I live to please."

He tugged on the binding. "Is that too tight?"

"No. I'm as happy as a dog with four mickies."

"I'll take that to mean it's fine. I'm from Tallav, not Ireland."

"Amhail is dá mba d'fhéadfadh mé dearmad."

Fingers gripping her face, he bent and kissed her long and hard, biting her lower lip as he pulled away. "Retribution will be sweet."

Her stomach quivered, but the rest of her craved another kiss. He slid up her body until his erection was tapping her chin while he secured each end of the strip of sheet to the bedposts. Patsy lifted her head and licked his cock, ending with a swirling flourish on the tip.

With a groan Trey sat back and gazed at her. She smirked and smacked her lips. "Yum."

"Like the taste? Let's see how good you are at sucking dick, *a leanbh*." He tapped the plump head on her mouth.

She hadn't been exaggerating when she described his cock as big and brawny. Sure the length was longer than average, but its girth was greater than she'd ever seen. "Ya have a stout tool there, but I'll do my best." Mouth wide she swallowed as much as she could. He shifted, held her by the nape with one hand, and pushed deeper with rhythmic thrusts.

"Take more, *a leanbh*."

Tears formed at the backs of her eyes. She fought her gag reflex, wanting to prove she could satisfy him. The musky scent of aroused male filled her nose. Her hips rocked. Her pussy was ready for the action to move lower. The salty taste of his pre-cum slipped along her tongue. Above her Trey groaned, his chest rising and falling rapidly with each breath he took. He pulled from her mouth.

His voice gruff, he said, "I like your best."

"You're welcome."

He grunted. "I believe I owe you some retribution."

Patsy jerked at the sheet binding her arms above her head. "Do your worst. Ya won't get me trussed like a Christmas goose so easy in the future." She'd meant to sound impudent, but her breathing hadn't yet recovered, so it came out sounding husky and seductive. His chuckle, low and filled with gravel, sent an ache skittering from her nipples straight to her clit.

"If I want easy, I'm sure I can find it."

EVERY INCH OF Trey's skin was alive with sensation. The merest touch or brush against it stirred the desire pulsing through him. He'd gone longer without a woman than the three weeks since he'd last played at the Whip Hand. It wasn't the lack of sex that had need coiling tight in his core, ready to spring and take until he found release. Patsy O'Shaughnessy brought something out of him that wanted more, that believed more was possible with this redheaded vixen.

Wasn't it like a lady fox to lead him on a merry chase before allowing him to have his way? If that's how she liked to play the game of dominance and submission, he could oblige her, because ultimately he'd have her right where she was now, bound beneath him.

He slid down her body so they were face-to-face. "*A leanbh—*"

"I'm not a child." Her eyes glittered.

"No, you're not. And I'm not your instructor."

A smirk played around the edges of her mouth, the precursor to saying something pert, but the time for banter was at an end. When his lips touched hers, a breathy sigh met him. Then he was claiming her. Heat and fervor encountered an equal measure of passion. Male musk from his groin clung to her, mingling with the sweet, flowery fragrance that was pure Patsy.

The slip and slide of her tongue along his incited his need to penetrate her in every way possible. If his cock had been closer to her entrance, he would have thrust into her, but their difference in height spared him. Control now would lead to a greater reward. He wasn't a young man unable to restrain himself. Besides, there was a small matter of retribution to be meted out.

He ended the kiss and waited until she opened her eyes. "No more words unless they involve begging."

"What if I feel the consumin' urge to shout out 'yes, Master' or extol your godlike abilities?"

A half smile slipped past his guard. "That would be permissible."

"Oh, ya smiled. Don't hurt yourself."

"That kind of remark will only add to my vengeance."

"You're serious."

"I am. Now hush."

Not waiting for a response, Trey eased down, spreading her legs with one knee and trailing kisses and nips along her neck and collarbone. When he reached her breasts, he rose on his elbows and palmed both. "Beautiful."

"Small."

Trey glared at her and growled. "Hush. They're perfect." He swept his tongue over her nipple, sucking it into his mouth as it tightened. Patsy's mewl of satisfaction was all the affirmation he needed to continue his ministrations to one and then the other of her breasts.

"Trey, please."

Exhilaration swept him. She was already begging. He pulled the nipple he'd been lavishing attention on taut and released it, watching it jiggle, and grinned. "Please what?"

"Ya know what."

"I don't believe I do."

He alternated between breasts, making each shake in turn.

"Stop playin' with my tits and get on with it."

"But I like playing with your tits. Stop squirming. You're interfering with creating the perfect bounce."

"Feckin' man."

"Now, now, now. You wouldn't want to add to the retribution you're receiving."

"You're punishin' me by keepin' me waitin'?"

"I said you wouldn't like it. If you keep talking, it will get worse. I expect to be obeyed."

"Jesus, Mary and Joseph, and all the saints besides!"

"Won't help you. Hush and try to remain still. I'll move on when I'm ready to and not a second before." He sucked her nipple in and flicked his tongue over the tip inside his mouth.

"Unh."

Over the next few minutes he concentrated on lavishing attention on Patsy's breasts, which really were quite exceptional, rosy pink and so responsive. Their hue was a perfect match for the scent that inundated his senses. Roses were one of the few flowers he could identify. It was another measure of how flawless she was that her nipples made him think of scented rose petals, increasing his need to discover the color, taste, and smell of her pussy.

He moved his other knee between her legs and lifted back on his heels. Spread before him, Patsy was an exquisite sight. Her hair was mussed, lime-green tips pointing in all directions. She stared at him from a haze of arousal that brought a pang to his chest. His fingers tracing patterns over the soft skin of her abdomen, he said, "You're everything a man could ever want."

She dragged the tip of her tongue over her lower lip. Without speaking a word the woman could tax his restraint. But first she had a reckoning to face. After scooting farther down the bed, he bent and kissed every inch of Patsy he touched, avoiding the feast that awaited him at the juncture of her thighs, until she was undulating beneath him.

"Please, Trey."

"Please what?"

"I need ya to touch me."

He slipped his thumb over the crease between her thigh and hip. "I am touching you."

"Ya know what I mean."

"Tell me."

A sound of complete exasperation was quickly followed by a raspy retort. "My pussy. Touch my pussy."

"Here?" He dragged his finger in a line, parting her red curls. *No lime green down here.*

"Yes."

With a smirk he stroked her again, ending with a swirl over her clit. "Like this?"

"Yes." The word hissed through her lips.

"All right." Watching Patsy wind tighter, her whole body straining toward climax, was an erotic sight that gratified him to his core. He was giving her what she needed, but on his terms, in his own way. And then he pulled his hand back. Patsy slumped into the mattress.

"That's one."

"One?" Her voice cracked.

"I'm going to bring you to the peak five times. I think that should satisfy my need for retribution."

"You're a sadistic feckin' man."

"And you're an impertinent feckin' woman."

Over her head, she waved her fingers. "Get on with it then."

He placed his hands on his hips. Patsy stared at him for a few seconds before understanding dawned. "Get on with it when you're good and ready, Master."

Trey released a deep, gratifying sigh. "I'm not your Master. Yet." He dropped his legs off the end of the bed and buried his face between her thighs, inhaling the scent of her arousal. Her sex was as rosy pink as he'd hoped. Taking his time, he traced along each side before slipping his tongue inside her vagina. Her flavor was full of feminine tang. He inserted two fingers, curling them against her inner wall, searching for the spot that would spiral her excitement higher. Her hips thrust up, and a whimper escaped her lips. *Found it.* He applied himself until she was taut as a loaded rope. Then he pulled away and pinched her thigh.

"Shite!"

"That's two."

Patsy writhed and yanked at the sheets that held her wrists above her head.

"Settle down. You'll hurt yourself."

It was probably better that Trey couldn't understand what Patsy muttered back at him. He might not be able to handle an additional round of orgasm denial. His erection was rock-hard and leaking drop after drop of pre-cum.

With his fingers and mouth Trey brought her to the edge twice more. By the time he'd said *that's four*, his libido wasn't brooking any more delay. He moved up her body, the sensation of her soft breasts sliding beneath him tightening his nipples into stiff buds. After a short pause to plunder her lips with a deep kiss, he slid higher and thrust into her. One thought penetrated the fog of physical lust that was close to overwhelming him. *Five. I said five. I can't come until she does.*

Rallying his self-control, he eased slowly in and out of her, moving his hips in a circular motion to give her the full benefit of each penetration. She responded with cries of satisfaction, meeting him thrust for thrust.

"Trey, ya really do have godlike abilities."

He was beyond words and intended to get her to the crest once again. Space and time shrank to this tiny microcosm where his body moved into her. The smell of sex permeated his senses, and the slap of slick bodies punctuated the sound of lungs panting.

Her body tensed beneath him. He croaked out one word. "Five." And she was coming around his cock, sending him over the edge. With his hands planted firmly on the bed, he reared back and came in an explosion that made his head reel while his body pulsed in ecstasy.

Somehow he threw himself to the side so he wouldn't smother her. But it was a near thing. She'd done him in. His heart still hammered, and his lungs insisted he suck in huge drafts of air. But at his core he was warm and light. Generosity oozed from his pores. When movement became possible again, he rolled to his hip and explored her skin with his fingers, not to arouse her. It just felt right to skim the softness that was Patsy O'Shaughnessy.

When her own breathing returned to normal, she turned her face to him. "That was lovely."

He ran a finger down her cheek. "More than lovely."

"Hmmm."

They lay still for a moment. "Are ya plannin' on untyin' me or havin' your way with me again?"

"I'll need a break before I try that again."

Patsy jiggled her hands. "So…"

"Right." Trey roused himself, reaching to untie the sheet from one bedpost. He grinned to himself. "I didn't realize I'd enjoy sex with a cantankerous woman." He could almost feel the glare she aimed at him.

"Cantankerous! Pot meet kettle. Not only are ya as irritable as an old cock without any hens, ya scare all the women and children with the stern expression ya always wear."

Gods, it's fun yanking her chain. "It's my face. I can't change it."

"Smile a little more."

"I smile."

"Not often. Unless you're plannin' some devious, sadistic, sexual—"

Finished untying her from the bedposts, he thumped alongside her. "You enjoyed it." He helped her draw her bound hands down, rubbing her shoulders.

"That's beside the point. Are ya goin' to untie me?"

"Are you going to stop berating me?" Her scowl was all the answer he needed. Probably not. "Peace, woman. I'll untie you."

When the strips of sheet had been pitched away and her wrists thoroughly rubbed, he pulled her into his arms. With her head nestled under his chin, his whole body relaxed, and he drowsed.

"What next?"

The question whispered across his consciousness. He stirred back awake. "We spend the next few days having fun and then go to Beta Tau."

"And us?"

He nuzzled her hair. "Definitely."

"Definitely what?" She resisted the urge to poke him with her elbow.

"Definitely us. Together. We should explore this attraction we have for one another."

"Good."

"You mean we agree on something?"

Patsy shifted against him. "Yes. But…"

"The cabaret."

"Yes. I used my safeword. If you're no longer instructin' me, how am I supposed to get that inner knowledge of BDSM before we arrive at Beta Tau?"

"You won't."

"I won't?"

Trey sighed. "That was an impossible expectation. I have a better idea."

They lay in silence, and Trey drifted asleep until a slap on his arm woke him. "Do ya plan to share your better idea?"

"Oh. I thought it was obvious. I'll be your expert consultant. You tell me your ideas. I explain what's wrong with them. We'll argue, and I'll get to seek more retribution against you. In about three years, I might be able to train you to become a proper sexual submissive."

"Oh. Sounds perfect."

"Yeah." He pulled her tighter into his arms and said, "Now hush. I want to sleep."

"Anything ya say, feckin' man."

Trey was too exhausted to smile, but he did laugh inside.

PART II

THE CRASH

7

Trey yanked his shirt from the locker, grabbed his comm, and slammed the door shut. His leather pants had no pockets, just clips where he could hang his favorite toys, so he gripped the comm with his teeth and strode toward the exit while fastening his buttons.

Damn woman. This was the third time and by no means the charm.

It was the end.

He knew right where she'd be. Where she was every day and late into most nights.

The hall cleared before him. He slammed his palms into the slab of plasti-steel that secured the employees-only entrance to the Whip Hand, stepping out into the flawless weather that made each Beta Tau dome a luxurious oasis.

It was his own damn fault. And that more than anything chapped his brown ass. *Fuck.*

He'd known better.

Taught better.

Lived better.

Until he'd allowed that woman to snare him in a tangle of words and exuberance.

Worse, it had been fun. Until it wasn't.

He'd loved every minute. Until he hadn't.

And this was where it all led, inexorably, like an ungoverned tram, careening around a curve and sailing off the tracks.

He jogged to catch the ubiquitous slowly moving tram that would take him to Bistro Coquin, snatching the shiny metal pole at the end of the fourth row of seats that provided a handhold. Bistro Coquin, where Patsy O'Shaughnessy no doubt was spending her afternoon enjoying the camaraderie of her colleagues. Not where she should have been, tied in rope, submitting beneath him.

Muscles overloaded with tension, he remained standing on the running board, glaring off into the distance out of habit rather than unsettling his fellow passengers by making eye contact with them. Attempts at pleasant expressions had never garnered much success in preventing tourists from growing uneasy near him. The current look on his face would probably send them shrieking for security.

An equal measure of the frustration that seethed through him was directed at himself. Yes, he'd known at the outset back on *LS Quantum* that getting involved with the chatty bundle of Irish lass that was Patsy was a mistake. But the craving for her had overwhelmed his defenses before he'd been able to save himself. And so he, the epitome of all things Beta Tau, had fallen for a woman whose nature was the opposite of his.

Like the pleasure planet, he rigidly controlled all aspects of his life. The Beta Tau board of directors oversaw everything down to the height of the grass in a hidden copse. Their goal was to provide a self-indulgent paradise for the millions of visitors that came each year to let loose. Those who worked on Beta Tau committed to maintaining that unreal level of orderliness.

The Beta Tau lifestyle had slid naturally over him. He embraced it as an adjunct to the training he'd received to become a full-time Dom and eventual instructor at a top sex school. His existence had been one of peace and equanimity as the Whip Hand's dungeon master.

And then Patsy.

Fuck. The skin of his knuckles where they gripped the shiny bar strained tight. He closed his eyes and took a deep breath, counting to eight before he released it.

Sure, there were people that angered him. But no one like Patsy. No one who could irritate him as intensely as she could. Make him return to cursing like the hotheaded teenager he'd once been.

And the kicker was, he'd permitted her to get away with it. Any other submissive would have been long gone.

But no.

He'd allowed the pain that squeezed his chest when he thought of her to dictate a whole new set of relationship parameters. He hadn't been able to watch her leave his life for good.

Until today.

Something had snapped inside while he waited for her to finally appear. An hour spent attempting to ignore the side glances of the staff at the Whip Hand only added more heat to the conflagration her disrespect had ignited in him.

It was more than time.

He jumped from the tram before it reached the stop. An area of the street in front of Bistro Coquin was cordoned off. Workers were setting up heavy lifting equipment. To the side a large section of synthsteel pipe rested on a loader. It was unusual for construction work to occur during the day, but then the bistro was open into the early morning hours.

Trey strode around the work zone and slapped his palm to the bistro's lock. His access hadn't been revoked even though he no longer served as Patsy's BDSM advisor for Randolph's newest venue. He stepped into the darkened interior, making his way to an entrance that led to the offices. Expected silence billowed out when he opened the door.

She wouldn't be in her office. She wasn't working.

She'd say she was. But she wasn't.

Not really.

The door clicked closed behind him. He stalked through the foyer to the door of the auditorium that opened on its far-right side, flinging the swinging entry wide. But the built-in system that made it whisper quiet prevented the dramatic thwack he'd have loved. Instead his arrival went unnoticed.

One more reason to cut ties. She's turned me into a drama queen.

Three tiers below on the same level as the stage and to the far right, Patsy was seated at a pristine round, white table. She was leaning her shoulder into the overly handsome man whose arm was lying along the back of her chair. Her hand to her face, she was laughing hard enough that Trey expected to find tears in her eyes when he drew closer.

The man—Jovan was his name—wore a self-satisfied smirk, reclining in his seat, at ease. Whatever he'd looked like before micro plastic surgery, now his features were a little too pretty, verging on unnatural symmetry. It didn't seem to bother women as far as Trey could tell.

He knew the moment he was spotted. The smirk on Jovan's face changed into a sneer.

"Look who's joined us." His voice, that of a showman, filled the space. "It's lover boy." The others lounging around the table lifted or turned their heads, then resumed their positions as a tight-knit group, dismissing Trey immediately. All but Patsy.

She forced her chair backward, causing Jovan to remove his arm and straighten. "Bollix. I'm for it now." A note of apprehension was evident in her voice. Unaware that she'd caused Jovan's insouciance to slip, she dashed toward Trey, her hands held before her in entreaty. "I lost track of time. I'm so sorry. Ya know how I am. A feckin' idjit. Say you're not angry."

How many times had she said those exact words in the past? Hundreds, it seemed.

She suffered from one-more-thing-itis. There was always something that delayed her. Something small that morphed beyond a minute or two to thirty or more. He'd adapted, but it was on his list of habits he intended to break her of.

Or had planned to…

Pain flooded his chest. Breathing took effort.

No more plans. This was the end.

She flung herself against him, and his body tensed. Those sweet curves would not overrule his decision. The inflexibility of his stance communicated to her, and she too stiffened, pulling back and staring up, soft blue eyes wide, her gaze searching his face. "I am sorry."

"I know." Looking away, he dragged a palm over his bare scalp. "Let's go to your office." This shouldn't play out in front of riveted spectators.

The warmth from her fingers brushed his hand when he turned. "Let's go the back way."

That brief touch sent a spark through him that he squashed when he realized he had allowed himself to enjoy it.

"Right." The word came out with a harsh sandpaper grit to it.

Patsy winced.

Well she should. He wasn't the bad guy in all this. He'd bent over so far backward for her his head was between his legs, and this was what he got. Left with plenty of rope and no one to tie three times in a row. In. A fucking. Row.

Ahead of him Patsy's red head, no longer sporting the spiky lime-green accents she'd worn when they first met, bobbed through the kitchen as though she were hurrying on tiptoe. She probably was. Some dancer's holdover. Treading softly around him wouldn't change things now. Her voice trailed back to him.

"I don't know how I let time slip again. I was tryin' so hard. Jovan asked me a question, so I sat. It was an hour before I was to come to ya. I don't know what's wrong with me. I'm sure I deserve whatever punishment you're plannin'."

Trey didn't respond. The head of steam he'd been building had banked momentarily at the physical sensations her presence always evoked in him. It was restored in full by her excuses. The mention of Jovan's name alone would do that.

She shut the door and slowly turned to face Trey. "I—"

Stay calm. Get this over and move on. "This is the end, Patsy." He took a deep breath and released it. "I can't do this anymore. You obviously don't have the time or the inclination to put the work into our relationship."

"But—"

He raised his palm. "Don't." His tone heated a notch, the anger he'd attempted to constrain bleeding through his emotional control. "Don't give me any more excuses. It's clear you'd rather be with your theater friends. I get it. But I won't be relegated to an afterthought."

Her lips flattened. "My theater friends? They're yours too."

"You damn well know they aren't my friends."

"If ya'd just tried harder, ya'd fit in better with them." She crossed her hands over her chest, gripping the sides of her shirt. "They're great people."

He snarled. "They're Jovan's sycophants. I fail to understand how I'm supposed to enjoy being skewered by that asshat's snark."

"That's just Jovan." She jerked up her right shoulder. "He's like that with everyone."

How does she not see the truth smack in front of her? His voice deepened. "With you?"

"Sure." Her left foot slipped back, and she turned half away from him, aiming a glare at him.

He shook his head. "Be honest. He flirts and touches, cuddling up to you like you're his girlfriend, not mine. At least when I'm around. Is that all for my benefit?" Trey had no doubt that Jovan wasn't truly interested in Patsy. The man was a narcissist. He sucked all the attention in his direction and then preened, ruling over anyone caught in his thrall.

She thrust her hands high, slicing at the air with each expletive. "Feck. Feck. Feck." Turning to face him, she shouted, "He knows we're partnered. It's his way of bein' friendly." One finger jabbing at him, she added, "Ya have nothin' to be jealous about."

"You think I'm jealous?" He struck his forehead with his palm. "What a revelation. I'm the problem."

"Oh! Feckin' son of a..." Fists at her sides, she shifted from foot to foot and back. "I'm not sayin' that. This job has been—"

"No."

The word dropped like a thunderclap. He wagged his own finger in the air. "You can't fall back on that excuse anymore. The Bistro Coquin has been open to sold-out crowds for three months. You're not still finding your way. You're the creative director, not the stage manager. You don't have to be here every night. Half the time you don't even sleep with me at home."

She stepped back, her chin lowering, but in the next instant, it jutted high and her expression tightened. "I sleep on that couch right there"—she pointed—"and ya know it."

"That's not the point."

He lowered his head to the side, his shoulders dropping. It was as plain as her flaming red hair. She wouldn't, couldn't, he didn't know which, see the damage she was doing to their relationship. "We knew from the outset this was a long shot. I'm a Dom. I need more than you can give me.

This..." He waved a hand between them. "This whatever we've been doing is fucking with my mind. I can't..."

Her eyes had brightened to a feverish gleam. "I love ya. Does that not count for somethin'?"

A vise clamped on his chest, squeezing his ability to speak, to breathe. They'd never spoken those words aloud. Now when they were ending, she acknowledged what he'd admitted to himself months ago. He was in love. Understanding had punched him right between the eyes, revealing why he'd tried so hard to accommodate her, putting her needs above his own to his own detriment.

"It counts for a lot." His lips curled defiantly. "Aaagh!"

He clenched his hand, pumping it in front of himself before turning away. "It's not enough. You don't get it. Something's broken between us. Or maybe we built on sand and were doomed from the start."

His gaze connected with hers over his shoulder. "I'm sorry."

As he walked to the door, she leaped forward and grabbed his arm, staring up at him, unvoiced words seeming to play across her lips. He drew a finger down her cheek in a slow stroke. *I managed to make her stop talking. Finally. When it really doesn't matter anymore.* "Goodbye, *a leanbh*."

Patsy looked at herself in the glass she'd attached to the wall near her desk. Crying always turned her nose and eyes red, and she refused to allow the people downstairs to see a teary-eyed mess when she rejoined them. They'd know what had happened. How could they not with how Trey and she had been screaming at one another.

Oh, what the feck!

Over the months while the bistro was in the planning stages, and on through its spectacular grand opening, she'd nurtured relationships with the staff and the performers. They would be on her side. A thought tried to niggle its way into her forebrain that a "my side"/"his side" divide was the root of her problems with Trey, but she pushed it away. She left her office with a brisk stride, taking the stairs quickly.

The first tremor hit the building when she was slipping through the kitchens. Stacks of plates rattled. Racked glassware clinked. Three large stockpots lined in a row on the top of a tall metal rack slid, one precariously close to the edge. The thunderous roar that accompanied the second juddering quake swallowed the sound of the pots when they fell. She flew to the main floor of the bistro, where the others were on their feet nervously looking around, some with fear on their faces, others with excitement.

Jovan's gaze connected with hers. "There's been an explosion. Outside, I think, or the roof would be coming down on us."

She heard his words, but they didn't communicate sensibly to her. Her mind was frozen, thoughts trapped in squishy slow motion. *What's happening? I should do something.*

The oldest sister in a trio of cabaret singers—Patsy couldn't remember her name—panicked. "We're being bombed. We're all going to be killed." She snatched Jovan's forearm and pleaded with him. "What should we do? Should we leave? Are we safe?"

"Settle down, people." Jovan patted the singer's hand, his relaxed demeanor sliding off him, replaced by the in-charge general manager. "Everyone, sit. I'll investigate. If the building shakes again before I return, leave through the back by the loading dock. Alfonse, you know the way. Show the others. Above all, please remain calm. I'm certain this is not a bomb or attack of some kind." He slewed his gaze around, focusing on each individual. "Beta Tau security would never allow bombs in the streets."

A flash of heat engulfed Patsy. *The streets! Trey was out on the street.* The next instant she was running up the steps of the aisle to the top level of bistro seating.

Behind her Jovan bellowed, "Patsy, stop! Let me go."

"Trey's...there." She didn't look back, flinging the anguished cry behind her, not caring whether Jovan heard it. Breathing hard, she plunged through the double door at the center of the bistro and into the foyer. A chaos of dust and debris filled her view, spilling into the shattered windows and doors leading to the street. *Dear God. Is Trey out there? In that? Surely he got past whatever... I can't even see the other side of the street.*

She coughed on the grit filling the air, covering her mouth before pulling her shirt over her nose. She gingerly threaded her way through chunks of sidewalk and remnants of plasti-glass littering the floor.

The sight that greeted her when she finally reached the gaping entrance to the bistro sent liquid horror through her veins. Half of the sidewalk was gone, fallen into a huge hole. A worker in hard hat and coveralls was attempting to climb up a loader that had slid partially into the pit. It's vise-like claw still held a section of road paving, the interlocking teeth of the paving plate in perfect condition around its edges. The vehicle had landed on a large pipe, keeping it from skidding into the larger cavity in front and to its right.

Through the floating dust, Patsy could just make out another construction vehicle on its side wedged in the gap created by collapsed sidewalk and road plating. A jet of water hit a pipe secured to the vehicle's flatbed, sending a spray fanning wide, clearing a portion of the air. She slipped sideways through the broken door, inching ahead to peer inside the hole. *Is Trey caught in the disaster? Is he trapped? Crushed? Oh God, it can't be.*

On hands and knees, disregarding the pain from crawling over gravel-size chunks of rock, she crept forward. At a point where the sidewalk sloped steeply toward the crater, she halted, scanning the pit before her for any signs of a human being. "Trey! Trey!" Was that spot moving? Was it a hand? It blended in so well with the shadows. She couldn't tell. Her eyes were clogged with grit and refusing to focus properly. If he was there, Trey was buried. *No. Not possible. He left with plenty of time to get past the work zone. Hadn't he been gone before I got to the back stairs? Yes. There's no way he could be involved in this catastrophe.*

As she was backing away, her fingers nudged a piece of debris. She ignored it until a moment later it registered to her that this wasn't a chunk of sidewalk or the substrata on which all Beta Tau domes were built. She picked it up, wiping at the grime. *The shape... It's a shoe.* She rubbed it vigorously against her slacks until she could see it better and then sank to the ground. Her cheek resting against the pavement, she clasped the shoe, Trey's shoe, to her breasts. Her world condensed into a viselike anguish, squeezing her chest.

Body racked with sobs, her eyes too begrimed for tears, she lay there. How long, she never knew. She'd fallen into a timeless void of her own, full of despair and self-incrimination. *If I'd only gone to the Whip Hand today. I've been so self-involved. I shouldn't have argued with him. He would have left sooner. Now he's dead. He's dead, and it's my fault.*

"Ma'am. Ma'am, can you hear me?"

A sensation of hands traveling over her arms broke through her black miasma. A presence hovered over her. "Are you injured, ma'am? Do you feel pain anywhere?"

She scrambled to sit, coughing to clear her throat and giving the man squatting beside her a quick glance before turning her gaze to the devastation. "Help him." With one hand she grabbed hold of the man's arm and pointed with the hand holding the shoe toward the pit. "Trey is in there. Ya must help him."

"You say someone is in the hole?" He gave her a penetrating look.

"Yes. Yes." She forced down the scream that was boiling up inside her. "Oh, for feck's sake! Stop botherin' with me. I'm fine."

"Command for medic 615, we have a patient that believes her partner is in the hole." He directed his gaze to her. "Did you see anyone else?"

Grit clogged her throat, forcing her to swallow hard. "No."

"Did you see him fall?"

"No. But..."

His face revealed no hint whether he believed her. "Why do you think he's there?" The calm tone of his voice was beyond irritating.

She waved the shoe at him, shoving it into his hands. "I have his shoe. It was lyin' right next to the edge. He lost it fallin' in."

She struggled to her feet, resisting his attempts to keep her from rising, and bellowed at him as loudly as a hoarse woman could. "Do somethin'."

His response was yet again calm, but with an extra measure of authority. "Yes, ma'am. Equipment is already on its way to the scene. More med techs are standing by. My job is to get you to safety and medically evaluated. It's a requirement of Beta Tau law that you come with me. All victims—"

"I'm not a victim." *Beta Tau and its gods-be-damned cover-your-ass rules.*

Another worker pushed a hover stretcher toward the man, who she gathered by the patch on his arm was himself a med tech. *But he'd said that. Hadn't he? I'm so confused.* "I don't need that."

"Please, ma'am. I must insist. It's procedure."

She turned her gaze to survey the situation. What looked like a small crane was arriving. "Can ya be quick about it?"

"I can." He lowered the stretcher, assisted her to climb on and lie down.

He placed a mask over her nose and mouth. The pure air worked to clear her mind.

The man she was coming to think of as her personal medic explained, "This will assist your respiratory system to clean out the dust you've inhaled." Then he guided the stretcher to the second medic.

She lifted the mask and glared at him. "Stop. You're taking me away. My partner is trapped in that hole."

"I understand."

If he understands, why is he moving me farther away? She raised her head. They had arrived at an emergency vehicle. Her attempt to scramble off the stretcher was thwarted by the straps she hadn't realized restrained her. "Let me up."

The mask muffled her words, but by the frown on his face, she was certain he'd heard her. "You need to be a safe distance when they begin the rescue. If you'll lie still and let me make sure you're okay, you'll be ready when you're called."

"Promise." She cleared her throat. "Promise they'll tell me what's happenin'?"

He tapped a button on the headset he wore. "Command for medic 615, I have the buried victim's partner in EMV 102." He adjusted the mask over her mouth and nose. "There. The person running the scene knows where you are. He'll notify you of any news as soon as he can. Lie still, and let's get you taken care of." He slipped her left wrist into a cuff to assess her vitals.

THE HALL SEEMED LONGER than any other time he'd traversed its length. An urge pulled at him to retrace his steps and give his relationship with Patsy another try. *No. This is the right thing to do.* He plodded along, his heart beating in time to each footstep.

I need to get my life back. Peace and quiet. Order.

On the other side of the staff door he paused. Outside the bistro's entrance, construction workers stood behind a clawed loader while another man guided the operator to move it into position. Each person was doing their part, synchronizing their efforts, and the task was going smoothly. Soon whatever problem they'd come to fix would be resolved. That's what he'd wanted with Patsy. Harmony of purpose and effort. He would meet her needs, and by ceding control to him, she'd meet his. Perfect.

And impossible. A utopia that, fundamentally, Patsy didn't want. With a deep sigh he headed toward the center double doors. The loader was lifting the first plate. Trey exited the bistro, stepping out onto the sidewalk and closer to the roped-off work zone.

Unlike ordinary planets, Beta Tau's development had been planned. No odd streets twisting off unless management had desired them. Utility services were all underground so that inside the domes the public could play in pristine settings. Everything was monitored, so when even a slight blip was detected in the functioning of power, water, or sewer, it was dealt with before it became something big. Maintenance usually happened in the wee hours of the night. Curiosity pulled him to discover what lay beneath the street.

Within seconds of the plate being lifted free, the sidewalk under Trey's feet shuddered. He staggered. The man in charge of the crew yelled at the worker operating the loader to put the plate back in place. And then the world tilted, a maw opening before Trey with a thunderous growl. An explosion of dust littered with chunks of rock was flung into the air. Backpedaling against the pull of gravity, Trey tried to halt his slow slide forward. The grime under his feet offered no traction.

He dropped to his knees, scrabbling to hold on to anything that would stop his fall. Instead he rolled sideways, his foot scraping along a jutting slab of sidewalk before he tumbled into the pit that opened before him. His universe distilled into a hell of choking dust, his body no longer under his control. He struck a jagged outcropping, the teeth of a monster.

There were brief moments of sharp pain, but even the strike to his head didn't distract him from the impression that he was being eaten alive by the planet. He hit bottom, his lower back smashing against an unyielding rocky protuberance. His pelvis and back altered their natural configuration to conform to it like melting cheese.

Beta Tau's gravity had doubled or tripled, flattening him into a lead pancake. It wasn't just dust that made it hard to see. A large object was blocking the light from the hole. And it was moving. Rolling toward where he lay. Adrenaline zigzagged through him, sounding an alarm of imminent death. He struggled to rise, to escape. Deadened arms flashed to life, pushing against the uneven surface. But his legs wouldn't move. The action sent a cascade of roiling agony through his entire body, overwhelming his nervous system. His vision went black. He could still hear, but his fingers wouldn't respond to the screams in his mind to move.

The screeching sound of metal scraping metal filled the cavern. Tremors shook the ground beneath him. He waited for the moment when his existence would end, life crushed out of him. Instead an eerie quiet descended. He glimpsed patches of brown in the darkness. His eyesight had returned. Perhaps... Yes. He twitched his tingling fingers, overcoming a rush of pain to turn his head and look where his hand lay in a puddle of water.

He tried to move his legs, but again they refused to respond. *I must be trapped under something.* His shirt dampened when he touched his hand to his side. Continuing to explore, he pushed lower, his fingers roaming. His belt. His slacks. Nothing else. He wasn't pinned in place. He pinched his thigh. Nothing.

I'm paralyzed.

Heat mushroomed from his chest, flooding his face. A switch flipped, and every nerve in his body that had been damaged in the fall flared with torment. Some with the mild hurt of a fresh bruise, but others with a devastating intensity that made him shout choked, harsh cries. His lungs stopped working. *There's not enough air down here. I'm going to... Oh gods. Get a grip. You're making things worse.* He held his breath for as long as possible and then slowly inhaled and exhaled to a three-second count. The world steadied around him.

Pain still racked him, but at least he could think again, could consider his situation and how he could help himself. He looked at the patch of water where his hand had lain. Light reflected off it. By some miracle a bit of brightness had pierced this abyss. *No. It's not that deep. They wouldn't build a street over a massive void. It must be a sinkhole. But that's impossible. Every dome was built on bedrock.*

It doesn't matter how it happened. Focus. You have to do something to let people know you're here. Help is on its way. Just hold on.

He stretched his arm out to the puddle. *If nothing else, I won't die of thirst.* The water covered his fingers. It hadn't been that high. And it was expanding. The staccato rhythm of his heartbeat filled his ears. Soon the liquid would overflow the depression it was filling, and he'd be lying in a pool. How long before it covered the bottom of this pit? Mere inches would find it overflowing his nose and mouth.

His victory over hyperventilation was short-lived. And then a cry floated on the dusty air to him. His name. Called twice. "Trey. Trey."

Patsy. Did she follow me? Is she trapped in this mess too? Spots frolicked in his vision, unconcerned with his need to locate her. He pulled his hand from the puddle and scrabbled to get a grip on the hard rock beneath him. *I have to reach her. She could be hurt. Fucking hell. This can't be happening.* He pushed forcefully against the ground, trying to lever himself into a sitting position. The slash of fierce pain his efforts caused made his eyesight darken again. Sight, sound, touch. All deserted him. He fell into a different kind of pit, blacker and all-encompassing.

8

"**M**a'am, your breathing is still faster than it should be. Do I have your permission to administer medication to help your system settle?"

Everything that made Patsy who she was had vanished. She was hollow like a peanut shell that was empty when you cracked it open between your fingers. Nothing but a disappointment to be cast aside. *It's my fault. Trey could be dead, and it's all my fault. I never listen. I do my thing expecting someone else to pick up the pieces or cover for me. And now Trey is probably dead. And it's my fault. And I'm just lying here like a useless pile of crap. I have to do something.*

She lifted her head from the stretcher. "I really can't stay here."

The medic's voice soothed the crazy buzzing radiating from her spine to her fingertips. "This is the best place for you. On your own you wouldn't be allowed even this close to the scene. You're shivering. Are you cold?"

Her teeth chattered. "I a-am."

The medic tucked a thin blanket around her. "Is that better?"

"Y-yes." *Of all the times for my body to betray me. Trey is dying or dead, and I can't do a thing.*

"Now the medicine. It may make you sleepy, but you'll remain clearheaded."

Patsy slipped her hand from under the cover to take the pill the medic held out to her. Once she popped it in her mouth, he offered her a cup of water. She drank it, swallowing the pill, alleviating some of the parched dryness of her throat.

"More, please." The words came easier.

The second cup brought additional relief, so she settled back, burrowing under the blanket, warmth seeping through her. Her eyes drifted closed, drowsiness overtaking her. She snapped them open when the emergency vehicle shuddered to life. "You promised I could stay here, close by."

The med tech was next to her, but now he was strapped into his seat. "I'm sorry if you misunderstood me, ma'am. I promised that the officer in charge of the scene would notify you as soon as he could. That still holds true. We've been asked to clear this area. They intend to bring the victim from the sinkhole to this spot. We're taking you to the ER at the BT Medical Center to be assessed by doctors. Any news will come to you there. Your partner will also be taken there."

"They've found him? Is he...? Is he alive?" Her lungs tightened around the breath she held.

"They don't know yet. A specialty unit has been brought in. They're trained to deal with disaster situations, to develop a plan to get to the victim, so he can be safely extricated and evaluated."

"How can you be so feckin' calm?" If she could reach the man, she'd shake him until she cracked his composed facade and made him realize how important Trey was. "Can't ya climb down to him? Somebody should be with him." *I should be with him. I should be in the hole instead of him.*

He craned his neck and glanced out the back window of the vehicle. "Not until the scene is stabilized. It looks to me like they're lifting a large pipe. Not sure. My view's blocked now." He patted her hand.

"Stop pattin' me."

"Yes, ma'am."

She gritted her teeth. *Yes, ma'am. Yes, ma'am. Feckin' man doesn't give a shite about any of this. Not me. Not Trey. Probably will be glad to get me off his hands at the hospital.*

He was still talking. "It shouldn't be long now. Once they have your partner in an emergency vehicle, they'll head straight to the Med Center ER."

The glare she focused on the tech didn't alter. "And I'll be able to see Trey then? At the ER."

"I can't promise that. It will depend on his condition and any treatment he requires."

Of course the feckin' man can't promise that. Why would I believe him if he did? I'll probably get better information at the ER. "All right." She settled back and shut her eyes again, pressing her eyelids tight against the ache of tears that struggled to fall. *Please let Trey be alive. Please.*

Her arrival at the emergency room was a whirl of impressions. She floated through the automatic doors and down a corridor, her spot on the stretcher an oasis of calm that heightened her disconnect from reality. The med tech communicated facts above her. Someone, a male voice, briskly snapped orders. Everyone seemed to be hurrying, each having something to do or someplace to go. She was left to struggle to make sense of it all as she was whipped along a route that ended in an exam room.

An instant after she'd been moved from the stretcher to an exam table, the med tech was gone. *Shite. I treated him awful. I should have thanked him.* Her gaze fixated on the grime covering her clothes and body. *I'm such a mess. Trey must be equally filthy. No, probably more. Please, God, they're already bringin' him in. Please, please, please.*

"Ma'am. Ma'am."

She glanced to the side. A nurse in purple surgical scrubs was trying to get her attention. "I'm sorry. I wasn't listenin'."

The nurse asked all the same questions as the med tech and rechecked everything he'd already checked. Interrupting by proclaiming she was fine did nothing to dissuade the nurse from executing her routine.

The woman's demeanor is identical to the med tech's. They must install that during their trainin'.

"The doctor will be here to—"

An efficient-looking middle-aged man in dark green scrubs stepped into the small room and pulled the curtain shut. "I'm Dr. Stangle. I understand you've been through a harrowing experience." He lowered his penetrating gaze to the tablet he was carrying. "I'm going to check your breathing." He moved a round metallic object above her chest and glanced at the tablet again. Without raising his gaze, he said, "Take a deep breath. Exhale. Again. Exhale."

Patsy complied. Moments later the doctor pocketed the monitor. He directed his next statement to the nurse. "Breathing treatment. Level one bronchodilator. A day and night cough medicine PRN. Base one nanite antibiotic infusion."

He turned his sharp gray gaze on Patsy. "Your lungs are clear. You have, however, inhaled a quantity of large particulate dust, which could lead to tracheobronchitis. To prevent this, I'm prescribing you two cough medicines to help clear the dust from your windpipe and bronchi. I'm also prescribing a breathing treatment to open and relax your airways and a nanite antibiotic as a prophylactic to avoid infection. The nurse will answer your questions."

The curtain swished open and closed, and the doctor was gone.

Patsy blinked several times. *All righty. At last someone with a similar need for speed. He's clearing the boards for Trey.*

The mindlessness inspired by the brief minutes of the doctor's detached examination was wiped away as the crushing weight of reality returned with hurricane force. A sob broke from her.

No, no, no. Keep it together.

She sat, scowled at the nurse. "I need to get out of here. My partner was caught in the collapse. They're bringing him here. Where can I clean up?" She looked down at her clothes. *How the hell am I going to do something about this mess?*

The nurse's voice was soothing. "Let me give you your antibiotic injection first. A respiratory therapist should come to give you your breathing treatment in about fifteen minutes. That will give you time to shower and change into a set of patient scrubs." She sent Patsy a weak smile. "You'll be out of here long before they'll let you see your partner if he's hurt as badly as we are expecting. Don't rush. Waiting takes longer when you have nothing to do."

Don't rush. Yeah right.

Her skin practically sang with relief as Patsy washed away the grime coating her. She scrubbed herself twice with the antiseptic-smelling soap provided in the shower dispenser and washed her hair three times before it returned to its normally silky texture.

The baby-blue scrub pants were long. Her fingers shook as she rolled the hems higher. The slippers they'd given her caught on her heel and wouldn't fit until she sat to put them on. The armpits of her scrubs were already damp by the time she wound her way to her exam room.

The therapist met her at the curtain, taking her by the arm to usher her to the exam table as though he could tell her shaky limbs were edging closer to giving way. Her thoughts were a disconnected mush. She'd been trying so hard to get to Trey's side, but the energy it had taken for that effort had drained her until she was empty, powerless, a mote of dust falling, aimlessly drifting on any breeze that came her direction.

It didn't take the therapist long to set up the treatment. Ten painful minutes later the machine stopped pumping medicated air into her, leaving an antiseptic taste on her tongue. Then the therapist was out the door. The nurse arrived with two bottles of pills, ran through her discharge orders, and had Patsy on her way to the ER waiting room. Bing. Bang. Boom. *Giving in is faster. Who knew?*

The ER family waiting room wasn't full. A cluster of tourists, all wearing the same shirts and pinched expressions, sat huddled, clasping cups of café, in one corner. A couple was speaking to the attendant at the desk.

High on the wall the vidscreen playing the Beta Tau news caught Patsy's eye. Nothing on the sinkhole disaster. An animated reporter was sharing the news of a sharpole born two days ago in the wildlife dome. *Naturally. They wouldn't want their guests to learn a street had collapsed and swallowed a man whole.*

The couple headed left. Patsy found a last surge of strength fluttering behind her breastbone. *Now. Maybe I'll get some answers.* She planted both hands on the plasti-wood reception station and addressed the attendant. "Have they brought Trey Johansson in? The man trapped in the sinkhole? He's my partner."

The woman scanned her vidscreen. "Only one victim has been admitted to ER, and she has already been released."

Patsy looked over her shoulder to the hallway that led to the ambulance entrance. An invisible corset tightened around her, stealing her breath for a moment. *Why isn't he here? Something's gone wrong.*

"Have they told you anything? The medic promised I'd be told what was happening."

Compassion shone in the woman's expression. "I'm sorry. I won't know anything until he's brought in. And even then, it will take some time. You're welcome to wait, but they won't let you back in trauma when he arrives."

"No." The corset cinched another notch tighter. *Please be okay, Trey.* "Of course not. I understand." She turned to find a seat, her toe catching on the rug, causing her to stumble.

Behind her the attendant asked, "Are you listed as the patient's next of kin?"

Patsy faced her again. "What?"

"Are you listed as the patient's next of kin, dear?"

"I don't know. I... We never discussed those things. Trey's"—Patsy swallowed a sob—"efficient. I don't know. Maybe."

The woman dipped her chin in a brisk nod. "Let me check. Spell the name."

"Trey. T R E Y. Johansson. J O H A N S S O N."

"And you are?"

"Patsy O'Shaughnessy."

A note of regret overlaid the attendant's voice. "No, I'm sorry. You're not listed. I can let you know his condition in general and where they take him, but you won't be allowed to see him until he's able to add you to the list."

The emergency vehicle entrance slapped open, and a stretcher surrounded by three medics was pushed inside and on through the automatic doors that led to the exam rooms.

The man lying on the stretcher was tall and muscular, and, underneath the grime that caked him, he was still wearing the black leather pants and remnants of the white shirt he'd worn the last time Patsy had seen him.

It's Trey. He must be alive because they're rushing.

"That's him. That's Trey." She rushed forward, halting abruptly at the invisible do-not-cross line between the waiting area and the hallway that led to the ER proper where doctors waged war in a no-weapons-barred fight to save Trey's life.

"They'll do everything they can for him. Why don't you have a seat? There's café, tea, and cookies in the alcove on the right."

Patsy's stomach churned, announcing its veto on food of any kind.

The attendant breezed on, this part of her job easily accomplished in automatic mode. "As soon as they assign him a number, I'll let you know. The tracking board will tell you where he's at in the system." She glanced at the vidscreen embedded in the desk. "Oh, there it is. TR1652. The board should show he's in trauma room 3."

"Thank you." *Okay. He's alive. That's good.* Patsy wrapped a hand over her middle and moved to an empty bank of chairs. She slumped into one and dropped her head, resting her mouth on her fist.

Mom? Every effort Trey made to move failed. His eyelids refused to budge. His mom's voice sounded indistinct in his ears. *This must be a dream. Mom's on Tallav.*

"He was always a good boy."

Definitely Mom. Mom? Mom? The dream disappeared in wisps replaced by the tantalizing embrace of sleep.

"He's awake. He just blinked. Trey. Trey, my love. How do you feel? Do you need something? Are you in pain?"

Trey grimaced, his gaze slowly focusing on the face of his mother, worry lines wrinkling her dark brown skin. *This isn't right. Where am I?*

She turned her face from him. "Peter. Get the nurse. Tell her he's awake, and he's in pain."

"Mom? Where am I?" Nothing made sense. *Why are my mother and father here? Why can't I move my head? What is going on?*

"You're in the hospital." Her fingers brushed at the hair he no longer had in a habit familiar from his childhood. "There was an accident, but you're going to be just fine."

Just fine! "I can't move. Why can't I move?" The heartbeat in his ears matched the sound pinging from somewhere near him.

Someone entered the room, and his mother backed away. "Mr. Johansson, we're glad to have you back with us." A petite nurse tapped the viewscreen on the cuff that encased his right forearm.

The effort to lift his head was futile, and besides, it hurt like hell. "What the fuck is going on? Why can't I move?"

Her gaze was both clinical and sympathetic, and somehow before she even spoke, he was reassured. "You're in traction to stop you from further injuring your spine. You were in an accident."

"What?" Trey examined his memories. "I don't remember anything like that happening. What about my spine?"

His mother had moved around to his other side and was plucking at the sheet draped over him. "Let the nurse explain. It's going to be fine."

"Nothing you can't handle, my boy." Trey flicked his gaze past the nurse, but his father wasn't visible. His voice had been gruff, full of the same rough assurance he'd given Trey during a variety of boyhood tragedies. This time it contained a hint of pain.

The thump, thump, thump in his ears was joined by a ringing that would surely deafen him if the nurse didn't answer soon. He brought his gaze back, imploring her with his eyes to hit him with the worst.

Her unwavering calm steadied him. "In addition to other injuries, you fractured your spine. The doctor will be in to describe your condition in greater detail and explain the treatment he wishes to pursue. We have you in a gel suit, suspended in a low gravity field. This is to keep your spinal column aligned and prevent further damage to your spinal cord."

"Damage?" The word came out with a raspy croak.

"Your spinal cord was severed."

No matter how soothing the tone was when someone told you that you were paralyzed, the blow was crushing. If it were possible to buckle, Trey would have sunk in on himself. *How? I...* The nurse continued speaking, her words not quite registering. His head spun, caught in a bleak, icy maelstrom that was pulling him into its depths.

"Most people who suffer such a trauma completely recover."

Trey latched on to the nurse's statement like a lifeline.

His mother brushed a finger across his forehead. "You're going to be just fine."

The nurse's voice became bright. "The doctor has an order for additional pain meds if you need it. On a scale from one to ten, ten being the worst pain you've ever felt in your life, how would you describe your pain?"

"What? I'm okay. Nothing I can't deal with." *Let me think.*

The nurse lowered her chin and leveled a stern gaze on him. "We don't want you dealing with it. You'll heal better if you're not experiencing pain. So what level?"

Trey grunted. "A three, I guess. But it's not that bad."

"Thank you. I'm going to up your dosage." She entered something on the cuff. "There. Let me know if you need anything. If you get hungry, I can get you something to eat."

"No. Uh, thanks, I'm not hungry."

On her way out the door she spoke to his father. "Call me if there're any changes."

"Unh." His father was a man of few words.

Trey shut his eyes, the only means he had to avoid his mother's worried gaze. "I'm gonna be fine, Mom."

"Yes, you are." Her voice was watery.

"No tears, Mom. Please." He slipped his eyes open to entreat his mother.

She swiped moisture from her cheeks. "No. No."

"Someone else is here and would like to speak with you." His dad had strayed closer to the bed. He looked pale. The roses in his cheeks that his mother had always made much over were absent.

"Trey? Can I come in?"

"Randolph? Sure."

His mother's reaction was typical Tallavan serving class when faced with a first-family aristocrat. "Peter, find Mr. Meryon a chair. Thank you so much for visiting. For everything you've done." To Trey she said, "Mr. Meryon flew us to Beta Tau. He's paid for everything." She brought her gaze back to Randolph. "We really can't thank you enough. Would you like some tea? I can fetch it."

Randolph, oozing confidence and charisma, smiled gently at her. "No, thank you. I've only done what any friend should." He turned his intense green gaze on Trey. "How are you enjoying being trussed up for a change?"

"I'm not."

"Never liked being tied up myself, much less for reasons like this." A broad grin swept Randolph's face. "I stopped by to see if you were awake yet, so I could take advantage of the short time that you would be. You probably haven't even thought of the details of your situation, so before you do, they're handled."

Trey scowled, attempting to lift himself only to be defeated by the gravity field. "Whatever you've spent, I'll reimburse you. However long it takes."

"Nonsense. I haven't spent a dime out of pocket." Randolph's eyebrow twitched up for an instant. He waited for a sign that Trey had heard him.

"Is that right?"

"Absolute truth." Randolph paused a moment before continuing. "Beta Tau corporate is picking up the tab, as they should. My lawyers are haggling over the minutia, but essentially they've secured you full coverage of your medical bills here on Beta Tau and wherever else you go to complete your recovery. You'll also have a substantial sum for pain and suffering."

Tension Trey hadn't realized he was carrying eased, the muscles in his shoulders and torso suddenly relaxing.

"The doctors will be in soon to explain your options. I urge you to consider returning to Tallav for your spinal surgery. You can be medevaced to Cahernamon, where your parents will be able to visit you while you are hospitalized. Adrianna, who sends you her love, intends to camp out in your room until you're completely recovered."

"I-I don't know what to say." He met Randolph's gaze with difficulty.

"I believe 'yes, sir' would be appropriate. Don't you?"

A grin played around Trey's lips.

"Oh, my dear, please listen to him. It would be ideal. Your father and I will have to return to work, and I don't think I could stand being away from you. I know the nurses and doctors will take good care of you. But... Please do as Mr. Meryon suggests."

Trey smiled softly at his mother. "Don't worry, Mother. I agree. It's ideal."

"Oh, thank goodness." She held up a hand to Rand. "And thank you again."

"That's settled then." Randolph gestured toward the door. "One other thing. I was asked to intercede for someone who would like to visit you. Patsy is outside. She's not allowed in because she's not on your list of next of kin or surrogates. You have to authorize it. Beta Tau is stringent on privacy rules."

"No." Trey's voice was curt, his reaction instantaneous. Visceral.

A line appeared between Rand's eyebrows, but it was the only change to his pleasant demeanor. Trey's mother, however, couldn't help but intervene.

"She's been waiting ever since the accident. Days, Trey. If this is some silly pride problem—"

"I don't want to see her. I… We're no longer together. Please tell her no." He gave Randolph a hard stare.

Randolph held Trey's gaze and soberly nodded. "Of course. I'll let her know how you are. That's probably what she wants. To check that you're okay. I'll pass along your status to Adrianna and Shane too."

"Thank you."

"You're welcome." Randolph punctuated an end to the matter with a slap to his thigh. "Well then. I need to make the arrangements for your transport to Tallav. I won't see you before you leave. My understanding is they plan to put you back under sedation as soon as possible. That low grav field you're in isn't conducive to healing bones. Mind the doctors, nurses, and your mom."

"Yeah."

"And you let me know"—Randolph gestured to Trey's mom first and then his dad—"if you need anything."

"Will do." Trey's dad reached out and shook Randolph's hand.

Exhaustion washed over Trey. His mind and body were disconnected as though he'd fallen into a wormhole and come out in a different universe. All that he'd known, assumed about his life had been wrenched from him in a havoc-filled event he didn't even remember. His eyelids slipped shut, too heavy to lift when his mother's touch brushed his forehead.

"You're going to be just fine."

His mother had faith, but even if he was physically healed, Trey wasn't certain he'd ever be truly fine again.

~

Patsy's whole body hurt as though she'd been the one to fall into the sink-hole. Her shoulders were knotted from vain attempts to relieve the ache in her back and a bum gone numb from days spent sitting awkwardly in hospital chairs.

Pointless.

Trey hadn't wanted to see her. Even from the hallway, his denial had been stark and immediate.

No.

Her throat tightened painfully at the memory.

Bigwig that he was, Randolph had obtained a VIP motorized cart. He'd brought her directly from the hospital to the Whip Hand.

People were still filing inside, employees and entertainers from Bistro Coquin as well as staff from the Whip Hand and others she didn't recognize.

Randolph held her back, recognizing that she was in no shape to field questions or acknowledge sympathetic remarks. It was impossible to hold high the boulder her head had become. Chin to fist, elbow on the frame of the vehicle, she propped it up, her gaze blurred on the distance until he spoke. "It looks like everyone has arrived. Let's go in now."

By the time she'd pushed to her feet, he was at her elbow. She'd never seen this solicitous side of her boss. But then Trey had always said Randolph was a gentleman first and sadist second.

The main floor of the large auditorium where the Whip Hand BDSM stage productions were held was half-full. Randolph led her to a seat on the front row before he mounted the stage.

She kept her gaze lowered, avoiding the tears that were bound to fall if she met sympathy in the eyes of her friends and coworkers.

She didn't want sympathy.

Didn't deserve it.

Trey had been right to refuse to see her. Thank God, he was going to be okay. But he had so much ahead of him. He'd need somebody. *But not me. He's made it clear he's done with me. The accident didn't change anythin'. Feckin' stubborn man.*

Randolph walked to the front of the stage. "Thank you for coming. Many of you want to hear how Trey is doing. I'll begin with that and get to matters specific to Bistro Coquin afterward. If you're not part of the bistro, you won't need to remain."

The rustling in the room grew quiet with Randolph's first words, attention locked on him. "I'll start from the beginning. A sinkhole opened in front of Bistro Coquin, and Trey had the bad luck to be on hand when it did. He fell in and suffered serious injuries. He broke his pelvis"—murmurs sounded—"and had other internal injuries that were corrected in surgery. His recovery is going well."

Several individuals clapped.

"But he also broke his back and damaged his spinal cord."

The hum grew louder.

"He's paralyzed from the waist down."

Behind her a man groaned, "Oh gods."

Randolph raised his hand. "I know. It's not good, but we're fortunate to live in a time when injuries like this can be repaired. Beta Tau corporate, as they should, is paying to have him transported to his home planet, Tallav, where he'll undergo spinal surgery and rehabilitation. It looks like six months before he'll be released. Nothing is definite except that I intend to make sure that he is taken care of properly."

"And Beta Tau? What are they going to do about this?" a woman on the other side shouted. A like-minded buzz skimmed through the auditorium.

"Don't worry. I have lawyers already working on holding BT corporate accountable. Any other questions?"

"Can Trey receive visitors?"

"No. He'll be under sedation until he arrives at Tallav. We'll set up a way for you to send messages to him without cluttering his private line."

He glanced at the man several seats away from Patsy. "Tom, can you take charge of disseminating that info when it's available."

Tom nodded.

"Great."

"How the hell did this happen?" A rumble of voices backed the question.

"The Beta Tau board of directors are as interested in that as you and I are. I've been told it goes back to the original foundation of that dome. The geological survey missed a small area of gypsum. Small being relative. Should have been filled in, but it wasn't."

The tip of Randolph's tongue was visible as though he were holding back his opinion. He shook his head. "A water main under the roadway sprang a leak, tiny enough that it created a high-pressure stream that washed out the gypsum over time, forming a void underneath the pavement."

"When things go wrong, they don't do it in ones and twos. A transport with a spare pipe was parked off to the side, which also happened to be right over the hole, and when the first pavement panel was lifted, the whole mess buckled into the sinkhole. Trey was caught in the collapse. No one else was seriously injured."

Conversations broke out as everyone tried to adjust to the idea of tragedy happening to one of their own.

"You'll want to discuss this among yourselves. Please do that outside the auditorium. I have further business to share with those who work at the bistro." Once the room had cleared, Randolph continued.

"Structural engineers have already evaluated the bistro. Their report should be available tomorrow morning. I've been through the building, and my uneducated eyes tell me that we aren't in serious trouble. Whatever is needed to make the bistro safe will be accomplished as rapidly as possible. Your salaries will continue to be paid until we reopen. Expect further information to come from Jovan Markovitch. Check your messages daily. This could take anywhere from a week to a month or longer, depending on the extent of damage. Any questions?"

"Can we get our stuff from the building? I could spend the time mending my costumes."

"Not until the engineers have declared it safe to do so."

Patsy stopped listening. Her eyes ached. Exhaustion oozed through her.

If only she could escape this bog of uncertainty, postpone life for a few days. Beta Tau was full of places you could take a mindless break, push hard choices away, and luxuriate in hedonistic pleasures.

Reality doesn't work that way. You're a big girl. Act like it.

Crawling under the covers and sleeping for the next twelve hours would have to do. Maybe her mind would work properly again. Maybe...

"Patsy?"

Drawn from the world that lies between awake and asleep, Patsy cracked an eyelid open.

"Damn, you look tired." The woman winced. "Sorry. I know I'd be falling apart. You're so strong. I—"

If she didn't interrupt, Viviana, one of the bistro's aerial artists, would keep talking and talking and talking. Patsy straightened and focused. "What did ya want, Viv?"

A light blush colored Viv's cheeks. Her hands fluttered as she spoke. "I wanted to tell you I'm sorry for how we… I… treated Trey before." The pouty frown she wore made her seem prettier.

Patsy's thoughts strayed. *Who looks pretty frowning?*

A touch from the petite brunette brought Patsy back to what the aerialist was saying. "We were really mean. I don't know why. He seemed like such a nice man, and well… Now he's hurt and all…"

"Thanks, Viv. He's goin' to be fine."

Viv sighed and smiled brightly. "That's wonderful to hear. I'm so glad. And I promise to be good. You can bring him to the bistro, and we'll all be friendlier."

"Yeah. Terrific. Thanks a lot, Viv." Patsy rose from her seat, pushing on the armrests to propel herself up and out. "I'm exhausted. I'm goin' home to get some sleep. I'll see ya in a day or two. Can ya tell the others I'm turnin' off my CBC messages?"

Viv's eyebrows knit together. "Sure. Is there anything else you need?"

"No. Just sleep." That was a bald-faced lie, but the truth was so deep and murky and filled with grief Patsy didn't have the will to look into that abyss.

9

Twelve hours of sleep had been reduced to seven, enough to wipe the worst of Patsy's malaise from her mind. But not all.

Tentacles wrapped around her thoughts and pulled the key from the padlock securing the invisible corset that encircled her ribs and abdomen, the corset that had at the hospital first stolen her power to breathe deeply. Tossing the key out of her reach. Ensuring she lacked the will to peel away misery's embrace.

She'd turned off message notifications from her EBC, so the pinging inside her brain shouldn't have sounded. The only person who had override privilege was Trey.

Trey?

Her stomach took wing. She thrashed her way out of the sheet tangled around her feet to sit.

A quick flick of her eyes to the lower left corner brought the message up to read. It was from Trey's mother.

Patsy, I probably shouldn't be doing this, using Trey's hand comm, but it's the only way I could reach you for certain. Trey is fine. He's under sedation again. They're preparing him for the journey to Tallav. We leave in a few hours. Mr. Meryon has hired a medical transport ship to take us. Mrs. Meryon will meet us to handle things on Tallav.

Well, that's neither here nor there. I'm rambling.

I'm so sorry you weren't able to visit Trey. I don't know what's happened between you two, but in the time you've known each other, Trey has never seemed happier. The vids and images of him in the last months have had more smiles than those from the last five years. And you were right there with him.

I shouldn't meddle. But here's my EBC address: SJ-TL-1092-375-1808. Call me anytime. Once Trey is feeling better, I'm sure he'll want to see you. Men can be obstinate about the silliest things. I want him to be happy. Take care.

Sylvia.

Huh. Patsy fell against the mattress, her head burying itself in its previous indentation in her pillow. She grasped the other pillow, wrapping it in her arms and snuggling it against her nose, letting the scent of Trey's aftershave curl around her awareness, invoking memories of past sensations.

Trey biting her earlobe and nibbling down her neck.

Trey sucking her nipple hard while using his fingers to bring her off.

Trey pinning her beneath him and…

A sob that had been building underneath the sensual responses of her body racked its way to the surface. *Oh God, I miss him so much.*

No more tears. Her gaze roamed the ceiling as she fought back the prickling behind her eyes.

Trey was leaving Beta Tau. If he didn't return, would she ever see him again? Not a chance.

The only man she'd ever truly loved. The only relationship that had ever been truly right. The only thing she should have truly wanted more than anything else. Gone. Obliterated.

And it hadn't been a sinkhole's fault. No. It was hers.

The real question was why. Why had she allowed a good man to slip from her life? It wasn't the dominance/submission thing. She'd come to enjoy that. So what? What made her sabotage her own happiness? Because the last few days had proven that life without Trey was the opposite of happy. It was miserable and bleak and god-awful lonely.

She lay baking in her own emotional desert, unable to return to sleep, her stomach nagging that it was ravenous after days of barely being fed.

I should get up.

Her body whined its aching complaints. Her skull drifted like a helium balloon, her neck a thin string keeping it from floating away. The non-contents of her stomach threatened to reappear if she didn't eat something, and soon.

Half dashing, half staggering, she arrived in the apartment's kitchen and wrenched open the cooler door. There wasn't much inside. Salad gone bad. Eggs. And individual containers of the sour-tasting health drink Trey consumed every morning. Orange mango. Strawberry banana. Or berry berry. She'd lived on earth. Knew how those fruits should taste. These were second cousins twice removed.

Beggars choosers and all that. Her mind was dribbling half-baked cliches. Berry berry it was. She drank it in one shot so the flavor wouldn't hit her until she'd downed it.

Gaaahhh. But her stomach loved it, settling and informing her brain that it was satisfied. Her head returned to its normal weight and landed in place on her shoulders.

Her system rebooted. Thoughts shuffled and organized themselves into a new order. And her course of action appeared fully formed in her mind.

There really wasn't any other way to go.

Her problems couldn't be instantly solved, but still the invisible corset released its hold, and a powerful surge—she wouldn't call it optimism, more like determination—straightened her spine and made her hands ache to do battle.

Her plan was simple. She would focus on two things.

First, do her job. Schedule the next year of Bistro Coquin's calendar with the best acts available, so she fulfilled Randolph's faith in her and could leave Beta Tau with her chin up. Because she'd have to leave Beta Tau to make the second thing even possible.

Get Trey back.

Funny. Trey's love of anachronism had provided her a hole to penetrate his defenses. He shaved with a straight razor and spent extra on the after-shave that she would forever associate with him. And he used a hand comm. He preferred not to clutter his brain or his eyes.

Now, even if he blocked her, which if he maintained his current atti-tude, he no doubt would. Even so, she had his mother's EBC address. Sylvia was on her side.

An insight popped into her brain like an EBC notification.

There that word was again. *Side.* Her side. His side. Somehow she had to make certain that when the opportunity to stand before Trey came, her side had become his side. No, their side.

Why sides to begin with? Did she have something innately wrong with her?

An accusation from her past surged to the foreground of her thoughts. *"You're so self-centered. Everythin' is about you, and only you. Don't ya care that you're tramplin' over the hearts of Mam and Da? Go your way then. Ya always have. Ya always will."*

Had her brother been right?

Things needed doing. She'd think about that later.

She reached for her grubbies, a worn set of pants and a bright blue T-shirt in the closet she shared with Trey. When she'd moved in with him, his clothes had been evenly spread out on the rod, no shirt or pair of pants touching any other. Now they hung as orderly as ever, but in one-third of the space. The rest was stuffed with her skirts and blouses and slacks and dresses.

What about Trey's stuff? Technically when they split, she would have been the one to move out. The apartment was originally his. She'd never availed herself of the housing that came with her contract.

Should I move out? Stay? Pack Trey's belongings and ship them to him? Will he continue to receive the housin' benefit? For how long?

She rubbed her forehead, turning and scanning the bedroom. Trey didn't have many things, but what he did own was important to him. *I'll have to ask Randolph what to do.*

Once she turned her EBC messages back on, her incoming queue filled. She ignored all but the tier one calls. That tier was limited to three people: Trey, Jovan, and Randolph. Four messages. Randolph's was brief, letting her know if she needed anything to call him. She opened the first of Jovan's.

Pats, sorry for the drama you've endured. Who knew that Trey would leave you and literally drop out of your life? Chin up. You're still my best girl. J

Wasn't that just like Jovan. Trey had been right. *What an asshat!*

The second message was worse.

Pats, if you've pulled yourself together, we need to talk. The entertainment side of the house are working themselves into a tizzy. Need you by my side, love. J

I am not his love.

Again Trey's words came back to her. *"He flirts and touches, cuddling up to you like you're his girlfriend, not mine."*

The true Jovan appeared in the third message.

Patsy, the bistro has been declared safe. You will be here and settle things back in order so we can open in two days. Be the professional you claim to be. Jovan

Trey had complained about Jovan's snark, and here it was aimed straight at her.

Why didn't I see this before?

Heat invaded her body, magnifying the thrum of her pulse. If only she could run from this apartment and never look back. Escape the thoughts hammering at the fortress walls she'd constructed to protect her inner self.

Trey had been right. How many times would she find herself admitting it? Love proved a potent battering ram.

Don't lie to yourself. Ya did see what was happenin'. And ya closed your eyes to it. What were ya afraid of? That they wouldn't like ya? Approve of ya? That Jovan would turn his acid comments on ya? That ya needed them to cover when you eventually screwed up?

Is it selfish to want to succeed?

Success required her to become indispensable to her colleagues. What was wrong with that?

And then Trey had dispensed with her.

This is the end. It was as though his voice in her head was accompanied by the knell of a bell tolling.

The approval of her peers had been all important, trumping her relationship with Trey. She had put them first. And he'd set her aside, claiming something was broken between them, that from the start they'd been doomed.

No more. Continuing to think about this would drive her back to bed, hiding under the covers. She had work to do, and like the professional she was, no matter what anyone else said, she would take care of business.

She marched out of the apartment, down the street to the tram, making her way to the bistro. Outside the entrance the paving, the sidewalk, the glass windows and doors… Everything appeared as it had the first day the bistro opened.

Her stomach muscles tight, she held her breath as she stepped lightly across the area where the hole had been.

It didn't give, not even a millimeter.

Inside, she didn't go to her own office. No sense in that. Jovan wouldn't be there. She found him standing behind his desk, punctuating his commands to the head chef with a thump of his fist that set his collection of dirty coffee mugs rattling.

"We have a contract with them. You will assure we have all the supplies needed for our regular menu. No substitutions."

The chef bobbed his head. "Yes, sir. Everything but the onions will be here. I can source them elsewhere. Sarah is picking up our order for broken equipment and glassware. We were fortunate that very little fell. The kitchen staff and servers are cleaning as we speak."

"Good. You may go." He flipped his fingers toward the door where Patsy stood. "About time you got here. Walk with me." He strode past her in full expectation that she would follow.

Her lips pressed tightly together, holding back the stream of epithets she'd like to send his way, she struggled to keep up with his longer stride. The coin had definitely flipped to the other side.

He led her down the back stairs to the dressing rooms. Farther along the stage manager was working with members of the props department to check for any damage on the show's set pieces. Many of the entertainers were flitting between the dressing rooms and the costume shop, while others filled every seat in the men's and women's dressing rooms, gossiping and bemoaning their travails over the last few days.

Everyone fell silent save for one aerialist whose back was to Jovan. "I will not have it. I want my act rigged exactly as it was before. This new man, this Josh, he says it is safer. I do not…" Her shoulders drew back, and she turned. Her mouth dropped open. When she spoke, her voice was muted, no longer strident. "Excuse me, Mr. Markovitch."

All eyes on him, Jovan lengthened his spine an impossible inch, faced Patsy, and thrust a flat palm toward the cluster of entertainers.

"This is what I've been dealing with because you have failed to do your job, wasting days at the hospital mooning over a man who didn't even want to see you. If you're done wallowing, please deal with your entertainers. I've already had to set the performance schedule. I don't have the time or patience to do your work for you."

Everyone remained frozen in place while he raked a final glare across them. Once he'd disappeared up the stairs, a sigh ran through the group as they relaxed in concert, turning to one another with pinched expressions, bringing their heads close to speak in hushed tones.

Patsy had stood rigid throughout Jovan's dressing-down. Professionals did not reprimand staff in front of underlings. And he claimed she wasn't professional. Well, she'd show him.

The feckin' man doesn't know who he is dealin' with if he thinks I'll allow him to treat me like this. I've earned my way at the bistro and deserve respect.

She stalked over to the aerialist, fisting and releasing her fingers to bleed off excess energy that wanted to explode from her. "Marta, explain what's troubling you."

The woman glanced around before beginning. "Well..."

Patsy reached out and touched her arm. "It's all right. I'm here to help."

Visibly relaxing, Marta explained her worry about the change in her rigging.

"I can understand how changes would concern you. Safety is our top priority, as it must be your own. Josh is new to the bistro, but he's not new to rigging. He's won awards for exactly what you're worried about. That's why when Bart left, we hired Josh. If that doesn't ease your mind, I'll ask him to take you through the reasons he's changed your rig."

"Thank you. I would like that. I get nervous. I've seen others fall. Not here, of course, but in other shows. I can't afford to be laid up because of an accident."

"No. I agree completely. I'll talk to Josh." Patsy turned slightly to speak with the other entertainers, but Marta drew her attention back, her voice tremulous.

"Ms. O'Shaughnessy—"

"Patsy."

Marta gave a slight smile. "Patsy." Then her forehead wrinkled, and she lowered her voice. "He shouldn't have talked to you that way. We all think you're wonderful. And for goodness' sakes, we're all so sorry for what happened to Trey. None of us blame you for trying to be with him. Mr. Markovitch can be such a bastard."

Although she was in total agreement, Patsy didn't say so; instead, doing what a consummate professional should, she backed up her boss.

"Mr. Markovitch is under a lot of stress overseeing the reopening. Once things settle back into routine again, I'm sure he won't be barking orders and scowling all the time."

She turned to address the others who had moved to cluster at the dressing room entrances. "Please bring all your problems with the reopening to me. Let's stick to getting the bistro up and running. Leave other issues to the side. I'll deal with those as soon as possible. I'll be in my office. My door is open. I appreciate every one of you. Please use an extra measure of charity with your coworkers. We all need it."

Four hours later she slipped her shoes off and put her feet on her desk, legs crossed. It was a toss-up which of them groaned louder as she settled back, her or the chair. But she'd dealt with the troubles of the various singers, dancers, comedians, and cabaret artists. Most were small. Entertainers, or at least a goodly percentage of them, needed a personal touch from the boss during a crisis. Thank goodness not all of them, or she would be here for another eight hours.

She ought to get something to eat, go home, and go to bed. More sleep was needed to make up for days spent dozing in hospital chairs. But her body was comfortable for the moment and refused to concentrate on thoughts of what it ought to do. She covered her eyes with her fingers, rubbing at the itchiness along her lashes.

Trey would have loved her coming home early. But he wasn't waiting for her.

She stifled the sob that welled up in her chest. Time to stop crying and bemoaning the situation.

The path through the debris clogging her life was obvious. It led straight to Trey Johansson. How she'd overcome all the obstacles to force him to listen to her beg for forgiveness wasn't clear. Yet.

But she had to make him see that he needed her as much as she needed him.

For now she would be the buffer between Jovan's testiness and the sensitive morale of the entertainers and artists. She'd fulfill her contract and earn the funds to follow Trey, even to Tallav if necessary.

Jovan had commanded her to be a professional. So be it. Who the hell wanted to be his sycophant anyway?

10

O*ne Month Later*

The fiery ache that had run the lengths of his legs immediately after his spinal surgery no longer affected Trey. He'd endured stoically, relieved when he first felt a flicker of muscle contraction in his toe and two days later in his thigh. One week after that an electric shock had struck his pelvis, leaving behind a painful burning that had taken extra pain meds to endure.

His doctors had congratulated him on his faster-than-normal recovery. For which he'd woozily thanked them.

Five daily rounds of upper and lower body range-of-motion exercises had begun the day after he'd had surgery. He'd advanced from sitting with assistance to walking with assistance over six weeks, and today had walked by himself for the first time.

Rehab on Tallav was nice, at least for those who could afford the elite hospital where he was ensconced in a recliner, king of his limited domain's sitting room. Adrianna was on the short pale-pink visitor's sofa, her daughter, Katrina, quietly pretending to feed her doll at her mother's feet. Experience declared that the peaceful scene would not last much longer. *Rambunctious* could have been Katrina's middle name.

A trace of amusement tickled a smile from Trey. Adrianna was sternly remonstrating with him, former submissive mentee to Dom mentor.

"You will stay with us at Gleann Millis. I don't want to hear another word about how you'll be fine in an apartment here in Cahernamon. You need fresh air and sunshine. Early summer at the estate is heavenly. Shane and I both insist."

"It's really not—"

She narrowed her eyes at him, resembling a hawk about to strike its prey. "I want Katrina to spend summer at Gleann Millis. And I won't abandon you to a dim little apartment no matter how many times your mother and father may visit or your mother brings you home cooking. We will nurse you back to perfect health."

"Mmm. I am not a child that I need to be babied—"

Katrina's head popped up, and she clambered to her feet, lifting her doll before her. "Baby." She thrust the doll onto Trey's knee.

He grasped it to keep it from sliding to the floor. "Thank you." A tendril of delight curled through him when a smile as bright as her mama's broke across the child's face.

Then she snatched the doll back. "Mine."

Adrianna chuckled. "Thank you for sharing."

The expression Katrina gave her mother, the doll clutched tightly in her arms, was enigmatic. Then she grinned and sat to resume her play.

"She doesn't share with just anyone. We're working on it, but for now you're one of the privileged few."

He gave Adrianna a knowing look. "It's all part of the conspiracy to bend me to your will."

"Is it working?" She combed her fingers through her daughter's dark ringlets.

Katrina admonished her doll. "Share."

Again soft delight threaded through him. "It is."

Who'd have thought I'd be such a pushover for a child? But it was true. By the end of her first visit, Katrina had embedded herself in his heart. Not many visits later, she had him wrapped around the tiny little digit of her right hand. The one she used to point at him when making demands. *Up. Kiss. Share.*

"You hear that, Katrina. Trey is going to come to Gleann Millis. Won't that be nice?"

Her expression solemn, the little girl spoke one word replete with meaning. "Horsies."

"Yes. Where the horsies live." Adrianna returned her gaze to Trey.

"Shane has promised her a ride on a pony. She's very excited." She paused, looking thoughtful. "You know horseback riding would be good therapy for you. Your balance, posture, even flexibility would improve." Her eyes widening, she feigned a look of wonder. "Another reason that you should stay at Gleann Millis."

He raised his hands and acquiesced. "Enough. It's still weeks away, but I'll come. At least for a little while. Who can refuse horsies?"

Katrina lifted her head and gave him a piercing look. "Horsies. Go horsies."

He smiled with the ease that Katrina fostered in him. Even so, an ache persisted in his chest since he'd ended things with Patsy. It wasn't as sharp. More like the afterimage that resulted from a flash of light.

Fading.

As time passed, it would be gone, and he would be healed from the anguish of leaving her. Heart and body fully restored.

Eventually.

That's what he told himself anyway.

To Katrina he gave a definitive nod. "Yes. Go horsies."

Adrianna slipped forward in her chair. "Katrina! Oh, baby girl." She scooped her daughter onto her lap and covered her with kisses. She met Trey's curious gaze. "That's the first time she's put two words together in a sentence." She returned to kissing the little girl, murmuring between each peck, "Wait till I tell your papa."

Twisting to avoid her mother's shower of kisses, Katrina giggled, patting Adrianna's cheek. "Mama. Eat. Go eat."

"Oh my goodness! That's two." Her face radiant, she turned to Trey. "Time to go before the hungry monster arrives."

Trey had met that bad-tempered ogre. "Feed the beast."

In less than a minute Adrianna had planted her daughter onto her hip, handed the girl her doll, slung her bag over her shoulder, given Trey a quick kiss goodbye on his cheek, and scurried from the room. A moment later she reappeared.

"I forgot to give you this." She slapped a folded piece of paper on his knee. "You should let her message you directly."

Katrina pointed her finger at Trey, her expression stern, but she didn't speak. Then the duo was gone until tomorrow.

He sighed. These visits were the highlight of his day, but they exhausted him. Proof that he wasn't fully recovered, if the fact that he could barely walk on his own wasn't sufficient. He shut his eyelids, his mind drifting but inevitably returning to that piece of paper. He was accumulating a collection.

But he wasn't ready to read what Patsy had to say. He had enough on his plate without getting tangled up with her again.

"Hey, bud."

His eyes snapped open.

"Hey."

The neurological physical therapist's presence thrust itself into the room on a wave of confident athleticism. There weren't many sports the guy hadn't at least tried if not excelled at. His physical fitness was both an annoyance and an inspiration. "I hear you walked on your own today. Good job!"

Trey grimaced. "I did."

"Don't look so overjoyed."

"I'm happy about it. But it's not enough. I'm still so far off from where I want to be."

"I'd say you're doing great"—he grinned his lack of regret at Trey's look of aggravation—"but you don't want to hear that. You're closer than you were last week, which means it's time to reassess your muscle strength." He tapped Trey on the shoulder, handing him his cane. "Let's go."

Trey followed him into the bedroom where the therapist converted the bed into an exam table. "Just legs and back. Docs are satisfied with your arms, shoulders, and neck."

"Lucky me." Trey climbed on, following the therapist's instructions to roll over, lift his leg at the knee, or resist pressure. His days had become a routine of therapy and exercise, eating and sleeping, and not much else. It didn't require planning on his part. Or worry about where his next meal would come from or which of his workers were slacking on the job or how he would spend his spare time. A little pleasure reading and a lot of sleeping. Patsy-free.

Maybe Gleann Millis would be different. Maybe he would find himself there. Maybe he'd figure out where he was headed in life. Maybe, maybe, maybe.

Absent Adrianna, Shane, and Katrina, would he find happiness? When he looked ahead, he didn't see answers to questions of where he would live or what he would do. Before him lay a panoramic bleakness that extended to a flat, featureless horizon.

PATSY LOOKED up from the calendar that displayed the Bistro Coquin's show schedule for the next three months. The male half of a contortionist act she'd booked for four weeks had broken his leg asteroid climbing. She'd been eager to see in person the bondage routine she'd developed with the pair. It involved one team member being bound and escaping behind the other's back.

Finding a replacement was made more difficult by the short timeline and the more general lack of acts that could mine the humor in BDSM. It had turned out to be easier to educate those who knew nothing of the life-style. Proven comedy acts skilled at the rhythm and timing of telling a joke could be taught. But that took time.

Jen Meryon stood in the doorway of Patsy's office. "I hope I'm not interrupting something important."

"Yeah, but I'm pleased ya have. There's nothin' more I can do to solve the problem I'm wranglin'. I'm waitin' on responses and none too patient." Patsy rose from her desk and waved Jen over to the sofa stuffed into the far side of the room.

"Are ya hungry? I've worked straight through lunch. I can have the kitchen staff bring us a bite to eat."

Three steps into the room, Jen hesitated. "We could go out. My treat."

Patsy flipped her shoes off and curled her feet under her. "That's kind of ya, but I'd rather stay in. The tourists may be our bread and butter, but they're a mite too fun lovin' for my current mood."

"Sure. That's fine. I'm not much for crowds either."

The quick smile Jen flashed at Patsy, combined with the way her eyebrows were squeezed tight, gave Patsy the sense that the boss's wife wasn't comfortable. But shouldn't Patsy be the one wearing that shoe?

A finger to her ear, Patsy commed the kitchen and put in an order for a platter of varied sandwiches. "Iced tea okay?"

"Yes." Jen lowered herself to the opposite end of the sofa, sitting with her knees together and hands in her lap, only slightly more easy than a treed cat.

"If you're on Beta Tau, then Randolph must be too. Will he be stoppin' by the bistro?"

Jen turned toward Patsy. "I'm not sure. He's dealing with problems at the Whip Hand; juggling staff changes from afar hasn't worked out well. The next week he plans to spend on the premises, evaluating the issues and setting things to rights. After that we have to head back to Tallav for some family events."

"It was nice of ya to come by for a visit." Patsy leaned toward Jen, ready to prod the woman if she didn't satisfy Patsy's curiosity.

She'd met Jen several times, but always with Randolph present. They'd stopped by the bistro during rehearsals before the grand opening. And they'd accompanied Beta Tau corporation executives on many occasions to performances, inviting Patsy to join them twice. But she and Jen weren't friends.

She didn't touch Patsy with the tentative hand she stretched out, but that was more a result of the distance between them. "I'll come clean. I was sent on a mission by Adrianna Tiernan."

Patsy clapped her mouth shut when she realized it was hanging open.

That Adrianna would approach her wasn't a surprise. She'd paired with Trey's mother in a plot to make Trey talk to Patsy, giving Trey her letters.

Over the last month she'd sorted and stacked her emotions in various configurations, poked and prodded at the rationalizations she dabbled with, and ultimately had come to no answers that either appealed to her or bore a tight bond to the truth.

What went wrong, and how can I avoid it happening again?

Perhaps Jen could help her sort through the mess. "A mission? That sounds ominous."

"Oh. No. No. Let me start over." Jen pulled the cuff on her long-sleeved blouse, straightening it. "Adrianna is a very good friend of Trey Johansson. She and Trey's mother have been discussing his relationship with you." She raised her hands before her. "I know. I know. What business is it of theirs? I'll explain."

Before Jen could continue, Patsy raised her hand between them. "Trey's mom, Sylvia, and I have been messaging each other since right before they left Beta Tau. She's let me know how Trey's doing and hinted, broadly, that she thinks we should be together."

"Adrianna does too. She believes he loves you and is pining for you. Even though he won't admit it to himself. She wants to bring the two of you together, if you're willing."

Patsy pushed back into the sofa and leaned her head to stare at the ceiling. The arrival of a member of the kitchen staff with their tray of sandwiches and iced tea gave her the time to consider her response.

Yes, she wanted to work things out with Trey. Had been trying to come up with a scheme of her own to meet him in person. But how would he perceive this level of meddling? And her bigger worry, was she setting herself up for another round of heartache? The odds she'd get a real chance of reconciling with Trey were so remote she'd been able to stuff into the back of her mind thoughts of the potential devastation that rejection would bring. Those thoughts were now clamoring for attention.

"Thanks, Ray."

He settled the tray between them, extending a glass of tea to each lady before leaving.

Patsy placed her cup in a holder in the sofa's arm, helping herself to a chicken salad sandwich after Jen took a ham and cheese.

Chewing slowly, she weighed her answer. "I am willin'. At least I think I am." She dropped her chin to her chest, her brows furrowed, her lips pressed tight.

Jen seemed to be one of those people who was not afraid of silence. The patient expectation on her face when Patsy finally looked up tipped the balance toward her asking the question that was tormenting her.

"Can ya love someone and still not be right for them?" Patsy glued her gaze to Jen, awaiting a confirmation that all was lost.

Instead Jen's gaze turned inward, her eyes rapidly blinking, making it obvious she was honestly contemplating Patsy's question, giving it due consideration.

Jen lifted the tray from between them and placed it on the floor, scooting closer to Patsy and taking her hands. Her gaze was direct, confident, and gentle. Patsy's stomach fluttered as a willingness to believe that maybe, just maybe, Jen could provide a solution rose within her.

"Love is powerful and can accomplish a great deal, but it has to go both ways. Adrianna is certain Trey is deeply in love with you. And it seems you love him too. So there is hope." She paused for a moment, silent and thoughtful. "Help me understand why you don't think you're right for Trey?"

The story of her life with Trey came pouring out of Patsy. Together she and Jen laughed at the funny parts, commiserated over the foolish parts, and hugged their way through the sad parts. Jen related her own history of discovering she was a masochist and the struggles she and Randolph shared in resolving issues both carried into their relationship.

For Patsy it was cathartic. At last she'd met someone who understood her journey from sexual naivete to immersion in BDSM. Had experienced something similar.

By the time the storytelling ended, they were both sitting cross-legged facing one another on the sofa. Jen patted Patsy's knee. "I think I've got some advice that will help you figure out what to do."

Patsy straightened her spine. "Spill."

"First, if you haven't figured this out, you ought to take it into account every time you interact with a man. Men don't always share what they're thinking or feeling. Some are worse than others. You have to remember that actions speak louder than words to some men. What you say isn't as meaningful as what you do. And it's definitely true that you need to pay attention to what he is doing if you're going to understand him. Especially if he's the kind to clam up rather than argue."

"I get that." Patsy swallowed the last chunk of ice from her tea. "Mmm. Trey sometimes does a lot of talkin', but it's usually instructin', not revealin' his innermost thoughts. The man's a meditator, so I know he has them."

A rueful expression twisted Jen's lips. "Yeah. Randolph is an excellent communicator, except when he isn't."

Patsy giggled. It was odd to be thinking of her boss as less than perfect.

Jen's demeanor grew serious again. "This next part I'm going to explain is something I believe I had internalized, but it was Trey's mother that gave it voice, who made me appreciate its importance."

The fluttery feeling returned to Patsy's stomach. Would this be the key that would ensure she and Trey reclaimed their relationship on the right terms?

"It's really simple. You can't control your partner's choices. Their decisions. How they see things. What they do or don't do is up to them." Jen made a slashing motion with her hand. "You can try to influence them, badger them, or emotionally blackmail them into doing what you want, but even if it works for a while, it won't work forever. And if it does, you have a piss-poor relationship."

Patsy slumped against the sofa. *Isn't that exactly what I'm considering doing? Forcing him to meet me so I can beg him to take me back?*

"What's the matter?" Jen's expression showed only concern. She didn't get that what she'd just said destroyed Patsy's hope.

Even to her own ears Patsy's words sounded dull. "No second chances then. Everythin' I've been considerin' is manipulatin' Trey to do what I want."

Jen gave Patsy's knee three sharp taps. "No, no, no. You can't force him to take you back. And from what I've heard of him, you can't manipulate the man. Asking him, in person, to reconsider his choice isn't underhanded. Adrianna believes he needs an opportunity to change his mind and that he's halfway there already."

A jolt went through Patsy, producing a quivery sensation in her stomach that usually meant she was going into chatter mode. Locking her hands together in her lap, she tried to steady herself.

"I'm close on to babblin' foolishness. You'll have a tough time shuttin' me up if ya don't finish what ya intended to say before my tongue breaks free. Ya still haven't told me how I'm to avoid splatterin' my heart and his all over the floor again."

Jen swallowed a laugh and rearranged her features, the picture of solemnity once again. "Unfortunately this next bit is the hard stuff. Even when you think you're following this advice, you might not be. It requires a lot of honest self-reflection. Honesty being imperative.

"If you can't control your partner's choices, you can control your own."

She paused, looking hard and long into Patsy's eyes.

Patsy's nerves jangled. She wanted to tell her to get on with it. *There isn't anythin' earth-shattering about controllin' your own choices. I've been doin' that for years.*

Jen pressed her lips into a line, gave a quick dip of her head, and spoke. "What I'm about to tell you might sound like I've stepped back into the good old days of misogynistic relationships. That's because I'm a woman addressing you as a woman. I'd counsel a man to do exactly the same. Got it?"

"Got it. Ya don't have to worry. I'm not a matriarchalist like ya have on Tallav."

"Good. Neither am I. But I started life that way, so I'm sensitive to making patriarchal arguments. Have you heard the expression 'what goes around comes around'?"

Patsy pulled her knees up, wrapping them in her arms. "Sure. Be sure your sins will find ya out."

"Yeah, it's always used to describe negative situations. But it holds true for positive things too. Mostly. Truly self-centered people like sociopaths never get it." Jen waved her hands in the air. "But most people aren't so lost that they don't want others to love them. Trey is a wonderful person. Remember that."

"Trey is a wonderful person. Always has been."

"Right. Here's the bit that drives the Tallavan matriarchal elite nuts."

Patsy tucked her legs under her chin, her focus riveted on Jen.

"If you put your man first, before yourself, he's very likely to respond by doing the same for you. Not a tit for tat kind of thing. And you're allowed to share what he does that bothers you. But he gets to do the same. It's a balancing act that works when you each try to do what's best for the other person."

If it were possible for Patsy to make Jen magically disappear, she'd have done so. Her throat was heavy with a lump she couldn't swallow. If she had time alone, this crazy feeling of defeat would dissolve.

She didn't want to be this vulnerable before a woman she was just getting to know. A woman who had let loose the genie in the bottle. The evil, nasty genie who bopped her on the head and nattered at her about her selfishness.

Maybe it was time she refused to deny that label. *Selfish. I'm selfish. And probably too far gone to make a difference with Trey. No, don't think that. If he's willin', ya can still put things right.*

How to explain it to Jen without losing a new friend?

Her gaze lowered to avoid Jen's eyes, Patsy began. "Before I left Earth, my brother accused me of bein' selfish. And I was. I was happy to be free of my family, to expand my world, and to live in exotic places. All children go through that. But I was usin' that same way of thinkin' with Trey. I'm not always the brightest bulb on the fairy light string."

Jen reached out and tapped Patsy on the ankle. "Hey, don't put yourself down. We all have flaws we see clearly and others we ignore."

Lifting her gaze to Jen, Patsy forced a watery smile onto her lips. "You've given me the most encouragement since Trey survived fallin' into that hole. Ya have a gift for makin' people perceive their true selves." Patsy wiped her eyes. "My new mantra will be 'choose Trey first.'" She snorted. "I should get a tattoo."

"See; there is hope. But if we're going to get you two together, there's planning to be done."

"Yeah." Assured by Jen's advice, Patsy's heart lifted. "We need ice cream. How long before Randolph will expect you back? If you're here all week and available, we could have multiple plannin' sessions."

Jen beamed at Patsy. "With ice cream?"

"What's your favorite flavor."

"Dark chocolate brownie."

"Mmm. Don't have that. I'll ask chef to stock some. Will cherry vanilla do for today, or we have mint chocolate chip?"

"A scoop of both?"

"Both it is."

11

---

ix months later

Although Patsy had been an eager participant in the planning stages to become the latest Irish émigré to Tallav, when she stepped from the shuttle onto the actual planet, her legs nearly collapsed.

Why am I here? The center of a pet project for rich people. Powerful people. A famous designer. A heroic Tallavan marshal.

Luck? Fate? Serendipity?

Nausea attempted to double her over. From the fuzz in her brain, if she stuck her fingers in her ears, she was certain the stuffing used to fill plush animals and fat suits was waiting to be drawn out in tufts.

Really bad timing. If you're going to have a meltdown, you should have done it before you left the skillet for the fire.

On autopilot her feet moved her into the customs queue. The agent's stern visage brought back memories of rocky-countenanced guild masters who considered it their job to make sure no one passed board examinations.

The answers she provided to the fierce woman must have been correct. She was approved. No need to collect luggage. It would be delivered. Instead she was the one collected. By a handsome man, part-time marshal, and the husband of Selina Shirley, the famous fashion designer.

"Call me Maon."

He steered her toward a car. A private, drive-on-the-road motor vehicle. *Huh. Maybe Trey gets his love of the anachronistic from being born on Tallav.*

Since her mind refused more than cursory attempts at thought and her body had decided wobbly was its new normal, Patsy did what came naturally. She buttressed her lack of confidence with false smiles and immediately began chattering.

"Maon, thank ya for pickin' me up. Everyone has been so kind to me. Your wife. Ms. Meryon. Ms. Tiernan. I'm so excited about comin' to Tallav. I know you're not doin' this for me. Course not. It's all for Trey. I understand. I never realized Trey had so many rich friends." Her face heated, matching the chili-pepper color that invariably followed when her mouth got ahead of her brain. "I mean—"

The masculine laugh that interrupted her explanation was accompanied by equal merriment in Maon's navy-blue eyes. "It's true. We are rich. I won't deny it." He shrugged.

"You haven't met Adrianna in person yet, but she's the commander ordering us to play our roles. Oh. She'll want you to use her first name, not Ms. Tiernan."

The windows of the car were open partway, a breeze ruffling Maon's sandy-brown hair. He flashed a smile at her before returning his gaze to the road. "Although I suppose *the project*, as I like to call it—"

Ha. Me too.

"—started with Trey's mother. She probably thinks she spoke to Adrianna, but I suspect it was more prying on Adrianna's part."

Patsy wasn't inclined to label Adrianna a busybody. Trey's mother had been such a godsend. And a definite instigator. "I've been messaging his mother since the day he left Beta Tau. She's been so lovely, kept me up on how he's been doin'."

Her gaze wandered to the passing scenery. Buildings flashed by at an alarming rate. She gripped the armrest next to her. *Wouldn't it be ironic if I were to die when I'm finally gettin' close to bein' face-to-face with Trey?*

"Try not to rip off the armrest when I make this turn."

She wrenched her gaze from the unnerving motion out the window to Maon's. His eyes were again filled with laughter.

"I'm a good driver. You're completely safe."

"I'm sure ya are. But do ya have to go so fast? I'd like to arrive with all my parts in the right arrangement."

"Trust me. If any harm came to you, I'd be toast with butter and jam slathered on and tossed out a third-story window. I assume the ladies haven't given you much backstory to why they're meddling with your and Trey's lives. You deserve to be armed with full knowledge with that trio plotting a romantic crusade."

Patsy peered at him. If she kept her focus on Maon, it might help her ignore the conflagration of worst-case scenarios that the swiftly moving traffic alongside them ignited. It might.

"I'm listenin'."

"The short version. Adrianna and Trey go way back. He helped save her from an evil megalomaniac. Bad guy struck back by kidnapping Trey to force Adrianna into marriage. The marshals rescued Trey. Shane helped Adrianna save herself. And the villain lived happily ever after on the planet where he's dictator for life."

"Wow. Trey never told me any of this. Just that he'd been Adrianna's mentor at the Opio Institute."

"Yeah. Randolph stole him from the Opio to be his dungeon master at the Whip Hand." He spread his hands wide. "The rest is history."

Her stomach dropped, seeming to roll into the footwell where her right foot kept rhythm like a snare drum. "Ya should keep your hands on the wheel."

Maon's easygoing manner urged her to smack him despite only having just met him. That and the brash tone of his voice.

She didn't.

What is it about alpha males? Do they all have a jackass gene?

"Not to worry." He rotated the steering wheel sharply left then right several times. "The car is easy to control and doesn't go off track unless you yank on it."

This one certainly has a full measure of asshat. "I'd prefer ya keep your hands where they belong and save any more demonstrations of your drivin' prowess for someone who enjoys your lunacy."

His grin was mischievous. "You're going to fit right in."

"I've no intention of fittin' in. If things don't work out, I'll keep my part of the deal like I did at the Whip Hand. That's all."

The we'll-see look he sent her direction was like alcohol applied to a paper cut. *Were all rich people so damn sure of themselves? Irritatin' man.*

Maon ignored her outburst and continued. "Randolph, Shane, and I have known each other since we were kids. Our friendship stuck over the years. We all married bossy women who attempt to run our lives. Mind you, I'm more than willing to allow my wife to dictate to me, but Rand and Shane are not as compliant. Put the three women in the same room, and they're soon plotting to salvage other people's relationships."

"Bein' bossy is your idea of fittin' in then?"

"Part of it." He smirked but didn't explain.

"Hmph."

"I'm completely on board. Selina explained it to me, and although I don't know you or Trey, I take her word that it's for the best. Trey is something of a father figure to Adrianna. I'm sure she's the one who got Jen, Randolph's wife, involved too. That's all that was necessary for this little female cabal to proceed. Besides, they have the blessing of Trey's mother."

He flashed another smirking grin. "If they needed the heavy guns, they'd have called in Selina's mother, Audrina, but they seem to think the battle has already been won. Trey just doesn't know it yet. Or that a surprise attack is coming."

"You're enjoying this."

"Definitely. Female magic at its finest."

Patsy's stomach soured. "Without them, I had no clue how I was going to get Trey to meet me, let alone restore our relationship. But this is real for me. It's my life. I don't want to screw up this one chance."

The expression on Maon's face sobered. "We know this is serious. It's not a game to us. Especially to Adrianna. We can help with setting Trey up, but you're the one who'll have to pull a rabbit from a stocking cap. Selina figures it will take about two weeks to sign the paperwork and finish on-scene preparation."

On-scene preparation. Is that the marshal coming out in him? On-scene. Who talks like that?

Her quiet laugh earned her a speculative look from the rascally man. "Then you'll be on your way north. A blizzard could come at any time and stall things."

Waiting longer than I already have? Not going to happen if I have anything to do with it. She sent him an anxious glance.

"Not to worry. Rand has shuttles capable of getting in and out, but most pilots won't fly in a storm except for an emergency. If things don't go well, you won't be stuck in a snow-covered lodge for the Tallavan winter."

Maybe getting snowbound would be perfect. Trey at her mercy.

THE SHUTTLE PILOT who'd dropped Trey off at the hunting lodge the day before had said it smelled like snow. A few inches had fallen overnight, adding to the previous snowfalls that had transformed most of this side of the Giant's Tit into a white crystalline-drenched land that would turn more fanciful minds to notions of winter fairies and snow elves. Someone like Patsy.

Damn. Adrianna had nudged him constantly to face his feelings for Patsy. Finally Shane, who was never nonplussed by his wife, had shoved Trey to get on with it.

The months spent at Gleann Millis had been good.

But he couldn't shake the sense that he was marking time, making no headway on his plans for the future beyond a generic idea that he should involve himself in the Tallavan men's movement. The lack of opportunity to freely choose his future and the relegation of all men to second-class citizens had driven him off planet. Fortune—or misfortune—had dropped an immense sum of money in his lap. He didn't want to fritter that opportunity away.

He was completely recovered. Well almost. And no matter how easy life was without responsibilities, he needed to get moving before he stewed too long in his own self-indulgence and turned permanently into Katrina's cardigan-wearing, raggedy-eyebrowed Uncle Trey.

And there was Patsy and her letters. What was he going to do about Patsy?

Randolph had offered the lodge on Rathlin Island, home of Briarcliff, his family estate. The hunting camp was isolated, a place where he wouldn't be disturbed by anything but his own thoughts.

As with most Tallavan first-family residences, it wasn't bare-bones.

Seven bedrooms, state-of-the-art kitchen, fully stocked larder with preserved foods that would last a year.

From his spot on the second-floor balcony that ran the length of the backside, Trey could see for miles down jagged slopes that met a tree line of birch and stunted pines. At lower elevations the variety and height of the trees increased, providing the best hunting.

Randolph had said that earlier in the fall, gamesmen would cull the wild goats and the deer herds that tended to overbreed. Birds and small game were in abundance because the island was predator-free except for its human population.

The air was sharp and had a taste of wet that Trey interpreted as the smell of snow to come. Up here where little grew or lived, it was supremely quiet. An occasional creak from the house and his own foot-steps, muffled by the sound-absorbing white layer blanketing everything in sight, were his only company.

Icy damp penetrated his bulky wool sweater. Time to stop stalling.

Inside he set the mood, aiming for emotionally comforting. His expecta-tions ping-ponged between a revelation of all he desired and Patsy in her usual mode, same-o' same-o'. After pressing a few buttons, he had the fire-place in the main living space burning and Bach's "Prelude No. 1" drifting in the air. Boots shucked to the side, he settled into an oversize armchair and picked up the first letter from the pile he'd left on the end table earlier.

It was a quick read.

The next too.

Third, fourth, fifth. All much like the first. Different details, but similar.

He pulled the most recent from the bottom of the stack. It too was written in the same vein.

His hand holding the letter dropped to his lap. Staring into the flames of the fire, he was flabbergasted. These were nothing like what he had imagined, good or bad.

They were missives from a kid sister, detailing her activities. How things were going at the bistro. Descriptions of new acts. Funny jokes she had heard.

Nothing about them. Their relationship.

No begging him to see her.

No demands at all.

And she'd maintained this veneer of... Not indifference. What?

Where was the sass?

It didn't seem right. What was she up to? Had to be something. Patsy ran on high-octane scheming. Not in a malicious way. She just couldn't keep herself from meddling or insisting others help her with her latest plan.

It occurred to him he was the focus of a monthslong Patsy project. A tingle of excitement hit his groin. He flicked the letter to the side and cupped his cock through his slacks. Damn if it wasn't getting hard. He sat perfectly still, allowing giddiness to play along his nerve endings. The import of what this meant flared in his brain, and a slow grin spread.

This was what he'd needed to proclaim himself fully recovered. That he had nothing to test its full efficacy on but his hand did not detract from his jubilation.

He squeezed and reached for his zipper.

A knock at the door, more an insistent rapping, disrupted the first attempt Trey had made to pleasure himself in more months than he had ever imagined possible. Who the hell was invading his privacy? Randolph had assured him the closest neighbor required a shuttle to visit.

The staccato drumming did not relent. He twisted his lips and growled.

Nothing had prepared him for the person standing on his doorstep, stamping her boot-covered feet, the only distinguishable parts of her body swathed in artic weather gear.

No hint of flame-red hair.

No hint of a dancer's body.

Not even a glimpse of her cosmic blue eyes through the long fringe of fur encircling the hood pulled tight around her face.

And yet he knew who it was. Perhaps because his thoughts were consumed with her.

No, that wasn't it.

Recognition had swelled deep inside him from the place he'd stowed each detail about her that he treasured. His heart reacted, blowing wide open.

Triumph filling his voice, he shouted, "Patsy!" And snatched her from the doorstep, depositing her in the foyer, fingers frantic to release snaps and zippers and buttons, to get to the woman beneath all that cold-weather gear. The desire to caress her skin, to skim her lips with his, to push his need into her, rushed outward in wild abandon.

PATSY HATED THE COLD. She'd grown accustomed to Beta Tau's perfect climate to the extent that winter in the northern reaches of Tallav represented her own version of hell. The exact opposite of the standard fiery-hot abode of flaming demons.

The shuttle pilot hadn't given her time for second thoughts, taking off once she and her luggage were clear of the landing pad.

By the time the door of the lodge swung outward, she was moments away from freezing solid despite the Irish dance steps she was shuffling through to keep warm in the dusting of snow.

Plucked from the wicked clutches of icy death, she heard her name bellowed and a shuddering slam. Trey appeared to have lost his mind, but the feckin' man was a joy to behold. More fit than she remembered. At least another ten pounds of pure muscle.

His fingers were roving over her, uncinching, unbuckling, undoing anything he could on her clothing. And growling between frustrated curses.

"Trey. Stop. Ya feckin' idjit. Let me do it. It'll go faster."

His hands dropped to his sides, and he stared at her, his chest rising and falling like a sprinter who'd run a record-breaking hundred-yard dash.

"You're really under all that?"

"I really am." She shed her coat, pulled her stocking cap off, and unwound the muffler covering most of her face.

The next instant his hands clasped either side of her head, warm fingers rubbing her cheeks, verifying the reality of her existence. He lowered his mouth to take hers in a kiss that didn't merely make her toes curl but made every strand of her depressingly straight hair kink.

His tongue slipped between her lips, and the taste that was distinctly Trey blossomed on her palate like a fine wine: broad and rich, the taste of dark fruits, and a finish that lasted until the next deep swallow.

He yanked her off her feet, crushing her to him, and consumed her as though a Patsy-free diet had left him starving. Lacking his physical strength, her response wasn't as obvious.

She was beyond anything save total surrender.

His to do with as he pleased.

A whimper slid from that swelling, achy place in her chest and between their joined lips. He groaned and yanked his mouth from hers.

"Take your boots off."

Her foot stuck halfway out. She staggered, grabbed onto him, and allowed him to wrench the recalcitrant footwear from her. Between both of their fingers flying, twisting, yanking, they peeled her from her clothing. Before the last piece had hit the floor, he had her against the wall, the still fully clothed length of his body pressed against her.

Every inch of skin he touched came to pleasurable life, fueling a greedy desire for more. He sucked her nipple into his mouth, giving it the attention it had never forgotten, sparking a need centered at the convergence of her thighs.

She wriggled her hands between them and worked at his belt, an occupation that required more thought than she could give to be successful. He brushed her fingers aside, wrenched, and unbuckled it. Snap and zipper opened in quick succession.

His cock exposed itself, straight and true, pressing against her. Solid. The tip damp against her belly. She found it with her fingers, caressing it in long strokes. Her reward was a gasp from Trey.

And then he was inside her. Twice he shoved into her in mind-blowing thrusts. "I-I'll make it good for you next time. I... Oh gods. You feel so perfect."

He came, a wall of hard muscle, plastered against her, shuddering in three mighty surges.

If Patsy could speak, she might have called it epic. But it was beyond that. Rampant happiness made her brain fill with butterflies and flowers and dancing sprites. And the single word whose essence pervaded every cell in her body.

Trey.

Face buried in the undyed wool of his sweater, Patsy clasped Trey's heaving sides. She stretched her right arm around his waist and trailed her finger down the center of his lower back, tracing a drop of sweat to where his buttocks swelled into the luscious golden-brown orbs she remembered. He had such a fine ass.

"Mmmph." His kiss found her forehead. "I..." He grunted, picked her up, draping her legs over one arm, and carried her to a massive black leather sofa. He settled her on his lap and dragged a dark blue throw off the back, wrapping it around her, tucking her feet in but leaving the side to fall free so his hand could slide beneath to stroke.

She burrowed into his chest, oozing contentment, and then lifted her face to seek his gaze, hoping to find a glowing smile.

She didn't.

But what she discovered was better. Trey stared steadily into her eyes, his expression soft, tension-free, no longer searching to find something inside her, instead savoring what was already present. His hand pulled away from her thigh so he could run his fingertips along her jaw. He claimed her lips again, and the taste of him burst upon her tongue, sending fireworks to her nipples and clit.

No no no. She resisted her body's insistent *yes yes yes.*

Before they went further, she needed to explain. Not to defend herself, but to offer him a new foundation, a reason to take her back. Which it seemed he was doing. But it couldn't be based on sex. That was such a small part of the truth.

In the brief pause he took to snatch a breath, she whispered, "Trey." Her voice sounded husky and seductive to her own ears.

"Mmm?" And he was kissing her again.

So she spoke against the caress of his lips and tongue. "Trey. Please. I need to tell ya somethin'."

He responded but without removing his mouth from hers. "What?"

It became apparent to him she had stopped returning the kiss, so he lifted his head. His eyebrows knit for a few seconds before his expression smoothed. "You're right. This is not how we should begin."

She attempted to sit, but he refused to release her. "Stay on my lap."

His voice, direct and solid and unwavering, dotted her skin with goose bumps. *Yeah. He's just goin' to have to not talk. Otherwise it'll be days before I finish ridin' him.*

"All right. But ya have to keep your hands still."

His smile had enough smirk to it to warn her she'd eventually pay in sensual currency for forbidding his fingers from roving her body.

"This is serious."

He pressed his lips to her forehead. "Tell me."

Safe, secure in his arms, she stepped off into the void that would become her future. His future. Their future if God listened to the prayers of a part-time believer.

"I've discovered some truths about myself. Truths I've done a bang-up job of overlookin' most of my life." She brought her gaze to meet his, looking deep into his eyes, seeing beyond the gorgeous brown flecked with gold around the edges to the inner man, to his magnificent spirit.

"I love ya, Trey Johansson. I said it before, but now I know it deep at my core, that you're the only man I've ever really loved. The only man I'll ever really need. Ya are my everythin'."

"Patsy—"

"Don't interrupt. There's more."

He lifted his chin, looking down his nose at her, and grunted.

"We were never an *us* to me. Not truly. There was your side and my side but never our side. And that was part of the problem. Part of my problem. Because of that, I had no trouble puttin' myself before ya. And I did. All the time. It was wrong. And I see exactly why now." She swallowed hard. "But not then when it would have made all the difference."

"Patsy—"

"No. Still more."

She heaved a sigh, shedding a bit of the tension she'd carried to reach this point. But this had to be said even though it proved she was a complete puddin' head.

"I put the bistro and the performers ahead of you because I was tryin' to prove myself. Not to them. Or you. Or even Randolph. To people I'll never see again. Back in Ireland. All the stuffy, hidebound members of the guild that stood between me and my dreams. As if I was a nonentity. A nobody. A daft girl who should let her betters think for her."

She thumped her fist against his chest from under the throw. "Damnation. I was creative director for a major show on a sophisticated pleasure planet. What more did I have to prove? Still I made everything about me. About what I wanted. What I thought I needed."

"I've"—she dropped her chin to her chest—"been doin' just what my brother accused me of before I left Earth. What I've done all my life. Puttin' myself first. Actin' selfish. Not carin' whether I was hurtin' anyone else by my actions."

Trey rubbed her upper arm, seeming ready to hear her out.

"Jen's the one who helped me see it."

"Jen Meryon?"

"Yeah. She came to Beta Tau with Randolph on business, and we spent some time together. Anyway, she let me spew my whole life out before her in one massive tear-jerking girl-talk session. We even ate ice cream."

She peeked at him to see if he caught the joke. Nope. Dead serious.

No tryin' to charm your way out of tellin' him everythin'.

"She explained relationships to me in a way I'd never heard before. Or at least never understood before. Things like actions speakin' louder than words when figurin' out men. And that you can't control your partner's choices, but ya can control your own. That if you put your man first, before yourself, he's much more likely to respond by doin' the same for you. Held a mirror up to me, so to speak."

Pain burst from her in a sob. "I'm always after callin' you an idjit, but the bigger fool is sittin' here in your lap, hopin' ya still love her enough to start over. Am I daft?"

"Daft? No more than I am. I miss hearing you call me an idjit. Is that daft?" He rumpled his face into a fierce frown.

The giggle that bubbled out of Patsy like an orange fizzy brought the smile he was hiding into the open. Was it too early to feel the edge of joy? Two of the building blocks of their relationship still existed: passion and humor.

"*A leanbh.*" He lost all expression.

Her heart trembled, beating a skittering rhythm.

"I appreciate what you've told me. More than you can know. Especially since I left you with no way to address everything I threw at you that last day. For that I'm deeply sorry." He drew his palm along his scalp. Then brought his hand to where the throw covered her, searching atop the fabric for her hands beneath. He captured one and squeezed.

"I have my own confession to make. This was my first try at love too." He moved his gaze from her eyes to where he clutched her fingers. "Sex. Power exchange. BDSM relationships. Plain unadulterated lust. I was a master."

His chest rose and then slowly fell in one of the calming breaths he used for meditation.

"But love? Not a clue."

His lips tightened into a line as though he were sealing in his next words until he got them just right. "My mother has been on a mission to amend that lack in me."

"What? How?" *Sylvia never told me this.*

The corner of his mouth lifted in a dry grin. "She took advantage of my inability to escape to read to me. Love poems by all the greats. She even tried Shakespeare, but Standard did not do justice to his stature. It was flat."

"But you like poetry. Right?"

"I do, but this wasn't poetry reading. It was my mother's never subtle way of reinforcing her point, stressing particular lines, squeezing my hand after passages she found profoundly valid."

He shook his head, his eyes closed as if in disbelief. "And then she started reading love letters written by famous lovers. I begged my father to make her stop. They made me miss you. And I didn't want to miss you. I had enough pain. The letters were excruciating."

Patsy drew herself up and took Trey's cheeks between her palms, waiting until he finally met her gaze. "I'm so sorry. I never imagined we were both emotionally tormented. I pictured you stalwartly soldiering on."

His lips were so close, but she resisted kissing him. It wouldn't bring back his smile. Her own struggles had proved you weren't finished until you got to the root of your problem. Trey hadn't reached that point. More was written all over his face.

"Tell me the rest."

He slipped his thumbs between his cheeks and her palms, taking hold of her hands and pulling them down between them. "My mother's love barrage did nothing but make me more pigheaded. When I left rehab to stay with the Tiernans, I thought I'd gained a reprieve. But one thing she read stalked my thoughts whenever I wasn't properly distracted."

Patsy relaxed against him, so he didn't have to look her in the eye if emotion overwhelmed him.

His gaze remained riveted on her. "I don't know how religion plays out in modern Ireland, but on Tallav there's a substantial number of Reformed

Catholics. My mother included. So she also read to me about love from the Bible, which has quite a lot to say on the topic. Somehow I missed the graphic nature of the Song of Solomon during my catechismal education."

A quirk of his lips pretended to be a smile. "I don't really remember much of what she read from the Song of Songs. What attached itself to me, clinging like chewing gum does to the bottom of your foot, was a section later on known as the love chapter. Even atheists thoroughly insulated on nontheistic planets have heard bits of it."

"Thanks to my mom, it's emblazoned on my mind. 'Love is patient, love is kind. Love does not envy, is not boastful, is not conceited, does not act improperly, is not selfish, is not provoked, and does not keep a record of wrongs.'"

"My reaction was… well, the term 'idjit' is more than appropriate. I saw myself in those words. For months, to my regret, they epitomized my understanding of how I had behaved during our relationship. I remember telling myself how I'd bent over backward to assure your happiness. That I was the perfect example of a noble and true lover."

He rested his forehead against hers, his eyes shut, his expression pained. His words were soft, fragile. "I didn't do any better with the next bit."

"'It bears all things.'"

"Check. I'd done a lot of bearing things."

"'Believes all things. Hopes all things.'"

"Double check. How could I have put up with all I had if I hadn't believed and hoped for the impossible? But the last phrase, three words that should have forced me to face the truth, had the opposite effect on me.

"'Endures all things.' That was where I drew my own thoroughly reasonable, self-serving, pristine line. Love did not have to endure all things. I did not have to endure what you put me through. Every time you left me hanging at the club, I lost respect. No man could or should accept such humiliation. I'd tell myself *no more enduring* whenever the love chapter gummed up my thoughts."

Tension wound its way through her, tightening a muscle here and there until her whole body was taut. "Is that what you still believe?"

He lifted his head, his eyes haunted and unblinking. "No." The word squeezed from his throat. "No. I don't."

His gaze lowered, and he winced. "I was so fucking proud. Too proud to see the truth even though it stared me in the face. Did you know Shane Tiernan, about as dominant as a man can be, lets his daughter play with his hair, put bows in it even?"

Patsy waited, not clear why this was relevant but certain it was.

"He came to dinner one night with pink, red, blue, yellow bows covering his head, and asked us if we thought he looked pretty. His mother, father, and Adrianna showered him with compliments. His daughter, not quite two, sat between her parents, radiating delight. Then she said, 'Papa pretty.' And the look that passed between them. It…" He huffed out a breath. "It was pure love. Pure, ridiculous love."

His gaze found hers, but from the side, not straight on, a twisted smile on his lips. "Not that I had this huge aha moment. I was obtusely steadfast in my refusal to appreciate the plain truth. It took more than that, but it was a beginning."

Her throat tight, Patsy swallowed hard, remaining as still as possible despite the increasing urge to escape Trey's torment. He had listened to her. She would do the same for him, for the man she loved with a ferocity that seeded her with courage.

Trey's gaze went unfocused as though he were seeing into the past. "In the months I spent with them, I witnessed Shane routinely set aside his plans, his wants, his needs for the sake of his wife without a drop of irritation. And not because he was a man and she a woman whom the Tallavan matriarchy declared should take preeminence. She was just as likely to cede to his wishes. But I never once saw him cause her distress.

"That's the core of a D/s relationship, a true D/s relationship. The dominant is to put the submissive's needs first. His come second, fulfilled only when hers are met. I understood that intellectually. Rule number one when I played with women, especially anyone I scened with regularly. I couldn't understand why it was different with you.

"I'd been blaming you all along. But I knew, Interpersonal Relationship 101, problems are almost never one-sided. Both parties play a role. I finally took the time to look at myself, to look beneath all my pat answers. What I found dismayed me. Not pretty, but worse, it was as obvious as a smack with a sledgehammer. I should have known better."

His hands cupped her face, and he stared into her eyes long enough for the silence to unnerve her. She searched his gaze, wanting to speak. Tell him he was forgiven. But she held back. Trey had to reveal the root of all his misconceived notions. Anything she said now could distract him from draining the last of the emotional infection.

Then the words spilled out, his voice gruff with pain. "I was afraid. Afraid you'd grow tired of me. Leave me. More than anything, that you didn't love me in the same blinding, heart-slashing way I loved you."

A dip of his chin dropped his gaze from hers, but then his eyes were once again directed at her, piercing with a ferocious need for her to understand. "*A leanbh*, I've discovered that pride doesn't provide happiness. It steals it."

She gripped his wrist. Her voice was soft, not with kindness but with shared distress. "Yes."

"I love you."

His lips captured hers in another hair-frizzing kiss. She rode a wave of exhilaration. They'd each traveled inner paths that penetrated to the centers of their beings and encountered at their very cores a nexus where the other stood waiting to love and be loved.

There was more they had to discuss. More they needed to work out if they were truly going to be together. Those issues could take a back seat to what was happening between them right now, in this moment.

He lifted her in his arms and took the stairs to the second level and his bedroom. Her gaze never left his face. Written there as it was written on her own heart was the result of his struggle. A sure knowledge that love endures all things.

Not much later her mind gave up pondering the philosophical to revel in the clever way Trey used his fingers, his mouth, and eventually his cock.

12

At some point Trey would have to release Patsy from his arms, if for no other reason than to wrap her in rope, not just because he loved the control it gave him during sex but because it soothed him to know for at least those hours she wouldn't be able to leave him.

Which was nuts. He'd done the leaving, not Patsy. She'd come to him. And from all she'd said, intended to stay.

He'd been on the cusp of deciding to go to her, and then she'd appeared on his doorstep. The explosion that had gone off in his mind, his heart, his cock had turned him into a rutting animal, taking her hard against the wall without consideration of anything but the pulsating need to fuse his whole being with her.

The door to his bedroom was half-closed. He nudged it with his foot. In three long strides he was at the unmade bed. No maid here. What a pampered ass he'd become. Patsy clamped to his chest, he yanked the bed coverings away and flung them onto the floor, centered a pillow, and lowered her as though she were fragile, made of elegant tracery that would crumble at the slightest touch.

Hands on either side of her, he stared, satisfying himself with every detail of her face, delicate nose, creamy skin, and scattering of freckles.

Her gaze clung to him, a glimmer in her eyes that seemed to see all of him to his core, penetrate his heart, and approve of what she found there. The smile that billowed from deep inside him shattered his face, slabs of reserve falling and breaking into shards, piecing them together again an impossibility.

"You're mine."

"Always."

The throw he'd wrapped her in downstairs had slipped, exposing one pert breast. He tongued the nipple, extracting a squeaky moan from her that went straight to his cock.

Relief, giddy and full of gratitude to the gods of manliness, swelled through him, making him tingle in more than just sexual response.

The doctors had said that his injuries should not cause him any problems sexually. And yet he'd had no erections since the accident. Not even morning wood.

He'd ignored suggestions that he visit a psych. Nonsense about psychosomatic symptoms? Impossible. Depression? If ever he'd fallen into a funk in the past, meditation had been the cure. But even that had failed him.

Save it for later, moron. The woman you've wanted for months is lying on a bed ripe for the taking, and your cock is ready and able for round two.

A swipe of his hand sent the throw flying. Patsy's reaction was a classic startle response. Perfect.

His laugh, tinged with the sadistic pleasure that occasionally seeped into his BDSM play, didn't elicit a verbal response from Patsy. That wouldn't last.

Strange. A year ago he wouldn't have believed that he'd miss her backtalk, crosstalk, talktalk.

"Put your elbows together."

She settled her body, shaking her limbs out before raising her arms, elbows and wrists matched. Her expression was solemn, but the barest of trembles assured him she wasn't calm.

The chest next to the bed, made of a dark, almost black wood, was tall on one side and short on the other. Both a nightstand and something else. In this case a toy cupboard. He selected a length of rope, formed a bight, and used it to tap her wrists.

"I should invest in colored rope." He raised the rope for her to see. "White is basic. Useful. Gets the job done. But prim. I think I should buy green for when you're sassy. Blue for when I intend to look deep in your eyes and bind our souls." His lips didn't part to show his teeth, but the smile that eased over his face was dangerous, predatory. "Black for when my mind is overflowing with all the dirty things I want to do to you."

Slowly, methodically, he wrapped her wrists, crossing, pulling under, looping, twisting. Finally tying off. It was torture. For them both. Nothing else would happen until he was done. Hands busy, he didn't touch her other than the graze of the backs of his fingers as he manipulated the rope.

Patsy lay meek, a kitten who'd chosen to keep her sharp milk teeth and needlelike claws to herself. Her usual barrage of provocation was missing.

Who is this woman?

Is she trying to prove she's changed with this total compliance? If she is, it's a mistake. I'm not buying it.

Sure, in the past he'd gotten her to where she was incapable of speech, but it took a lot more than binding her wrists. Did she believe unresisting submission was what he wanted from her?

The scent of her arousal beguiled his senses.

He scanned her eyes while dipping his finger into her cleft. A sizzle of desire sparked, quickly covered when she lowered her lids.

Was the change she'd spoken of only superficial? As much as his heart swelled to be with her again, uncertainty impeded his breath. Most unwelcome when he was in the middle of making love to the woman who was his other half. Call it self-preservation, but he hated it.

He shoved aside his doubt. He… she… they were starting over, and so he would have to return to first principles. A Dom always met his sub's needs before his own.

Trey's gift to her would be the undeniable certainty that he loved her as she was, feisty, demanding, and given to tempests. This time he wouldn't fail her, and he arrowed a prayer to his mother's God that she had truly conquered the demons that kept her from going all in on their relationship.

First. First he must discover what motivated her current extraordinary passivity. The Whip Hand was full of women who lived and breathed compliance. Over the years, pre-Patsy, he'd played with a good number of them. But none had fired his soul the way she did. It wasn't her nature to yield, so when she finally attained that moment of total submission, when she gave herself up to him completely, it was like the sun blazing, sweeping away storm clouds, a sea change reached only by passionate perseverance.

Her eyes flashed open at his low chuckle, uncertainty flaring, followed by a slight squint but no smart remark.

Tucked behind a submissive facade, the real Patsy was still there.

She was not alone in her ability to unleash turbulence. He lifted her hands and attached the long end of the rope around her wrists to a convenient, unobtrusively placed ring on the headboard.

At the foot of the bed where she could easily see him, he began to strip. "Watch me."

His shirt dropped to the floor with a soft shush of fabric.

The tip of her tongue darted in a quick swipe of her lower lip, a slip in her composure. Again the squint.

Raising his arms, he stretched, long and languid. He was rather proud of the physique he'd been honing in Shane's gym. His jeans, zipper still open, slid down another inch.

Her lips parted.

He pushed his pants low enough to kick out of each leg.

Her nipples, ruched but not yet as hard as they would become, quivered with each breath she took.

He palmed his cock through his underwear. Clearly the damn thing only worked for Patsy. Heart and cock overruled the niggling doubt that continued to seep around the edges of his thoughts. If their future held pain, he'd cope with it because there was no going back this time. His pride would have to take a back seat.

"Spread your legs."

Red curls, darker than the hair on her head, acted as a veil, covering the tempting cleft beneath but not totally obscuring it. His erection leaped, knocking against his hand. Arousal pressed at him, urging him to claim her once again. As though fucking her mindlessly in the foyer hadn't already asserted his territorial rights.

Stick to your priorities.

He climbed onto the bed, sliding up the smooth pale blue sheet that contrasted perfectly with Patsy's ivory skin and flaming hair, until he reached the point of the triangle created by her thighs. Her heated scent drifted into his nostrils. He breathed in deeply, filling himself with an aroma more enticing than his mother's cooking, more lovely than any flower, and more addicting than bliss beads. His eyes closed automatically, eliminating that sense to focus on the glory flooding his nose.

Hands wrapped around her waist, he nuzzled his way through the curls, swiping his tongue along her pussy before narrowing in on her clit. One tap and her diaphragm jerked, a whisper of a gasp escaping her lips.

A cooling breath, blown right at the center of her moistness, made her squirm. Not much. She was still trying to hold back, confusing submission with passivity.

He tightened his grasp and tasted her fully, lapping like she was an ice cream cone and he didn't want to miss a drop of her liquid goodness.

Her hips lifted, pushing her against his face, muscles tightening beneath his fingers. His cock was a throbbing monster between his legs.

The bed creaked when he shoved up on his hands and backed off. The air caught in his lungs for a moment, staring at her, searching to find more of the true woman.

Her cheeks and chest were flushed a pretty red, a color that most women achieved only when thoroughly spanked. A color that spoke to the beast inside him, demanding he ravage.

Grabbing hold of his control like the horn of a saddle, he refused to be thrown by the lusting bull that twisted in wild gyrations to free itself and pursue its own pleasure. "Did you like that?"

"Yes." The words scraped past her clenched teeth.

"Is that all you have to say?"

A scowl crept onto her face like a house cat whose wagging backside gave away its intent. "Yes."

He raised his gaze to hers while placing an openmouthed kiss on her inner thigh. "Really? I don't want to overdo things. Go too fast."

"Fast?" Lips pressed in a tight line, she struggled and lost the fight to remain placid. "Feckin' man, get on with it. Ya know I've missed the mind-blowin' orgasms ya've given me in the past. Stop your dawdlin'. Ya've had your fun. It's been just as long for me."

Elation drummed its heady beat inside his chest. "I'm not sure I've had enough fun yet." He smacked her hip, his hand curved to create a popping sound. "You know a mind-blowing orgasm takes time to achieve. No skipping steps."

"Feckin' man."

He slid on top of her, his skin reveling in her naked heat, and kissed her, long and hard with a thoroughness that made them both gasp for breath when it broke.

"Say it again." He sipped at her lower lip.

Her eyes were dazed, awash in lust's rewards. "What?"

"Call me that again."

"Feckin' man?"

"Yeah."

"Feckin' man."

"No. Say it like you mean it."

He scooped her breast into his hand and pinched her nipple. Hard.

She reared up as far as her restrained arms would allow. "Feckin' man, you're interminably irritatin'."

"No. Just daft." His fingers found her clit and stroked.

"Oh that. That's lovely."

"Lovely?"

"I'm keepin' my verbal powder dry, holdin' out for more of your masterful masterin'."

He chuckled with a satisfaction that ran deep and true. "Just don't hold back. I don't know what motivated you to think I wanted you passive beneath me, but I don't. I want you in all your sassy, desirable magnificence."

Her body tightened with a tension that wasn't leading to ecstatic release. "Ya didn't want me before."

His finger stilled. The arrow flew straight and true, striking him in the chest, tainted with pain and shame. "I was an idiot. I'll not leave you again. If you want shed of me, you'll have to do the walking away. Every word that falls from your lips is precious to me. Every time you let me tie you in rope and control your sexual pleasure is precious to me. Above all, you are precious to me."

Eyes shiny with emotion, she spoke, her voice husky. "Show me."

Those two simple words snapped the tether that restrained the beast.

His kiss turned savage.

He ground his body against hers, his cock hardening, painfully throbbing with the need to be quenched inside her. He yanked down the remaining barrier between them, unleashing his cock, probed until he found her center, and penetrated her as slowly as overwhelming need and fading self-control allowed.

Her hips rose to meet him, matching the punishing rhythm he set, with an ardor that astounded him while it spurred him ever higher.

Patsy's gasping cries inundated him, an almost musical reminder that this wasn't just for his personal indulgence. If he continued instinctively thrusting, he'd break his promise to himself. She must go first.

Determined, he gritted his teeth hard enough to make his jaw ache. The pain served to brake the orgasm that was barreling at breakneck speed toward completion.

He reached between them, searching her folds until he found her clit. It wasn't necessary to stroke. Pressure and the movement of their bodies were all the stimulus required.

Pleasure mounted, increasing until it filled his mind like an oncoming train. His movements became erratic.

Her breathing turned shallow, her voice low with inarticulate exclamations.

She tightened around him, gripping his cock as though she would never release it.

The slender thread of control tore.

Sight disappeared behind clenched eyelids.

Hearing faded in a heavy blankness.

All was drowned in the devastating intensity of an orgasm that rocketed through his cock and up his spine.

A thought pierced the ecstasy. *I'm whole again.*

Consideration of the revelation was postponed.

Unable to do anything but collapse, he melted into her, fighting to breathe while his body continued to somersault inside in heady acrobatics that none of the artists at Bistro Coquin could ever execute.

Finally he slid to the side, fumbled to untie her wrists, and drew her to rest with her head on his shoulder.

"That was…" The stream of air that accompanied her words stilled.

"Masterful?"

"You know it was, feckin' man."

A CLUNK SOUNDED, discordantly invading Patsy's dream of Trey making love to her. She turned over, pulling away the blanket that covered her face when she'd rolled into it. Trey had placed a mug on the bedside table. The aroma of coffee was sublime. Real coffee. Not café, a substitute that was both affordable and nowhere near to duplicating the original.

"Morning, *a leanbh*."

She took hold of his fingertips, intending to pull him into bed. "Come here."

Resistance was unexpected. His appetite for her had been that of a man ravenous from starvation, waking her multiple times to bring her to release, often without finding his own. Wrapping her close when he'd brought her to the peak and falling asleep again.

He sidled toward an armchair and draped his muscular body and long legs over it. Damn, even fully clothed, the man was so feckin' sexy she'd be wiping her chin if she kept looking. Too much of his delectable smoky-topaz skin was hidden under another bulky sweater, this time a forest green. He resembled a woodsy outdoorsman. And hiking boots. He was wearing hiking boots. *Is he planning to stay in this frozen wilderness?*

"I brought your luggage in."

"Oh. I forgot." She sat, pulling the covers around her but allowing them to settle and expose her breasts.

A smile crossed his face in slow increments and stuck. "Temptress."

"Feckin' man."

"Blizzard outside. Could last for days."

She jumped from the bed, arms wrapping her torso to dispel the chill that smacked her skin, and scampered to the double doors that led to the balcony.

It was snowing. None of the great fat flakes she'd seen fall yesterday for about fifteen minutes. The view was obscured by billions of wind-borne icy crystals, swept into drifts that were soon scoured by blusters and blown away to pile into new temporary formations.

A shiver skittered through her, signaling goose bumps to spread over her arms and shoulders. She dashed back to the bed, burrowing into the blankets, clutching them under her chin.

"If you get in bed, we could keep each other warm." Lips parted, she bit the tip of her tongue and lowered her lids to hood her eyes.

Amusement danced in his gaze, proof that the fist pressed to his mouth was holding back a laugh. "We have things to discuss."

"Can't it wait?" She attempted a puppy-dog expression, hoping it would succeed where seduction had failed, but wasn't sure she'd done it right because he didn't respond.

He sobered. "I told Shane I needed time alone to decide what I was going to do next in life. I've been toying with the idea of becoming involved in the men's movement here on Tallav. It would mean living on Tallav. That's one issue.

"And I intended to formulate a plan to get you back. Adrianna made sure I received your letters. I'd refused to read them. Until yesterday. You showing up was a miracle of timing." He scowled at her, narrowing his eyes, allowing suspicion to land with a splat between them. "Or was it?"

Her brain went into dither mode. *The moment of truth. How to explain? How to explain?*

She'd known this was coming but still hadn't come up with a surefire justification, one that would have him chuckling his gratitude and agreeing that the plot fulfilled his every hope and dream, and when she revealed it, they'd embrace, content to proceed into a perfect future.

Fantasy met reality.

Trey's face held the look that cowed lesser beings, which included about ninety-nine percent of anyone he confronted. How weird was it that her reaction was perversely the opposite? Sure, she was intimidated, but equal if not greater parts of her lusted for him to bring his own special recipe for chastisement.

The things he could do with his long, agile fingers. The power that he demonstrated in every flexing muscle. The sweet sin that oozed from his pores, intoxicating and sublimely wicked. All part of the inevitable aftermath of any punishment.

When they played.

But they weren't playing.

He'd said he wouldn't leave her again. But that was before he'd known the magnitude of their...no, her, ultimately her manipulation. Adrianna, Jen, even Maon had assured her the plan was not selfish at heart. But it was far down the path of implementation, and Trey had not been consulted.

The smile she flashed at him refused to stay in place and had the effect of making his scowl deepen. Her mind raced through an extensive list of things she could say to appease his anger and stalled after she discarded each as self-serving, ridiculous, or irrelevant.

I might as well be hanged for a sheep as a lamb.

"We planned it." She let the words drop between them, flat and leaden.

He narrowed one enigmatic eye. At least it wasn't a frown. "Who is we? You, Adrianna, my mother? Who else?"

She gave a slight shrug and kept her expression bland, picking at an imperfection in the sheet.

"Everyone. Shane too. And Randolph and Jen. Selena and Maon. Even your dad."

And then a grin broke across Trey's face, like the sun rising and reflecting off a still morning lake. Patsy's heart skipped a pattering beat to begin a new assured rhythm. The sheet slid from fingers whose tingling rendered them nerveless.

"I didn't stand a chance, did I?" His smile took on a disparaging tilt.

Her chest swelled with an enormous bubble of relief. She might have floated over to Trey if exuberance hadn't sent her dashing out of the bed and into his lap. The bubble grew with great puffs of happiness. She tipped her head back and scanned his face. No need to hunt to find what she knew without reservation in every quivering, overexcited nerve in her body. Trey loved her.

"You're not mad." It wasn't a question.

He brushed his lips across her with a tenderness that would normally exasperate her desire for domination but was perfect for this moment.

"How could I be mad when the results are exactly what I want? Besides, I wasn't a blind pigeon all this time. Neither Adrianna nor my mother are good at hiding their scheming. Whenever I asked Dad what Mom was up to, he'd shake his head and say, 'You know your mother.'"

Patsy snuggled into his neck, seeking the warmth of his skin and the reassurance that his scent always produced. "The tricky bit was getting you here. Adrianna got Shane and Rand to do that, knowing you'd balk if she was involved."

"I would have. Balked. But I can't imagine that this"—he pecked her lips, a less fulsome explanation of what he meant than she desired—"is the culmination of their grand plan. So what's next?"

"Well…"

He pinched her thigh, grunting when she squeaked. "I know there's more. How much of my life and yours has Adrianna planned?"

The transgressions she'd admitted to were faits accomplis. The revelations to come dealt with the future, his and hers. And not just their relationship. Arrangements had been made. Money had been spent. Contracts had been signed. All without his input. He wasn't a man given to allowing others to make decisions for him.

This would be delicate. She'd stay in his lap, but the cuddling, while lovely, had to be put on hold. Pulling away and straightening brought her eye to eye with him.

"I've turned in my resignation to Randolph. No more Bistro Coquin."

"But that's your dream job." The tone of his voice was startled.

She clutched a handful of his sweater. "It was my dream job. And I made a damn fine creative director. But that's the past. I have new dreams. Ones that involve you if you're prepared to take on new things yourself."

Her gaze dropped to his chest where her fingers were pleating rows of knitted stitches.

"Maybe I should have waited until I was certain we would be together again before moving ahead." A shake of her head denounced that thought. "Adrianna, Jen, and Selina have created an opportunity for me that I couldn't refuse."

Trey's head tipped back, his gaze roving over the ceiling, his expression attentive. Patsy sat still, trying to catch whatever he heard.

A distant whine sounded outside. It grew louder until a powerful boom resounded, shaking the lodge. She snatched at his sweater again, this time her fingernails snagging like briars. Alarm slammed through her. She bleated, "It's happening again."

Trey flattened her even harder against his chest. A moan, equal parts terror and pain, shot from him. They clung to one another until it dawned on them that no cataclysm had snared them.

Voice taut, Trey muttered, "It can't be an avalanche. Not enough snow."

"Then what?" Initial alarm had passed, to be replaced by the drip, drip, drip of worst-case scenarios building in her mind, nasty speculations.

"I'll have to find out. Go and look."

The hairs on the back of her neck and arms stood at attention. A single command flew from her lips. "No."

The kiss he planted on the top of her head did nothing to refute the certainty of that liquid dread that had seeped into every nook and cranny of her soul. He must not go outside.

The death grip he'd held her in eased, softening the muscles of his arms. "It'll be okay. I promise not to fall in any holes."

"Feckin' man." Her power of speech froze for a moment, throttled by panic. "Don't joke."

He stroked her shoulder. "I wouldn't."

A sob slipped from deep inside her, a match to the many that had racked her days and nights after the accident. He tightened his embrace around her again, physical evidence that he was here and to be relied upon this time.

A shuddering sigh eased the tension in muscles that had gone tight. The change was apparent to Trey, so he released his grip but continued to stroke her arm. She oriented her gaze where she clung to his sweater.

"It sounds like something has fallen. Not rocks or a tree. Something higher than that. Something that had to have come from the sky. I'll be careful." He traced a finger over her hands. "Can you release me?"

"I really don't want to." Her voice sounded petulant in her own ears. "Can't someone else figure this out? We can call for help."

He tipped her face up with his knuckle. "Look at me." Honor, courage, damnable decency shone from his eyes. "Not if there's someone out there who needs us. I'm not letting someone suffer. I can't."

"I'll go with you." The words burst from her before she'd had time to consider them. She couldn't let him out of her sight.

He stood and set her on the bed in full Dom mode. No alternatives required. He'd decided on what was best. For her. For whomever might be out there. For himself because he could do nothing less.

"You'll stay here. Get dressed and comm Randolph. If you can't reach him directly, then try Shane or Adrianna." Overcoat donned, and in rapid succession hat crammed onto his head and gloves jammed onto his hands, he strode to the door. "I'll be back as quickly as possible. See if you can find the med bed. We may need it."

"You think it's a shuttle?"

He looked over his shoulder, face tense. "I don't know what else it could be."

Patsy rushed to where Trey had left her suitcase beside the closet. She opened it, flinging garments aside as she searched for more of the winter outdoor clothing she'd picked up in Cahernamon. Fingers flying, she dressed, rapidly buttoning and zipping. She dashed to the foyer to pull on her boots.

Sending a direct voice-to-voice comm without messaging a request was impolite, but this was an emergency. Thank Mary, Joseph, and all the saints Randolph answered.

"Patsy?"

Trey came thumping back inside and raced upstairs.

"Patsy?"

"Yes. I'm sorry to comm like this, but something's happened here at the lodge. We think a shuttle has crashed near us. Trey's goin' out to check." Sudden fear froze in her veins, an icy slush that chilled her entire being. "No one was coming here, were they?"

"No. Adrianna gave us strict orders to leave the two of you alone for a minimum of three days if we didn't get a comm before then. If a shuttle has crashed, it's not anyone I know. There shouldn't be any shuttles flying on that side of the Giant's Tit. Not at this time of year. The lodge is the only winter-capable shelter."

Her mind stretched to suggest other possibilities. "Maybe someone got lost in the storm."

"With a shuttle? Not likely. I'll call the authorities. As soon as you know anything more, comm me."

"All right."

Trey reappeared, waving a tangled mass of rope at her, and dashed back out.

Jittery from a need to do something, Patsy replayed Trey's instructions. *What was the last thing he said? Oh, the med bed.*

She ran through the house, moving from room to room until she discovered it tucked away in a small alcove at the back of the lodge.

Standard unit. A few taps of her index finger had it fully prepped for patients.

Next she explored the cupboards lining the opposite wall, finding a generous supply of first aid and emergency medical supplies. She was as ready as possible for whatever Trey found. *Please, not dead bodies or anyone critically injured.*

13

The snow fell unabated, lashed in all directions by winds that slammed into the upper slopes of the Giant's Tit from off the sea, at this altitude undeterred by trees or man-made obstacles. Trey moved a few feet from the porch through drifts that reached his thighs, scanning, searching for some visual hint of disaster.

Nothing. The scene before him was silent, swirling white and gray.

Screeee.

He yanked his head in the shuttle pad's direction. Had he heard…? Was that…metal protesting?

Silence descended, hanging on tenterhooks.

And then came a muffled thump. Trey leaned into the wind.

Another thump.

Louder.

Someone was out in that freezing death.

So close, but the distance was compounded by the blinding blizzard that separated the lodge and the shuttle pad. The porch was barely visible even though he was only three feet distant.

I need a guideline. Tie it to a porch column. Play it out as I go.

Trey mentally chuckled. *Thanks to Randolph, the lodge has plenty of rope.*

He thumped up the steps of the porch and threw open the door. Patsy was talking on her EBC comm. He sprinted upstairs and raced room to room, gathering rope as he went. On his way back through the foyer, he waved the rope at her rather than interrupt her call.

Puddles of melting snow decorated the foyer when he arrived with his armload. He took several calming breaths to slow his heart rate and keep jangling nerves from impeding him and then tied each length end to end, coiling the final product over his shoulder.

Outside, winter's snarling attack remained unrelenting.

The lifeline didn't require the elaborate knots that Trey was skilled in tying. Instead he made short work of a basic tie, securing the rope to the column closest to the path he'd churned. A path even now filling and smoothing with fresh snow.

How am I going to get someone seriously injured back through this? Maybe whoever's out there won't be badly hurt.

He plowed forward, stamping each foot to assure that he was still on the concrete walkway, the sole civilized track between shuttle pad and lodge.

I can at least get them into the shelter of the hangar. It's heated. Maybe I'll find a med kit.

Toiling to break a trail foot by laborious foot, Trey relentlessly scanned the featureless obscurity that cut him off from anything familiar. He concentrated his hearing and his vision, attempting to refine the location of the accident.

He hadn't been paying close attention when he'd been dropped off by Randolph's shuttle pilot, and so the map in his mind was low on detail. From what he recalled, the hangar was on the far side of the landing pad. The walkway that connected the lodge was located equidistant from each end of the long slab.

Gravel crunched beneath his feet, throwing him off-balance. *Fuck.* Now he remembered. The walkway turned at an angle at the halfway point. He stomped around until he felt pavement again, fighting his way through drifts that had grown waist-high.

The search for a spot to tie the rope and mark the change in direction was futile. The land between the lodge and shuttle pad was barren. No decorative trees or symbolic hunting statuary or a signpost with the name of the lodge.

He plowed forward, muttering, "You'll manage," on repeat.

Ahead and to his left a red light flickered. He stopped, straining his eyesight until he saw it again. Slogging onward, he paused every couple of feet to reorient on the now steady beacon.

He was close.

If his memory was correct, the pad was built on an outcropping of rock, but he couldn't recall how steep the drop-offs were at either end. Somewhere between a mild slope and a plunge to your death. Situated where it was, that crimson beam was guiding him toward a potential precipice.

In this blizzard, how would I even know I was near the edge?

The hike through the snow had been enough of a workout that he was breathing heavily. But his mind, overwhelmed with memories of the ground opening before him like a giant maw, didn't notice his lungs had switched to short, rasping intakes until his chest seized with pain.

Standing stock-still, he grew dizzy, fingers numb, but not from cold. He resisted the urge to turn and flee to the lodge.

Don't be an asshat. You're not going to fall again. A human being needs your help. Stop hyperventilating before you pass out.

He slammed a gloved fist against his thigh three times and squatted, putting his head between his knees.

His brain cleared as his breathing stabilized. *Okay. Okay.*

The wind carried the tattered sound of a moan to his ears. He lifted his chin and stood, his nose tipped as though he were a dog scenting a trail.

Get moving, Johansson. Someone definitely sounds injured.

A brief lull in the scouring frozen gusts gave him his first unobstructed view. A small shuttle, probably not even spaceworthy, limited to atmospheric flight, lay broken with the front half angled off the shuttle pad. The slope was sharp enough that Trey's chest hitched. He shut his eyelids and struggled against the urge to return to hyperventilating, focusing on other aspects of what he'd seen.

Someone, by his height most likely a man, had been leaning against the side of the shuttle, scrabbling his way up to the safety of the pad.

Trey opened his eyes. The storm had once more roused itself to obscure the scene, but the break had been sufficient to confirm he could move straight toward that ominous red light.

Thrusting ahead as rapidly as the deep snow allowed, he redoubled his efforts.

The back end of the damaged aircraft reared before him. He leaned one-handed on the vehicle's side and peered along its length. The cover of snow on the pad had been flung away from the body of the shuttle by the impact, clearing the pavement about a foot's width from the fuselage.

It didn't appear to have slid, landing like a spoonful of jelly thwapped onto a piece of toast without the landing gear deploying. Would have had to have been a terrific crash for the front end to have snapped. An engineer's enigma. But at least it hadn't gone careening down the rock face.

Trey sped to where he'd spotted the man.

Splayed from his hips up on the pad, his feet wedged on the slope at the spot they'd gained traction for the final push past the rim, the man lay melted as though the distance he'd traveled from the cockpit had burned through all his energy.

Ignoring the drop-off as best he could, Trey maintained tight control on his respiration. "It's not steep. It's not steep." Still his heart scurried as though it sought to outrun the fierce winds whipping across the heights.

He dropped to one knee, placing a hand on the man's back, discovering his slender frame was racked with ragged breathing. The man craned his neck, twisting it so he could stare at Trey. A balaclava hid most of his face. Wide-eyed, a moat of white around his hazel irises, he seemed incapable of speech.

It took Trey less than a minute to pull the man fully onto the shuttle pad.

"Where does it hurt?" Even as he spoke, Trey was probing for broken bones or other wounds through the man's reflective silver ski suit.

Trey skimmed the right leg from hip to ankle. Then the left leg. The man shifted, trying to avoid the examination of his left leg, screaming when Trey reached the ankle.

"Holy shit. Stop touching it." The mouth hole of the balaclava revealed a fine set of clenched, perfect teeth.

"Sorry. Gotta do this. It'll hurt me more than it hurts you." *Right. Now the guy thinks you're an idiot.* The man's low boot didn't allow Trey to assess with certainty whether the ankle was broken. They'd need the boot off for a proper determination. *Better keep it on for now.*

He brought himself nose to nose with the victim. "I'd like to get you to the lodge where we have a med bed. Do you think you can try walking on one foot with me holding you up through the snow? It's not that far."

The man's gaze darted back and forth, attempting to see past him, to judge the difficulty for himself. Or so Trey thought until the man's eyes refused to settle, gazing anywhere but straight at Trey.

Odd.

Trey shoved aside the niggling mote of apprehension. Who was he to question someone else's response to trauma? After all, the idea of going near a steep drop turned him into a quivering mass of hysterical fear.

"How about it?"

The man scrunched his eyelids shut. "All right."

"Up you go then." Trey assisted the man to rise and lean against the shuttle. "I'm gonna tie this rope around you. The other end is lashed to the lodge's front porch. If we're quick about this, we should be able to follow the path I made to get here."

Once the rope was securely looped around the man's waist, Trey pulled the man's arm over his shoulder and induced him to move forward.

If Trey had been returning to the lodge by himself, the return trek would have proved easier than the outgoing with a trail already blazed. Two made a wider path necessary. He also carried more and more of the other man's weight.

The blizzard hadn't slackened its howling ferocity. If anything, its rage had once again increased. He was swallowed in a swirling white where past and present hid from the now. The immediate need to propel one foot ahead and then another, dragging his companion along with him, was the sole focus of his world.

His toe thumped into the first step leading to the porch, the surprise nearly sending him backward in a heap. The thousands of crunches he'd strained through at Gleann Millis confirmed their worth. Abdominal strength and a better-than-average sense of balance rescued him from a fall that would have brought the man next to him to the ground too.

Patsy had been watching from the door. She dashed toward them, sliding in place on the man's other side. Together they lifted him to the top of the steps. Trey removed the rope and then carried the man through the foyer and onto a couch in the living room.

The warmth of the air that Trey sucked deep into his lungs was welcome. He slumped on an oversize ottoman, observing as Patsy pulled the balaclava from the man's head.

Dark blond hair sprang out every which way, adding to the man's startled expression. He shot a look at Trey, then back at Patsy, his face filling with wariness, his brows lowering and his eyes narrowing. "Wh-where am I?"

"You're at the Meryon huntin' lodge on the backside of the Giant's Tit on Rathlin Island. Are ya injured?" Patsy cast a glance in Trey's direction but didn't wait for a response from him. "Ya look colder than an ice cube. That ski suit isn't near warm enough to have been out in that blizzard. A hot shower is what you're needin'." She fired a glare at Trey. "Don't just sit there, actin' like you've done some manly feat that took all your strength."

Trey grimaced, stopping short of snapping at her, softening his voice before speaking. "Let a man catch his breath." Both he and the stranger could use the space to collect themselves.

The man's gaze had been locked on Patsy while she'd rattled on, but now he was clearly focused on Trey. Despite an ankle that hadn't been able to bear his weight on the trip from the shuttle to the lodge, the man appeared to be preparing to sprint for the door. Trey knew he often scared people with his unwelcome resting-thug face, but he'd all but carried the guy to warmth and safety.

Maybe I'll look less dangerous if I remove my coat. So he did. The man didn't relax.

"I'm Trey Johansson. We need to tend to that ankle of yours."

Patsy pointed. "Med bed's back there. I prepped it. I'll get ya a nice soft blanket to wrap up in. Those medical plasti-covers are the worst." She dashed away as soon as the words left her lips, running up the stairs.

"Let's get you to the med bed. We'll take off your boot there." Trey wrapped an arm around the man's torso and assisted him to rise. "So I'm Trey, and you are?"

"Danny…uh, Dan."

Without the balaclava concealing his face, Trey realized Dan couldn't be more than in his early twenties. Was he a runaway? That would account for the wariness.

But how had he ended up here?

His shuttle wouldn't get him to the space station. Where else would a runaway head?

If he was a first family son, was he stealing away to marry a woman his mother deemed unsuitable? The ski suit was expensive. And shuttles were almost the total purview of the Tallavan aristocracy.

Or was he fleeing the law?

"Can we comm someone for you, a friend or family member, or have you already done that?"

"No." The answer was snapped back. "Uh…I'll do that."

"Okay." Trey helped Dan climb onto the med bed and settle. "You'll need to roll up your sleeve so your arm will go in the analysis unit."

Dan unclasped the closures of his ski suit at the wrist. The fabric was stretchy, so it was a simple matter to push it above his elbow. He slipped his arm into the unit, and in less than a minute the results proved reassuring. His blood pressure and heart rate were elevated. Not a surprise. But BP 140/90 and a heart rate of 110 weren't problematic. His oxygen level was 97, normal.

The good news Trey relayed understandably didn't relax the young man. His leg still needed to be dealt with. But it eased the tightness in Trey's chest that had never quite released, a tension he hadn't been aware he was carrying until now, when he knew Dan wasn't suffering a serious internal injury.

Trey studied Dan's face as he first closed his eyes and then opened them, refusing to make eye contact. The analysis unit emitted a warning tone. "Don't clench your fist."

"Oh." Dan made a weak effort at clearing his throat. "Sorry."

"Don't worry. You'll be out of pain soon. Just a little more to do and the med bed will prescribe you something that will make all your troubles fly away."

Dan responded with a hard swallow. *So much for my friendly bedside manner.*

"Do you hurt anywhere besides the ankle?"

"Uh. Not from the crash. I fell climbing out. I'll have bruises down my left side."

Trey pursed his lips and nodded. "I'll run a full body scan to be safe. First, I'm gonna take that boot off."

Trey moved to the end of the med bed, freeing the right foot first. It was a low boot, meant for lounging around an indoor fire, drinking hot buttered rum, much as the ski suit was not designed for outdoor sports. A sturdier boot with a taller shaft might have saved the guy's ankle. Nothing for it but to get it off as quickly as possible.

The man's scream brought Patsy at a run, clutching a blanket and carrying a mug away from her body in a futile attempt to keep the contents from slopping onto the floor. "Oh for goodness' sakes, you're killin' the poor boy."

Trey glared at her and then the floor where a line of coffee marked a trail. "His boot had to come off." He didn't mention the mess.

"Course it did." Her voice turned soothing. "And me standin' here with coffee ya can't drink cause your lyin' flat." She set the mug on a counter, shoved the blanket at Trey, and grabbed a wad of paper towels from the dispenser, bending to wipe up the spill.

Tucking the blanket around Dan reminded Trey of after care. Except that when he played with people, they didn't end up with injuries. He lowered the scanner to within a foot of Dan and initiated the sequence for a full body scan.

Patsy popped up at the head of the med bed. "We're goin' to take good care of ya. No worries. I'm Patsy O'Shaughnessy. I'm new to Tallav. Never been in a blizzard like this before. It's amazin'. Ya can barely see anythin'. It's like we're livin' on a giant snowball of a planet. But then, you're probably used to this. What should I call ya?"

The stunned expression returned to Dan's face. He blinked slowly, his gaze flat. Patsy had that effect on others, especially introverts.

Trey placed a hand on Dan's shoulder and looked pointedly at Patsy, hoping she'd dial back her garrulous chatter. "This is Dan." To Dan he said, "You can tune her out if you want to. I do."

Thwack. Patsy's instant response was to smack Trey on the arm. "Ya do not.

"Dan, it's nice to meet ya. Sorry about the circumstances. How'd ya end up on this side of Rathlin Island? I was told there's nothin' here of much use in winter and nothin' further north but icy sea. Did ya get lost?"

His gaze darted from Patsy to Trey as though he were watching two tennis players volleying. "Uh…"

The scan completed with a chime. Dan shifted on the bed, rubbing his upper arm with his free hand. "Wh—" His fist to his mouth, he gave a short cough. "Sorry. What's it say?"

Trey read the diagnosis. "You've got a sprained ankle. Fortunately no torn ligaments, just strained." He tapped the screen for treatment instructions. "Patsy, can you get a bottle marked SP24 from the med cabinet." To Dan he said, "It's a concoction of nanites and pain relief that should have your ankle back in working order by tomorrow. Meanwhile it recommends an ankle wrap."

Patsy handed him the medicine. "I'll find a wrap." She rummaged through the cabinets, and Trey flipped the lid off the bottle and slid it into the med slot of the analysis unit.

"We'll let that take hold a few minutes before I deal with your ankle."

The tightness around Dan's eyes eased, and his lips softened from a harsh line. "Thanks. I'm feeling better already."

"That's good." *SP24 must include an antianxiety med or relaxer. All to the good. The kid's clearly in trouble. He's too damn nervous. If it was just me helping him, I might understand it, but Patsy's here, and she's the least terrifying person I know.*

From behind him, Patsy gave a whoop of victory. "Found one. But ya better let me handle this. I've tended millions of sprained ankles."

Trey slung a cocked eyebrow at her. She knew he didn't like exaggeration.

"Well, hundreds at least." She let the words fall lightly, opting for an insouciant air.

And there it was. That sense of contentment that appeared at the most unlikely of moments. When Patsy was just Patsy. The round pegs were in the round holes, and the square pegs in the square.

He raised the scanner to get it out of the way. "Go ahead." The smile was in his voice as well as on his face.

But Patsy hadn't waited for Trey's approval. Of course not. She went straight to work, gently lifting Dan's foot so she could apply the wrap. Her fingers moved with a deftness Trey wouldn't have possessed. She really did know how to treat a sprained ankle.

Even so, the skin of Dan's face went blotchy.

"How old are you?"

"Twenty." Dan's voice had deepened, the word a croak struggling past a tightened jaw.

The kid didn't deal with pain well. Not everyone did.

"All done."

Patsy's declaration was like a key unlocking Dan from the shackles of torment. He blew out a gust of air, his shoulders relaxing, a thin smile appearing on his lips.

Trey released his arm from the analysis unit, patting his shoulder. "Rest a minute. Then we'll help you back to the living room. Patsy's dying to nurse you to complete health."

Beaming eagerness, Patsy flashed Dan the grin that always knocked Trey off his feet. In his opinion she was altogether too free in dispersing what he'd prefer she limited to him. But you couldn't constrain Patsy, at least not without good stout rope.

She bubbled with bright sincerity. "That I am. I'll have ya dancin' an Irish jig before ya know it."

Her reward was another slight smile. "Thank you."

It should have surprised Trey but didn't when the kid's brows lowered and his eyes narrowed as though he were returning to threat assessment mode. "You two aren't first family, are you? I don't recognize your names."

That's what's worrying him? Like I thought, the kid has to be a runaway. Trey chuckled, trying to lighten the mood. It came out more like a croak. Fake laughs weren't his forte.

"Hardly. My mother is a cook. My father, a butler. I've lived off Tallav for years until recently. And Patsy isn't even from Tallav." Trey looked at Patsy. "Which begs the question, Patsy. Are you here as Adrianna's guest?"

A self-satisfied smirk replaced Patsy's genial expression. "No. I'm a proper Tallavan citizen."

Both Dan and Trey looked as though they wanted to say *pull the other one.* Instead Trey grunted. "How's that possible? Did Adrianna get Shane's mother to use her influence?"

Patsy swiveled on her toes like a reluctant child, not ready to share her secret. "She didn't have to. Ya don't know the finer points of Tallavan immigration law. Anyone born in Ireland itself, on Earth, can apply for citizenship if they meet certain standards. Which I do."

Trey's head jerked back. "Huh."

"I'd escape if I could."

Both Trey and Patsy turned toward Dan, whose scowling face gazed into the distance at thoughts or memories he found beyond distasteful. Malice lurked in his eyes.

The silence that had dropped like a shroud over the room finally registered on Dan, as did the concerned stares of Patsy and Trey. "I'm first family." His voice was harsh with a bitterness no one his age should possess. "And I'd die to make it possible for men like me to live as they choose, own assets, manage their lives without requiring their mother or oldest sister's consent."

A slight chill ran down Trey's spine, more like a drop of cool water than an icicle. A manic glint flickered in the kid's eyes. Still, who knew what he'd been through. Some first families were abominable. "Yeah. I have male first family friends who'd agree with the sentiment. Not the dying part, but the freedom."

Trey patted Dan's shoulder again, satisfied when the kid visibly shook off his mood. "Let's get you out to the couch where you'll be more comfortable."

The trip to the living room was smooth, the meds and foot wrap making the journey less painful for Dan. Ensconced in a corner of the couch, side table at hand and foot propped on the ottoman, he fought to keep heavy eyelids from closing.

Patsy perched on the edge of the ottoman. "The coffee I made ya is cold now. I'll go get ya another. Do ya need somethin' else? Is there anything I can do for ya? Ya sure we can't comm someone for ya?"

"Coffee would be nice. Thanks." Elbow on the couch's padded arm, he rested his forehead in the crook between his thumb and fingers.

"Right."

Dan waited until Patsy was out of earshot in the kitchen before turning his gaze to Trey, who was leaning against the fireplace, his arms crossed over his chest. One glance and Dan's eyes jerked away. The floor became far more interesting than it ever had been, except maybe to the decorators Randolph had hired.

"Are you in trouble?" Trey kept his voice gentle.

His face turning pale, Dan wiped his hands down his pants. "N-no. My mother's going to be mad at me. I wrecked her shuttle. And I..."

He looked toward the kitchen where Patsy had gone. "I was supposed to pick up something for her. She's always trying to keep up with our wealthy relations. Harebrained ideas, most of them. This time she's on to making money growing a-a rare f-fungus. In a-a m-man-made environment."

The pace of his words went from a dribble to rushing one after another. "It's a delicacy that only grows in a cave on a tiny island out in the Northern Ocean. That's why I was out in the shuttle. Picking it up."

He flicked a sidelong glance at Trey.

"My flight computer told me to fly around Rathlin, but I thought it would be faster to cross it. The storm didn't seem so bad out at sea. But once I came ashore, it got worse and worse."

Immersed in harrowing memories, he rocked in place as much as his leg, counteracting the movement, allowed. Description that had flown from his lips now stalled. He crossed his arms, rubbing his palms along the upper sleeves of his ski suit. After clearing his throat, he began again.

"The shuttle was old and started shaking like it would fall apart midair. I asked the computer for a spot to land, and your shuttle pad was closest." His shoulders slumped, and he buried his fists in his armpits. "I screwed that up."

Trey allowed silence to hang between them. Silence bothered most people, pushed them to fill it, an early lesson Trey had learned when dealing with subs who lied.

One thing was certain. Dan was lying.

He hadn't been making up how the accident happened. The horror of that was written on his face and communicated by his body language. The stuff about the fungus? That was probably built on an element of truth, but fungus? Growing only on a tiny island in the Northern Ocean? *Yeah, no. I don't believe it. What was the kid doing out over the Northern Ocean? Not meeting a future bride, that's for sure.*

Dan flicked another quick look at Trey. "My mom is going to be so pissed. And I won't even have the fungus to make up for it. By now it's freezing."

Something might be freezing out in that broken shuttle, but Trey didn't believe it was fungus. He continued to stare at Dan, knowing that he'd gone past resting-thug face to his I-punish-liars face.

The kid plunged ahead.

"Unless… You wouldn't mind… Could you…"

"What? Go get it and bring it here?"

Dan pushed against the arm and back of the couch as though he were attempting to rise. His leg, however, remained stationary on the ottoman. "I guess I could give it a try."

Yeah, he's going to plow through all that snow. Really? I'll just go with it. Maybe get a look at what the kid's hiding for myself. Trey tried to lighten his expression unsuccessfully. Dan was still sitting tensed in preparation to stand. "How much is there?"

"A flat about this size." He made an approximation with his hands, his gaze fixing on Trey's eyes, still leaning forward, but more in eagerness that Trey might acquiesce than an actual bid to get up from the couch. "The flat is in a bin with growing medium on the bottom. It's not very heavy. J-just don't open it. The fungus has particular, uh, air requirements. H-humidity or something."

Trey didn't give the kid a break, continuing to use the tone of voice that cowed even experienced subs. "Uh-huh. Where is it in the shuttle?"

"In the front beside the pilot's seat." Dan edged closer to the side of the couch away from Trey. "I mean, I c-could go get it. Not a problem. Just loan me a coat." He patted his ankle. "See, foot's a lot better. But I'll need my boots."

Stepping carefully this time, Patsy reentered the room, carrying a steaming mug. "Here's your coffee. I commed Randolph. He'll call off emergency services now he knows no one was seriously hurt. He's arrangin' for a shuttle wrecker service to come once the storm clears." She set the coffee next to Dan, glancing between him and Trey. "What's up?"

"The kid needs someone to go get fungus from the shuttle. He's worried it will freeze." Skepticism dripped from Trey's statements.

Dan eyed Patsy as though she were a more likely prospect for convincing of his dire need. "Th-the door is ajar. I barely got it open. And then I fell, so I didn't try to close it."

Like I'd ever let Patsy walk by herself into danger.

Trey ran a hand over his face. Dan wallowing through deep snow on a sprained ankle was nuts. *Which leaves me.*

Of course it would be dangerous.

Damn.

Of course it would require him to climb down to the crew door to get to it.

Double damn.

Of course his body rebelled at the mere thought, kicking off the paranoid reactions he didn't need clawing to life again. His stomach roiled and the back of his throat tightened with an ache he couldn't relieve by swallowing.

Damn. Damn. Damn.

"Fungus?" With one word, Patsy inserted herself in the middle of Trey's decision. The question wasn't directed at Dan. And it implied far more.

If anyone could read him, it was Patsy. She knew he was rooted in place, not calmly standing still. She was really asking, *What the heck is going on with you? What is this fungus you're talking about, and how am I going to help? Because I am going to help.* That she'd communicated that in one word must be a record, but Trey was in no shape to draw it to her attention despite the desire to laugh hysterically.

"We should both go." Patsy planted her fists on her hips, rotating her torso in the same way a cat wiggles his bottom when preparing to spring. "You went out there once by yourself. It's not safe. Don't go actin' the maggot."

"I am not a fool. Which is why you should go nowhere near that wreck." He turned his glare on Dan. "None of us should."

Dan threw his leg off the ottoman, grimacing when his foot hit the floor and folding his lips to muffle a cry. He struggled to rise, shoving himself to the edge of the couch. Balancing on his good foot, he sidled along the ottoman, released his handle hold on the arm of the couch, and limped in the direction of the room with the med bed.

Clump.

Whimper.

Clump.

Whimper.

"Stop it." Patsy hollered, rushing to aid Dan.

Dan swayed, sagging against Patsy and accepting her assistance to return to his seat.

"We'll go get your fungus. Never you mind. I can see you're as stubborn an idjit as the wally over there." She tilted her head in Trey's direction. "Sit yourself down, and don't think about liftin' a finger until we get back."

She sashayed toward the foyer.

Trey waited a moment before throwing his hands in the air and following her, gazing at the glorious way her ass twitched.

Damned if this wasn't exactly like his first meeting with her. He'd followed her onto *LS Quantum,* enjoying how her marvelous bum moved when she walked, and into a situation that had Patsy apologizing multiple times in one day for unwise decisions. It seemed fate had a multiuse formula for his life.

That worked out.

Let's hope this does too.

A multitude of terrifying possibilities flooded his thoughts, poisoning his courage. But not his determination. No way was Patsy going into danger without him along to rescue her when fate's formula for her life flung unanticipated modifications into her plans.

14

Patsy's winter outdoor gear was neatly positioned on hooks and in cubbies in the foyer thanks to Trey. Her handsome neat freak had surprised her though. He'd given in so easily. Here he was, beside her, quietly sealing his overcoat while she pulled on her boots.

Finished prepping for the blizzard, he helped her put on her coat and handed her hat, muffler, and gloves, pulling her hood up and snugging it so she could just see out the small hole left from his tight cinching. He removed his own gloves from his pockets and donned them.

He loomed over her, big dominant male that he was, and wrested back the control she thought she'd gained. "It's colder now than when you arrived. The wind is so fierce you can't see more than a foot or two in front of your face. I'm going to tie one end of the rope I used before to you and wrap the excess over my shoulder. I'll go first. If you run into trouble, jerk on the rope. Understand?" That last question came out sounding more talking grizzly bear than human.

The man's peeved, but I'm glad he's comin'. "I understand."

If it's as bad as he says, it'll take both of us to succeed. If it's as bad as he says, shouldn't he be demandin' I stay inside?

He turned, moving toward the front door, but stopped when she yanked on his sleeve.

"Why aren't ya tryin' to stop me? I can tell you're not wantin' to go out in that mess again. Why d'ya give in so easy?"

He met her gaze, his eyes intense, unblinking. "We both know you'd stew over Dan's fungus, drive me crazy, and I'd have to try eventually. I love you. I'd do anything for you. Apparently that includes going out in the worst snowstorm I've ever seen, tied to a rope, to help someone we've just met, someone who crashed our reunion and will be a third wheel until either this blizzard blows us into oblivion or comes to a halt."

For a second he looked away before returning his gaze to hers, his eyes twinkling with a smile she couldn't see with his lips covered. "I'm doing it because I love you, so don't forget that. You owe me for this." He headed to the door.

Well, didn't that just bake the cake. He loved her. More than just physically, but all the way to now and forever. A fact she'd known. He'd made it unmistakable yesterday in words and deeds. But as a million butterflies—no, hundreds, hundreds of butterflies—cavorted in her stomach, she embraced a certainty down to the DNA that determined she'd have red hair and freckles. He loved her. It was written on the strands of life from which she was created. She felt like she could float away, which was a relief since her knees were wobbly.

"Are you coming?" The question growled at her in full Dom mode sent a blast of arctic air to freeze her euphoria. It shattered, shards falling around her when he opened the door and the blizzard smacked her back into reality.

"Comin'." *Sweet mother Mary, protect us. This is goin' to be cold.*

Outside, Trey secured the rope to Patsy, pointed out into air thick with whipped snow, and trudged forward. He seemed to be following a rumpled track that slashed through smooth drifts on either side.

I knew we could do this.

The storm carried on around the bubble that seemed to surround them. Inside it she felt safe, secure that Trey would get them to the shuttle and back with the fungus that Dan and his mother so desperately needed.

It isn't so bad out here.

Trey blocked any view she might have had of the shuttle pad and hangar or the wreck, but she could see much farther than Trey had claimed. The peak of the Giant's Tit was obscured, but closer to her the wind ruffled banks of confectionary white into an ethereal, forbidding beauty of spiraling, dancing crystals.

They came to a turning point, and she tripped, falling and sinking into snow that was deeper than she expected, laughing at her own ineptness. Trey offered her his hand, yanking her back onto her feet, and bellowed, "Be careful."

He's right.

Be serious.

This isn't a lark.

Even though it feels like a lark. So much delightful snow.

Blizzard, idjit. You've read about people gettin' lost in them and freezin' to death.

Hard to remember when she was so full of frolic. She was with the man who loved her as relentlessly and as deeply as she loved him. Frolicking was the least of what the effervescent champagne that had replaced the blood in her veins encouraged.

They'd take care of Dan, send him on his way when they could, and return to eating, sleeping, and loving. Not so much eating and sleeping. Take care of Dan…

Shite. She mentally whacked herself. *I'm at it again. Takin' care of others. Puttin' them first.* It hadn't taken long for all her good intentions to be swamped by old habits.

She smacked into Trey, who'd stopped, blocking the path. The shuttle was plainly visible to either side of him, but she'd been focusing on her feet, so she missed it.

Trey dumped the remaining line on his shoulder beside the fuselage in an area scoured free of snow and worked at the knot to disconnect Patsy from it. "I want you to stay here. Right here. Don't move from this spot." He played out a length of rope and then tied it to the shuttle, lashing the other end around his waist. "I'll use this to climb to the open door in the cockpit, go inside, grab the bin, and get back to you as fast as I can."

The slope he intended to descend didn't seem that steep to Patsy. There was a definite grade to it, but it was nowhere near difficult, and it went on for quite a way before the cliff dropped off in a sheer wall. Not that she was an expert, but she'd hiked worse at home in Ireland. Perhaps if the ground was icy, but it wasn't. A little slippery, but more of a worry for bruising your knees or spraining your ankle if you fell. No plummeting to your death.

And yet Trey stood solid as an ice sculpture, staring off in the distance. Where was the take-charge, I'll-deal-with-this man who would already be down the slope and climbing into the shuttle?

Something was wrong.

He'd been standing just like this when she'd interrupted the conversation between him and Dan. And that had been about getting the fungus from the shuttle. Trey had been here, so he knew what he faced. And something was scaring the shite out of him, because he still hadn't moved.

If he hadn't been wearing an overcoat, he might have jumped out of his skin when she reached out and touched his arm. "Feckin' man, ya have things turned about. Suppose ya get stuck? Or ya trip over your enormous feet tryin' to walk over those rocks, sprainin' your ankle like that lad whose feet aren't half the size of yours. Why, one of your toes would dwarf his whole foot. Monstrous big they are. And then what's to be done? Are ya plannin' on me to haul ya back up here? Only an idjit would conceive of such a simpleminded way of doin' things."

Trey's eyes never left her as she rambled on, watching as she untied the rope from his waist. An internal quake shook him, freeing him from the mental ice that had locked him in its grasp. He reached for her hand when she tried to fasten the guideline around her middle. "Patsy. You can't. It's far too dangerous. You're a slip of a woman. I should climb down there and—"

"Exactly." She shook free of his grasp and continued tying the rope. "I'm the right size for sliding through the door. The bin isn't heavy."

He grasped her arms and shook her.

"You can't. You could fall." His voice was hoarse, heavy with gravel.

She bellowed at him. "I won't fall." Clapping a gloved hand to the side of his face, or what appeared to be the side of his face under his muffler and hood, she glared straight into his eyes. "And if I did, ya could pull me up. Besides, you feckin' behemoth, ya haul your bulk in that shuttle and the cockpit might slide right off."

What she could see of Trey's face went ashen gray.

Fool woman. If there was any more shite to scare out of him, ya just managed it.

"I'll be fine. I hardly weigh a bean. Ya know that." She patted his muffler one more time and trotted backward a few steps before turning and hurrying to the pad's edge. If she did this quickly, he wouldn't have a chance to stop her.

A tug on the rope around her waist brought her up short. She gripped it and turned, prepared to melt the snow off Trey with a blistering reproof. He waved her on, playing out more rope. Instead of scolding him, she settled back on her heels. Just as well she couldn't see his face. *Certain it is he's scowling, his own way of sending a blistering reproof.*

All right then. The rope continued to tug at her, but it didn't impede her as she moved lower, stepping carefully amid the rocks she'd claimed would trip Trey up but could do the same to her. The pull of the guideline was a potent reminder that he was behind her. She had no doubt that if she got herself into trouble, he'd rescue her, no matter the neurotic fear of falling that had him terrorized.

The cockpit door was two feet above where she stood. No wonder Dan had sprained his ankle. He'd probably been in shock and didn't even realize the drop was there until he was already falling.

The first toehold she could find would be a stretch to reach, but it was doable. *Fate be damned. Break a leg. The show must go on.*

One hand on the shuttle's side and the other gripping the door, she heaved herself up.

Her foot hit the bottom of the doorway and slid off.

She caught her balance, settled herself for a second attempt, and leaped. Missed.

Shite. Ya get up there before ya wear yourself out.

Putting all her might into it, she sprang, her right leg straining to force her foot high enough. And she had it.

Wobbly from the effort, she perched on the rim, her head partway inside the shuttle.

A jolting thought came to her as she squeezed to get the rest of her through the uncooperative doorway. *What if the bin won't fit?*

The cabin was dark, sunlight barely penetrating the interior. How was she to find the bin in this murk? She could hear Trey sermonizing one of his I-told-you-so lectures.

Not to worry. Ya can still do this. Returning empty-handed would be a galling defeat.

Gradually she saw more of her surroundings.

Idjit, you're snow-blind. Give it a moment.

To the right, the opening that led from the cockpit to the passenger section was filled with the debris of collapsed ceiling panels and other interior shuttle components. That direction offered no avenue of escape if the bin wouldn't fit through the partly opened door.

She moved around the back of the pilot's seat. A console filled most of the area between the pilot and copilot's stations. Its size made no sense considering its function seemed more about providing cup holders and access to entertainment systems.

Vidscreens looked to be the primary tool for piloting a craft that was most likely one of the idiot-proof shuttles marketed as vanity rides for the rich and famous about eighteen years ago. The buttons, dials, and thruster controls she'd expected from action and adventure vids were in a narrow space between the vidscreens.

The bin was not where Dan had described. It was strapped into the copilot's seat. *I guess that counts as beside the pilot's seat.* She struggled to unclasp the five-point buckle. It was jammed, but in her attempts to force it to release, she turned the bin. At that angle, it might slip between the straps. She wrestled with it until one end broke through the restraints, allowing her to pull it straight out.

It was both taller and longer than it was wide, which she estimated was twelve inches. Dan had been right. It wasn't heavy. She levered it behind the seats and brought it close to the door, depositing it on the floor before scanning the width of the exit.

Not twelve inches. Closer to eleven.

But close.

If she could get the door to slide farther on its track, the rest would be easy. Balanced on the rim of the entrance, her back propped on one side, she shoved at it with her foot.

Nothing happened.

She'd needed more force. A sledgehammer would be nice. She reentered the cabin, looking for anything that she could use to strike at the door's edge with greater power.

Possibilities were scarce. A suitcase, which on opening she discovered contained clothing that probably belonged to Dan. A trash bag with empty snack containers. And an ancient piñata, a hole torn in its side and candy gone.

The suitcase is narrow, so I can at least get that to the lodge. But nothing she found would help unstick the door.

Then she noticed a recessed latch in the floor. It opened easily, revealing a cavity with a jumble of tools. A ten-inch adjustable wrench offered the only real heft. She snatched up the telescopic mirror too, figuring it might come in handy.

Once again perched in a birdlike pose, she slid forward to get a better look at the apparatus that was supposed to allow the door to skim along the plane and out of the way. It had cleared about one-third of the track before jamming.

The hardware that opened and closed it was hidden from view. From her knowledge of pocket doors, she imagined a hinge attaching the door itself to the rolling mechanism and track on the side of the plane. Try as she might, she couldn't slide the extension mirror through the crack to see whether these were functional or busted.

Shite. Whatever she did, however she shoved at the edge of the door, she couldn't get it to budge that extra inch she needed.

Sweat trickled down her back. Her jaw ached. If she kept clenching it, she could crack a tooth. Everything in her wanted to throw the wrench and hit something breakable.

Instead she gave the flat inside panel of the door a resounding kick with the bottom of her boot.

It moved.

Broken free from whatever had blocked it, the door nearly closed, but gravity interfered to slow it. She caught hold and rammed it in a desperate effort to keep from getting trapped. The result? An extra six inches that even Trey might have squeezed his hulk through.

Thankfully she hadn't thrown the wrench; it wedged perfectly into the door's bottom track to keep it stationary. She returned to the cabin, grabbed the suitcase, and shoved it out in the direction of the shuttle's pad.

Next she pulled the bin into her arms, sat on the doorway's rim, and eased herself to the ground, one arm securing the container to her chest and the other with a death grip on the door, flexing her knees as she hit the rocks. *That's how it's done to keep from takin' a hopper. Too bad Dan had to fall and hurt his ankle.*

Trey had edged closer to the slope, not right on the brink but closer. She sent him a thumbs-up. The muffler covered his lower face, so she couldn't tell if he was grinning like a loon too.

The ascent was considerably easier, even carrying the bin, because he was boosting her along, pulling on the rope. She extended the container to him so she could grab the suitcase.

It required him to inch forward another foot, but he did it on his knees.

Sweet mother Mary, I love that man. She whooped and hollered, "Atta boy. That's my feckin' hero."

"Get the hell up here."

The growled words were vibrant with taciturn love, fluently emotive despite the unsuccessful use of anger to obscure their true meaning. Trey had his own love language.

She tossed the suitcase onto the pad and scrambled past it, flipping to sit and catch her breath.

"Feckin' woman. Get. Away. From the edge."

"Ah. The mating call of a dominant human male. I come, my love." A case of the giggles overtook her while she rose and latched onto the suitcase's handle. Life couldn't get better.

The suitcase was heavier than the bin, but still easy enough to haul after years of dealing with recalcitrant stage sets. She lugged it toward Trey and was snatched off her feet, held tight in his arms, his face buried into her hood to rest muffler to muffler.

She let the suitcase fall. "Whoa, big man. I'm safe. You're safe. We got the bin. Let's look inside."

"What?" Trey dropped her to the ground. "What about the fungus needing a protected environment? Now you want to kill it?"

"If there is fungus in there, we'll make it up to him. But that's the dumbest thing I ever heard. Ya didn't believe it, did ya?"

"No. I thought you did."

"Somethin's goin' on with that boy, but it has nothin' to do with fungus. I figured we needed to find out."

Trey plucked the bin from the snow-covered pavement and held it between them. "Open it."

The latches opened with a snap. Patsy dropped the lid. "No fungus. What is it?"

"Good God! This looks like…"

"Like what?" Patsy leaned in to peer into the bin, blocking Trey's view. "Looks like the kinds of fiddly bits my cousin kept in his workroom."

"I doubt your cousin had any of this stuff in his workroom."

Patsy tipped her head to stare at Trey, chilled not by the blizzard but from a nameless dread that blossomed on hearing the weighted tone of his voice.

"Supplies to make a bomb."

She rapidly backpedaled until she was blocked by the shuttle's fuselage.

"A bomb?"

His response was whip-crack sharp. "No. Not a bomb. Not yet. Nothing is going to blow up." He wrapped his arm around the bin and sifted through the contents with his fingers. "Detonating cord, blasting caps, and packs of explosives."

His gaze rose to meet hers. "Enough to do a lot of damage. What the hell is Danny boy into?"

Patsy didn't have the slightest idea. Wasn't Tallav a stable society? Irish history had its own share of terror bombings, complicated by the intertwining of religious and secular aspirations. A loony cult maybe?

She moved back to where Trey stood with the bin. "What should we do?"

He pulled out his hand comm. "You comm Randolph. I'm calling Shane. Tell him what we've found and that I'm putting Shane in the loop."

A jittery sensation slid along her nerves. "Right."

Patsy dropped her unfocused gaze to the snow-trampled pavement and stilled her feet. *This is serious. Damn serious. And that kid doesn't look like he has serious in him. But hadn't he said he'd die to make it possible for men on*

Tallav to live as they chose. Is that it? Men's rights? Still, he can't have done this on his own. Someone is helping him. Maybe even using him.

I'll see about that.

"Right."

The comm to Randolph was quick. He fired off a series of questions, getting the essentials, and advised her to follow Shane's instructions to the letter.

Trey snapped his hand comm closed and stared at her with unseeing eyes. His silence seemed to expand inside her, stealing into every nook and cranny until she felt ready to burst.

"What did he say?"

In a rock-hard tone of voice, Trey spit out each bit of information, flinging it into the face of the blizzard swirling about them as though daring it to spoil their plans. "Shane, Adrianna, and Maon will be on their way to Rathlin in the next hour. As soon as the storm abates, they'll come to this side of the island. In a shuttle far more capable than that wreck of Dan's."

Chest tight, Patsy jerked her head in a sharp nod. Questions would only muddy the waters when Trey was in succinct mode.

"Maon's doing background checks on Dan and his mother. We didn't get his last name, so that's not going to be easy."

"Right. Right. Maybe we can get that out of him," Patsy muttered to herself.

"Shane said not to do anything that might spook him. He could be dangerous. Dangerous, Patsy. At least we know he's not armed. That ski suit hides nothing."

"Right. Right." Dangerous and Dan didn't connect. The kid stuttered, for goodness' sakes.

Some of the rigidity left Trey's voice. "We're to act like we haven't looked in the bin. Natural. Go about our day. One night. And then they should be here to take over." That last was spoken with satisfaction.

The questions Patsy had been holding back could no longer be denied. Trey might be satisfied, but she wasn't.

"What about the hunting weapons at the lodge?"

"Under lock and key in a gun case."

"What about his suitcase? He could have a weapon in there."

Trey frowned in consideration.

A solution popped into her brain before he could make up his mind. She waved her hands in the air. "No. No. I know how we can find out. He's disabled. Right? I'll carry his suitcase up and unpack for him. If he insists on refusing the help, it'll mean he's got something to hide."

Laughter spilled through Trey's response. "If you have to. But you could just open it up in front of him. Do you really think his mother would allow Dan to have a gun or that he'd even know how to use one? Let's do what Shane told us to do. You play caretaker, Patsy, and I'll chat him up."

Feckin' man. I'm still going through the suitcase. She laughed out loud and scoffed, "You chat him up?"

"I can carry on a conversation when I want to."

"Whatever you say. I'll fill in the gaps."

The grizzly bear returned, casting a huffy growl. Trey snatched the lid and positioned it on the container, holding it out for Patsy to seal the latches. He thrust the bin into her hands, revamped the rope's attachments, grabbed the handle of the suitcase, and plodded through the snow, leading the way and reeling in their guideline as he went.

The pace he set was faster than on the outgoing journey. Patsy found it harder and harder to match his speed. Fed up, she grasped the rope and gave it a violent yank. It didn't faze Trey, but at least he turned and checked on her.

"Feckin' man, my legs are shorter than yours. Ya think ya could slow down?"

"Yeah. Sorry." He stepped toward her and put his hand on her shoulder. "I'm running on adrenaline. It wasn't on purpose."

"I'm on edge too. Maybe if we take it slower, we'll both get our heads on straight before we face Dan."

He trampled a spot in the snow, set the suitcase down, and crushed her to him. "Right. We will do this because if we give it away, we'll need to be ready to take him prisoner."

Patsy let the bin drop to her feet and latched on to him, burrowing into his chest, wishing she could hear the steady beat of his heart through his clothing, pretending she could.

"At least ya've got experience in tying people up. But I don't want that to happen. I still feel sorry for the kid. He's pretty scared as it is."

Trey's arms tightened. "I won't let him hurt you."

"Course not." Patsy stopped herself from biting her lip. Despite the muffler, she'd been licking her lips, and they were badly chapped. *I'll brew us all a nice soothing cup of tea at the lodge. One of those relaxing ones. Maybe get the med bed to prescribe antianxiety meds and give us a dose in our tea.*

She bent and gripped the handles of the bin tight. "Steady on," she whispered.

15

Trey dropped the suitcase on the foyer tiles and shut his eyes, blocking out thoughts of the predicament he and Patsy were in, and heaved a slow sigh, grateful to be back inside away from the blizzard. The lull in the storm that had accompanied their trek out to the damaged shuttle had disappeared in a renewed ferocity of wind-whipped snow on their return.

Behind him, he heard Patsy stamping her feet and cursing the damnable feckin' weather. He stripped his outerwear, hopping on one foot after removing his right boot until he found a dry spot to step. Despite his effort, he lost his balance loosening the bindings on his second boot and ended up with soaked socks. Freezing toes protested.

He claimed the bin from Patsy, who was standing much as he had, eyes closed, soaking in the warmth and calm of this refuge from the bitter battle outside.

Their guest was stirring in the living room. "Did you get it?"

Trey found Dan propped against the side of the couch, holding himself up with one arm like a sapling trembling in a stiff breeze. His gaze locked onto the bin like his existence depended on its contents. Then he slumped, awkwardly folding in on himself, spinning to sit in a barely controlled tumble before Trey could slap the bin on the ottoman and reach him.

"Careful there. We got your fungus." Trey wavered on whether to place a steadying hand on Dan's shoulder, deciding against it because it would require him to lean over the kid. *Might think I'm going to throttle him.*

"Th-thanks. Really. I can't thank you enough. I know I put you to a lot of trouble. It may not seem like life or death to you, but for me... For me it is." Dan shoved his knuckles to his lips and shuddered. The smile he forced on his face was a sickly effort at gratitude, watered down by suppressed anxiety.

"Glad to help." Trey's stomach quivered with uneasy guilt. *Desperation is the only thing that could make this kid dangerous. We'll have to make sure he doesn't get desperate.*

Patsy clomped into the living room, boots covered in icy slush, hefting the suitcase toward the stairs that led up to the bedrooms. "I found your suitcase."

"You're tracking snow all over the floor." Trey waved an arm at the melting footprints she'd made. Per the advice Shane had given them, inane bickering between Patsy and himself was as natural as it got. Worrying about insignificant things would make them look clueless about the bin's deadly contents.

True to form, Patsy snapped back a response. "I didn't want my socks to get wet."

"What about my socks?"

"They're already wet. Dan, I'll take this up to a bedroom for ya and unpack your things. It's past lunchtime. We could all use something to eat. Trey, why don't ya see to that?" She headed toward the stairs, ignoring Dan's protest.

He didn't try to stand, responding over his shoulder. "You don't have to do that. You've done too much already. I shouldn't be here long." He turned his head and addressed Trey. "At least I don't think so. How long does this kind of storm last?"

The chance of a weapon stashed in Dan's luggage dropped to zero. One refusal to accept her help made purely for the sake of being polite. No stuttering. Yeah, no gun.

"Not a clue. This is only my second day on this side of Rathlin, but I gather weather here can be extreme. Somewhere around here there should be a control tablet for the vidscreen behind that wall panel." Trey rummaged in the side table at the far end of the couch from where Dan was seated. "Not in here. Maybe that one." He pointed.

Dan found it and held it out to Trey.

"Nah. Go ahead. You can probably drive that better than I can."

A flush moved up Dan's face into his hairline. *Damn. I didn't mean to remind the kid he's wrecked his mom's shuttle. If it actually belongs to her.*

Trey picked up the bin. "Where should I put this?"

The difference between Dan's reaction to Patsy hauling his suitcase away and Trey taking hold of the fungus bin was dramatic. On the stage a director might have encouraged an actor to tone down his over-the-top performance. Dan practically leaped from the couch in an instantaneous rush to lay hands on the bin.

"Calm down. I just want to get it out of the way so we don't trip over it. I know it's important to you." Trey set the bin on the side table beside Dan. "I'll put it here where you can keep an eye on it."

"Th-thanks. I guess I'm a little nervous about it." Dan settled himself back, adjusting his foot on the ottoman with a wince.

"I'll be in the kitchen." Before Trey left the room, he saw Dan lift his hand and touch the side of the bin. *Yeah, the only thing that kid is worried about is the bomb supplies. But if anyone can get his story out of him, that'll be Patsy, the woman of a thousand questions.* He grinned to himself. *No, a million.*

He grabbed a dozen vacu-sealed sausage rolls from the pantry, figuring two for Patsy, four for Dan, and six for himself. Peeled from its wrapper, the first roll wasn't as big as those his mom made, so he grabbed six more.

The lodge kitchen was equipped to cook for large groups with shiny commercial appliances and open shelves of cookware. The eighteen sausage rolls fit on a single sheet pan that Trey popped into the instant-on oven to warm. He opened two vacu-sealed bags of mixed fruits, filling a serving bowl, happy that whoever had stocked the kitchen and pantry hadn't expected visitors to be chefs.

Carrying the fruit and three sets of dishes and cutlery, he returned to the living room. Patsy was at the opposite end of the couch, her legs curled beside her in full interrogation mode.

"So you're an only child. No sister."

Dan's expression was a mixture of forlorn and anxious, as though he'd found the perfect person to strew his personal struggles before and receive the pity he craved. "No. My mother's line ends with her. Not that she's on the main branch of the family. No, she's a sad twig they'll throw on the fire when she's gone. Happy to be rid of her."

Sad twig? The kid talks like a poet. "Here's the first part of our late lunch."

Patsy jumped up and grabbed the fruit bowl, placing it on the side table at her end of the couch, taking the dishes and silverware when Trey held them out to her. "Sausage rolls will be ready in a minute. I'll get drinks too. Iced tea okay?"

He received a positive response from the others and returned to the kitchen, listening to Patsy make a big deal over how much fruit she served Dan. She'd be well on her way to pampering that kid into love with her before they finished eating.

He returned with the rest of their meal and sank into the center of the couch, easily filling his third and parts of theirs.

"Ya could have pulled over the armchair."

"Mmm. Could have." He lowered his plate to his lap and squeezed her knee.

Dan's eyes widened at the amount of food on Trey's plate, but Trey was used to that reaction. He bit off half a sausage roll in one bite. *These are definitely smaller than Mom's. And not as good.*

"So Dan was tellin' me that if he's not married by the time his mother passes, he'll have to live with one of his relatives, doin' whatever they tell him to like a servant but with no pay. Can ya believe it? Of course ya can. Ya grew up here."

"Mmm." Even without a mouthful, it was better to let Patsy keep on a roll.

She leaned to her right to bring Dan back into view. "Why haven't ya gone to school to learn a profession? Ya could become a doctor, a lawyer, a schoolteacher."

Dan mournfully shook his head. "First family sons are not educated beyond the basics. We're allowed to become marshals if we're unmarried and our mothers agree. Otherwise we are expected to marry and raise children. If we never marry, there are other possibilities…"

"Like?"

"Like caring for our relatives' children or elderly parents." He stared off in the distance, his face flat and expressionless except for the trembling slash of his lips. "And other things…"

Patsy held her spoonful of fruit midair, aghast. "They don't murder ya, do they?"

She ignored Trey's snort.

The sausage roll in Dan's hand went uneaten. He dropped it to the plate, his gaze riveted on Patsy, eyes wide. "I-I don't know. I never thought…"

His eyes lost focus on the here and now for a moment before continuing. "I suppose it could happen. A man sent to an estate and never heard from again. I just assumed they never allowed them to leave. I've had friends. Comms disabled… Oh gods."

Distracted, he tried to find somewhere to set his plate. Trey snatched it before the bowl of fruit slid into his lap. He nudged the bowl onto his own plate and slid Dan's sausage rolls over before sliding the empty plate beneath his.

The idea was ridiculous. Patsy should never have suggested it. "No one is that debased. The police, the government would know if that happened as more than a once off. Maybe some evil old hag might want to do it. But the more people in on a secret, the more likely it is to be discovered."

"You don't know," Dan snarled. His face had transformed, lips pulling back to bare his teeth and his cheeks mottling with hectic scarlet. "I've experienced the depths of their depravity. They're capable of anything."

Trey shifted sideways, turning himself into a broader barrier between Patsy and this dangerous side of Dan now fully exposed. The potency of his fury no longer lurked beneath his usual meekness. Thoroughly engulfed in rage, the hatred in his eyes was aimed at a specter only he could see.

It spewed from a wound inflicted by someone who should have kept Dan safe, if what Trey feared was true. And it had festered into a virulent alter ego, opposite of Dan's real temperament.

The kid turned his head aside, his jaw clenched, tremors shaking the control he was trying to assert by holding himself stiff.

"What happened?"

"What did they do to you?" The question burst from Trey, overlapping Patsy's.

It took a few minutes for Dan's breathing to slow and his body to calm. "I shouldn't tell you."

He sagged back into the couch, his neck bending and his gaze dropping to his lap where his hands lay palms up, passive.

Trey's voice was grim with the desire to right whatever wrongs had been committed against the boy. "If your mother or other relatives have been mistreating you, we know people who can help. The Tallavan Matriarchist Party may think they have a tight rein on Tallav, but they don't."

He put his plate on the floor. "You're among friends. Tell us."

Several moments passed, creeping by, the expectancy in the room held in a mire that wouldn't allow time to move faster. At last Dan lifted his gaze, searching Trey's face, weighing whether to trust, to reveal his secrets.

He didn't once look at Patsy, and Trey supposed that wasn't a native Tallavan. Whatever he was looking for, he seemed to have found it, or enough of it to believe he'd discovered a powerful ally in Trey.

"My mother sells me at house parties."

Patsy's gasp caught in her throat.

"Most times it's older women who want an escort"—his lips pinched together in distaste—"a lover and someone who will dote on them for the week."

His shoulders narrowed as he drew in on himself. "If that were all, I could handle it. I don't enjoy it, but as Mother says, it puts food on our table. It's the other times." Bitter overtones haunted his words. "Weekend retreats. Organized by the dregs of society. Even some of the cream. But always in out-of-the-way locations. Homes set aside for the use of women like my mother who are one step away from service themselves."

His story, begun in dribs and drabs, now raced as though if he hurried, he would limit the memories' claims on his soul.

"They cling to a tiny family stipend, too proud to avail themselves of the room and board offered by working on the family's estate or its business ventures. Living in genteel poverty, hoping for a daughter who will elevate their status if their families allow them a pregnancy."

Watery-eyed, he snorted.

"Instead my mother had me. Worthless except for the money she could make off me."

"No." Patsy's voice was filled with sharp sympathy. "No one is worthless."

Dan's gaze flinched toward the ceiling, his head shaking and his lower lip trembling.

"I was eight when the retreats began. Mostly I was assigned the role of nude page boy." He bit his fist, attempting to hide a sob.

Trey felt trapped by the need to hear Dan's story, regretting the toll it was taking to recount the sordid details. The inability to make things immediately right for Dan or the men and boys suffering at the hands of these evil women made Trey's gut clench.

Damn bitches. Making a mockery of the BDSM lifestyle. Holding all the power, so no matter if the men involved claimed they did so of their free will, no actual consent existed. And involving children is beyond disgusting. It's criminal.

For now he could listen. In the future? He'd just found a good use for the massive payment he'd received from the Beta Tau Corporation. It wouldn't be bomb supplies. What he was hearing from Dan would create a bigger explosion through Tallavan society than any terrorist blast.

But even if the political side of the issue turned in men's favor, there would still be men like Dan who needed a place to go where they could receive the help they would need.

Trey looked Dan directly in the eyes. "What happened to you wasn't your fault." His throat closed over a knot of frustration when Dan's gaze fled from the intimacy. Trey had worked with damaged subs in the past. Getting them to believe that they hadn't been responsible for their abuse was difficult.

His voice a monotone, Dan continued his story without acknowledging Trey, each statement peeling back layers of cruel injuries from years of exploitation.

"They liked to be surrounded by nude men. Boys too. S-sometimes they played with me. I was so embarrassed. They laughed at me." His shrug that relegated the painful memories to the past. "I knew the fate that awaited me when I got older. The humiliation. The games. It was all out in the open in the house and grounds.

"There was a punishment room. Anyone new to the retreats was taken on a tour and showed what happened to tattlers. My tour... A man had his"—he gestured toward his lap—"in a vise. He was in agony. It was an effective threat.

"I-I never had to endure the torture inflicted in th-there." He turned his head to gaze off into the distance. "I was always compliant. A trembling whiner, as the woman who used that room as her personal play space called me. No fun at all."

Trey fisted his hands, wishing he could spend time with that woman in his own personal play space or hand her over to Randolph. A sexual sadist would know how to rain retribution on those who perverted the lifestyle. Patsy covered his clenched fingers with her own, stroking them until they relaxed.

"Another retreat is scheduled in two weeks." Dan heaved a shuddering sigh. "Mother is planning to sell me permanently. Her gambling debts have overtaken her ability to pay."

Patsy leaned forward across Trey and grasped Dan's knee. "That's not goin' to happen. We won't let it."

"That's right." Trey wrapped his arm around Patsy's waist and pulled her to sit on his lap. She clasped Dan's fingers, a gesture of reassurance.

The tears welling in Dan's eyes overflowed, sliding down to lips lifted in a jittery smile.

"I can't... I can't believe... My fate... I didn't think I could change it. Can you really... Can you really save me?"

"Yes." Trey let the force of his belief fill that single-word response. "Men have rights on Tallav. What you've told us is criminal. Fuck. I knew that things like this went on in the past, but not now. It's been forty years since the Freedom from Sexual Slavery referendum passed. Overwhelmingly. Every woman on the damned planet was for it. What kind of corruption must exist for this kind of organized evil to be happening today, hidden from the public eye?

"Dan, our friends are all members of first families. Their mothers and mothers-in-law are all heads of family and powerful women. Two of the men are well-respected marshals. They are all moderate to liberal in their views. You're never going back to your mother again. Not if I can help it."

Dan cupped his hands over his nose and mouth, crying in earnest now.

A call to Shane was the first step in bringing the law down on both groups of extremists, misandrists and bombers. But first they needed to deal with Dan and the contents of the bin he had been so eager to recover. The plan to smuggle explosives couldn't have originated with the kid. Someone else was behind this insane shuttle trip. Dan just needed to be encouraged to throw the last of his burdens on Trey.

Trey waited until Dan relaxed and was wiping his cheeks to introduce that touchy issue.

"We know what's in the bin. We looked before we ever brought it back here."

Dan blanched, his entire body going rigid as though he feared they would turn on him.

"Don't get excited." Trey tried not to scowl. "I'm pretty sure you're a courier for a group that's talked you into believing that terror is your only weapon against the matriarchists. Am I right?"

"I-I..." Dan faltered, his eyes shifting from Trey to Patsy to Trey again.

"Tell us what happened. I can't guarantee it, but I don't think you'll be in trouble if you reveal everything you know about who got you involved and what they intend to do with the explosives in that bin."

Trey's reassurance didn't seem to help Dan make up his mind. His thoughts must have taken a fatalistic turn. His face went slack, and he struggled to form his next words.

"I-I..."

He cleared his throat with a harshness that must have caused him pain.

"I joined the MRM, the men's resistance movement. My cousin told me about them last summer. Gave me files to read. Said I should be ready. That someday, someone would contact me about playing my part in freeing all Tallavan men from subjugation."

Patsy repositioned her legs. That she'd remained quiet so far was a testament to her compassion. Lancing a boil was painful but often necessary. Interrupting Dan with questions would only extend his discomfort.

"Nothing happened for months, and then one day as I was walking to our local village, taking a package to the delivery office, a man stopped me. He gave me the pass codes for a shuttle that I would find behind the local med clinic. All I had to do was start it up and follow the preprogrammed flight plan to a smugglers station in the North Sea and pick up a bin. I didn't know it was bomb supplies. Not until I got there.

"Anyway, the day after I received the instructions, my mother planned to be gone all day. As soon as she'd left, I found the shuttle and set off. The route zigzagged all over, I suppose to avoid detection. The shuttle didn't have any problem landing that time. I was sure I was at the right spot until several men emerged from a cave. Rough men. One threatened me if I went to the police. That's when I learned I'd be carrying explosives.

"At that point I was willing to do anything to get home. I was to park the shuttle where I'd found it and walk away. I just wanted to get home and forget the whole thing." His chin quivered. "I told myself not to think about what might happen with the bombs they planned to make. Tried convincing myself that they would blow up some empty building and no one would be hurt.

"I changed the return flight plan because it would be faster to fly over Rathlin rather than go around, and I flew into the storm. The rest you know." His shoulders drooped, and he covered his eyes with his hands. Between his fingers, his voice plaintive, he said, "I'm sorry. So sorry."

"Ya poor thing."

Trey shifted Patsy and slid from beneath her. She wrapped Dan in her arms.

"I'm going to comm Shane. Then Randolph. They'll know how to handle matters."

"Oh." Fresh fear clouded Dan's face. "I was given a number to comm if I ran into trouble."

"And?" Trey didn't hide his fierce concern.

Dan pulled back farther into Patsy's embrace. The glare she sent Trey communicated her annoyance.

"I did. They're coming when the storm clears. To get me and the bin. Deal with the shuttle. They weren't happy."

"I expect not. Okay. I'll pass that on to Shane. He's probably already on the other side of the island. Good chance he'll get here before your friends." Trey allowed his anger to pack extra snark into that last word.

Whether Shane arrived first, Trey would be ready for the danger due to land on their doorstep.

THE NEXT DAY Trey was surprised at how well he'd slept. He'd set his comm alarm to signal him when the weather service declared the north side of Rathlin open to low-level shuttle flights. It hadn't sounded, so he'd slumbered undisturbed, Patsy draped over him after a heated round of lovemaking.

He trusted Dan. But he had locked the bedroom door. He woke to a morning erection, gratified that the solution to his throbbing dilemma was skin to skin with him.

Flipped to her back, Patsy smiled at him, hair rumpled and eyes full of a sexy muzziness that made his libido shift into overdrive.

Her wrists were pinned above her head in a trice. Interruption could be moments away, and he had no intention of suffering from blue balls if he could avoid it.

Patsy helpfully wrapped her legs around him, nudging him with her pussy, already damp with arousal. "Gettin' right to business, are ya?"

"Hmm." She trembled beneath him, a reaction that always stroked his ego. "Did you forget something?"

She arched, pressing the tight peaks of her breasts firmly against his chest, and responded in sassy minx mode. "Sir. Gettin' right down to business, are ya, Sir?"

"Better." Claiming her lips, he kissed and penetrated her in the same moment. Thrust for thrust, his tongue duplicated his cock entering her vagina.

Best way.

To wake up.

Ever.

The pace he set forced him to break the kiss to draw in savage lungfuls of air, his erection never ceasing its rhythmic plunging. "You can come, but not before me."

"Ya feckin' man." She wrinkled her nose at him. "Sir."

He traced the line of her jaw with his mouth, nibbling and sucking, moving lower until he reached the junction of her neck and shoulder, enjoying the breathy moans that escaped her in time to his thrusting.

The tricks he'd learned to stave off his release weren't on today's menu. His senses fully stimulated, his physical awareness at its peak, he reveled in the blatant eroticism that was pure Patsy.

The point of no return loomed. He freed her wrists, gripping her hips to pull her harder against him, penetrating her as deeply as he could. Her fingernails bit into his back, pushing him over the edge, his orgasm barreling through him in multiple spasms of sweet ecstasy.

The last of his cum was squeezed from a cock already growing slack as she joined him in release, pulsating around him. He collapsed atop her, unable to make even a half-hearted effort to keep from crushing her.

"Oh, Sir." Not an ounce of distress accompanied that murmur of satisfaction. "Don't move… please."

His chest swelled with a torrent of emotions. *The perfect start to a… probably not a perfect day. But who the hell cares? I'd wallow in this kind of perfect every morning for the rest of my existence.*

The one last kiss intended as the finale to their lovemaking took on a life of its own, shattered to an abrupt conclusion by the buzz from his comm. The blizzard had ended. Time to get moving.

He rolled off Patsy and out of bed. "Get dressed. Company will be here soon."

"Right." The thump of her feet hitting the floor brought his gaze around from rummaging in the dresser, sticking to her fluid curves as she padded toward the bathroom. "You want the shower first? You're faster."

"Yeah. Sure." She was between him and the bathroom. How was he going to get past her without ravishing her again?

Temptress.

Then she bent over, and the question was moot. Two strides, maybe three, and his hand was cupped over her breast, his thumb stroking her nipple. The other hand firmly planted on her bum, he hauled her against him, his cock semihard.

A stinging slap to his butt cheek didn't deter him from dropping his head to kiss her. She popped him again.

Her voice rang with authority and laughter. "Adrianna commed me a message. They're on their way. We have half an hour at best. Get your magnificent ass in the shower now."

He pressed his forehead to hers with a groan. "Yes, ma'am."

"Don't start sweet-talkin' me. Get."

By the time Trey was showered and dressed, the sound of a shuttle met his ears. He went straight to the foyer to pull on and tie his boots.

Patsy jogged down the stairs as he was throwing on his coat and cold-weather gear. "That was fast. They're already here."

"Yeah. You should check on Dan and get him up."

Dan's voice drifted down from the top of the stairs. "I'm up. I'll get my clothes on."

"Great. Patsy can work on breakfast." Trey swung the door open, still hollering. "I'll greet our guests." Turning to step outdoors, he was stopped in his tracks.

"Trey. You're looking fabulous." Adrianna, her grin bright enough to blind a person even without it glinting off the snow, attempted to wrap him in an embrace, but her arms wouldn't reach around him, so she settled for patting him. "I'd mistake you for a bear if I didn't know there aren't any on Rathlin."

The next instant she was pushing past him. "Where's— There you are."

The two women dashed together with such energy Trey thought they might hurt one another in the collision, but they turned the extra momentum into a twirling hug, accompanied by bursts of laughter, exclamations, and greetings. Patsy had obviously passed on her good news to Adrianna.

Trey looked outside for the others but didn't spot them. "I'll go check on Shane and Maon, shall I?" He didn't receive a response from either woman, but Dan, who was standing at foot of the stairs clutching the newel post, nodded. *Poor kid looks like he wants to run back upstairs. Can't blame him.*

At the shuttle pad Shane was parking the craft he'd flown in the hangar. Trey found Maon inspecting the damaged shuttle and shaking his head.

"That's about as close as you can get and still land. A few more feet and that shuttle would have been in the ravine." Maon bumped Trey's shoulder with his fist. "How are you doing? You get things straightened out with that Irish jumping bean?"

Trey ignored the remark about the ravine. He had no problem letting someone else handle the crash site. "Do they have jumping beans in Ireland?"

"Who knows?" Maon leaned forward, the focus of his gaze tight on

Trey's face. "Sooo? You look to me like a man who's figured out which side of his bread is buttered."

"I am, and I have." Trey shoved his hands into his pockets. He wasn't ready to discuss his relationship with Patsy yet. There were too many issues they hadn't worked out.

The hangar door lowered with a clacking sound, drawing their attention. Shane exited the walk-in door and strode toward them. He was all business. "Let's get inside."

On the walkway he asked, "Why didn't you turn on the automatic deicer on the shuttle pad? There's one for this too." He gestured to the path they lumbered to cut through the snow.

Trey threw his hands up in a just-shoot-me-now gesture. "Fuck. I didn't know."

"Why would you?" Maon clapped Trey on his shoulder. "How many times you been back and forth through this mess?"

"This is number three."

"Sorry," Shane said. "I thought Randolph would have told you."

"Nope."

"You and Patsy?"

That's what Trey liked best about Shane. The man didn't need many words to get his point across.

"We're good."

"Glad to hear it."

The foyer was empty when they entered the lodge, but the sound of Patsy and Adrianna's voices reached him from the living room. "I'll hide your coats in the mudroom." It took less than a minute for Trey to jog down the hall and pitch his load on a counter, acknowledging to himself that he'd taken on the role of Dan's champion and didn't want to leave him depending too long on the marshals' sympathy.

The scene was as Trey had expected. Dan was seated in the center of the couch, Patsy on one side and Adrianna on the other, looking like he was clinging to the edge of a pool after being told to put his face in the water and blow bubbles for the first time. Except his hands were gripping his knees.

"His last name is Mullan, Shane. I don't recognize it, but I'm sure your mother will. Audrina too," Adrianna added, looking at Maon as Trey came up behind the couch and gripped Dan's shoulder.

"Mmm. That'll help." Shane took over. "We're going to keep this simple." He explained where he wanted each of them when the terror suspects arrived.

"Trey, you'll be point. You think you can handle it?"

Memories of being beaten and bound by the Benefactor's thugs in an effort to extort Adrianna into marrying the bastard rose to taunt Trey. *This is different. You weren't expecting to be jumped. Besides, Dan says there are only two guys coming. It took four of the Benefactor's goons to take me down.*

"Yeah. I got this."

The left side of Shane's mouth lifted in a half smile. No doubt he remembered that ignominious moment too. "Let me repeat. Maon and I will make the arrest. If things get rough, you get down or out of the way. Everyone understand?"

"When do I come downstairs?" Dan asked.

"Not until we signal the all clear. Adrianna will know." Shane shifted his gaze to look at each of them, assessing their steadiness. "All right.

"Dan, would you come through to the kitchen with Maon and me? We'd like to get a preliminary statement from you and ask you some questions. The rest of you keep an eye out for another shuttle. As soon as someone spots it, we'll want to assume our positions."

"And don't worry." Maon's expression was solemn as though he were about to impart supportive advice. "If we need her, Adrianna will kick ass and take names."

Trey thought he was joking until Adrianna said, "Damn straight."

16

The tip of Patsy's nose was colder than she ever remembered it being, even on the one day in her childhood in Ireland when they'd awakened to snow and she'd played outside until every flake had melted. The mucus inside hardened into tiny balls that rattled around in her nostrils.

The rest of her remained warm. She'd decked herself in as much winter weather gear as she could and then swathed herself from head to toe in a down quilt to stand as their sentinel. A white landslide had cascaded onto her feet when she'd opened the door to the deck from the bedroom Trey and she were using.

She bounced on her toes, straining to hear anything besides the soft sighs of the wind grown peaceful again and the occasional cracking of ice. The sound when it came was so distinctly alien to the natural ambience of the Giant's Tit, it was immediately recognizable as man-made. She scanned the sky, concentrating until she spotted a speck. As she watched, it grew bigger.

The moment she was certain, she turned, dropped the quilt, and sprinted inside and down the stairs. Trey and Adrianna were in the living room. Their heads spun with a snap in her direction.

"They're coming."

The announcement was made at the top of her lungs. Her dash to the kitchen was precluded by the men there joining them.

"They're coming." The second statement wasn't as loud, but it was equally agitated.

Shane snapped commands. "Dan, you go to your bedroom with Adrianna. No matter what happens, do not come downstairs until I've called the all clear." He clamped his hands on Dan's shoulders and stared into his eyes. "Got it?"

Spine straight, Dan set his jaw. "Yes, sir. Got it."

"Good man." Shane slapped Dan's upper arm. "Adrianna, get him upstairs."

The pair headed for the stairs, Dan taking Adrianna by the elbow to guide her.

Interesting. Patsy mused. *The kid definitely has the role of gentleman drilled into him. It's his default. And that interaction with Shane. Dan's life would have been completely different if he'd had a man like Shane in his life from the start. Tallav is one messed up planet.*

"Patsy, get out of your coat and boots."

Jerked from her reverie by Shane's sharp tone directed her way, she reprimanded herself. *No time to be distracted.*

Shane continued. "You and Trey are vacationers. Nothing more. You don't suspect a thing. Dan told you they were coming. That's all. Maon and I'll be in the kitchen."

He pointed at Trey. "Your job is to get them there. Have them follow you in. Move to that niche that leads to the pantry door as quickly as possible. Got it?"

"Yep."

"Okay then. Let's do this." Shane and Maon left to take up their positions.

Patsy scrambled out of her coat, putting it and the rest of her gear away in the foyer. She rejoined Trey on the couch. He'd seated himself sideways on one end with his leg lined along the back. Patsy snuggled into the vee of his legs, drawing comfort from his enfolding strength.

Her throat was tight, but damned if she'd allow her resolve to falter. Hadn't she been afraid of Dan? *But this situation is worse. These men really are dangerous. And Trey will be right in the middle of the takedown.*

Worry put her in verbal overdrive. "Don't go actin' the maggot. Ya hear? And get your head down and your arse in the pantry. If ya get yourself shot, it'll be donkey's years before I speak to ya again. Do ya hear me, ya great lummox?"

Trey brushed her hair aside and kissed her temple. "I hear you. I'll be careful."

She twisted, throwing her legs off the couch to gaze into his eyes, sinking into shimmering dark brown pools with glinting golden flecks around the irises. *Sweet mother Mary, I love his eyes. He's not lying. At least I don't think so...*

"I promise."

Despite the sincerity in his voice, doubt hammered at her, raising specters of disastrous possibilities. *Trey doesn't need my doubts. He needs my confidence.*

She was on the verge of straightening her spine and smoothing the stress from her face when he brought his mouth to hers in a sweet kiss, its gentleness nearly breaking her. She wouldn't cry. *Not one damn tear.*

"Everything will be fine." His response was gruff and Dom-like in his attempt to convince her.

She lifted her chin, bristling with challenge. "It'd better be."

Offended by the chuckle that followed her pronouncement, she swatted at his chest. His hand engulfed hers before it struck him; his lips erased her annoyance, claiming hers with an intensity that sparked the passion between them, bubbling just below the surface, waiting for moments like this to erupt.

And then he pushed her away so he could he rise.

"Oh sure. Get me riled up and then leave me hangin'."

"Remember where we were. I'm going to meet our guests outside."

"Feckin' man. Be careful." She strained to transform the tension flooding through her into ordinary-seeming contentment.

TREY PULLED THE muffler more firmly across his nose. The icy outdoor temperature was one reason to conceal his face, but another was to keep their visitors from reading his expression as anything but welcoming.

Resting thug face, as Patsy called it, wasn't a good look on this occasion. His height was daunting enough.

He strode along the now snow-free walkway, watching as a midsize shuttle completed its landing. He waited until the engines shut down before moving closer.

The door to the main cabin slid open, and a staircase descended. This craft was in prime condition.

The wait for someone to appear ticked by slowly despite the staccato beat of Trey's heart. The beefy ruffian Trey imagined didn't emerge; the man was actually smaller than average, stout but short.

The second man, however, was everything Trey feared. Not as tall as Trey himself, but definitely as muscular.

His size is not a problem. Guns outmatch muscles. Shane and Maon are both armed and waiting.

Trey moved to the base of the stairs. The companion ignored him, sauntering several feet away before halting to focus on Dan's wrecked shuttle. *Proving what? He's the dominant male here? Cocky bastard.*

The taller man stopped next to Trey and glanced over at the other man before returning his gaze to Trey. "Hey."

"Hey. We've been expecting you."

A grunt was the only response Trey received.

Finally the first man turned, eschewing a greeting to get straight to the point. "Do we need to grab Dan's things from the shuttle?"

"No. It's all inside." Trey couldn't get a handle on whether these two were low-on-the-totem-pole first family members or serving class. Far more of the men on Tallav were part of the working class, especially since Tallav was a replica of an agrarian society of preindustrial earth. They worked the farms they or their wives could never own.

The first man returned to where Trey stood, holding out his bare hand. "I'm Mike. A friend of Dan's. We'll get this mess out of your way as soon as we can." He jerked his thumb toward the wreck.

Trey shook the man's hand, swamping it with the added padding of the gloves on his own. "Trey. Trey Johansson. Come on up to the lodge. Dan's still in bed. He hurt himself climbing out of his shuttle. All the stress of the crash and worrying about his mother's fungus wore him out."

The glance Mike flicked at his partner was so quick Trey nearly missed it. *The big guy must not know about Dan's cover story.*

The taller man looked at Mike, his brows knit slightly as though he were trying to suppress his confusion. Whatever he saw in Mike's eyes compelled him to drop it. Instead he scowled at Trey. "He's okay though, right?"

Trey answered the question with a light tone, brushing aside any possibility of worry. "Yeah. He'll be fine. Just a sprained ankle. The med bed prescribed a dose of nanites. He probably won't even be limping today." *At least one of these two is concerned for Dan.*

The second man rolled his shoulders and grunted. "Good." He waved his hand toward his chest. "I'm Gabe."

"Trey."

"Can we go inside?" Mike interrupted, rubbing his hands together. "It's cold out here, and we need to get going. Have to have this shuttle back this afternoon."

"Yeah. Follow me." Trey was determined not to seem as though he was in a rush, so he strolled toward the lodge, keeping his back to the pair behind him. Difficult, considering the phantom blade that pricked the nerve endings in his spine. Gabe didn't seem the kind of guy that resorted to violence, but Mike was another story.

Trey took their coats and hung them on hooks in the foyer. Patsy was sitting in the living room in an overstuffed buffalo-plaid armchair in the nook of a bay window. Her tablet was on her lap. She looked up slowly as though she were deeply involved in her reading when Trey entered the room, followed by the two visitors.

"Dan's friends, Mike and Gabe"—he pointed at each man in turn—"are in a hurry. Can you wake him up and tell him they're here?"

"Sure." Patsy leaped to her feet. "Time he stopped bunkin' off."

Trey gradually released the breath he'd been holding once Patsy left. "That bin of fungus Dan's given himself a wedgie over is in the kitchen. If you come with me, we can grab it and maybe something hot to drink."

He didn't wait for a response, figuring if he led, they would follow behind him. A quick glance over his shoulder told him he was right. "We have coffee. The real stuff. Or tea. Hot chocolate too, I think."

Their answers were simultaneous.

Gabe positive. "Coffee would be great."

Mike negative. "No. We're fine."

A sulky rumble was Gabe's acknowledgment that he wouldn't be drinking coffee.

The two-way door to the kitchen was usually propped wide, but now it stood shut. Trey palmed it open, increasing his speed.

By the time Mike, who was two steps behind Trey, pushed the door now swinging toward him in the other direction, Trey was on his way between the industrial-sized cooler and the center island to the niche that opened into the pantry.

His body moved with effortless precision.

The clarity of his vision had improved tenfold.

Every detail was crisp.

On hands and knees he poked his head out far enough to track the action. The thudding of his heart in his ears made the silence even more impenetrable.

Across from him Shane and Maon stood, feet apart, weapons braced in both hands, out of the direct line of sight from the door.

The instant Mike's steps brought him into Trey's view, the terrorist saw Shane and Maon. He backpedaled, running into Gabe, who was still unaware of the marshals ahead.

Shane rocketed along the far side of the island to stand opposite the door where Mike was being propelled forward by an oblivious Gabe.

Gabe's instantaneous reaction on seeing Shane pointing a gun straight at him was to raise his hands and exclaim, "Oh gods."

The pitch of Mike's voice rose to a screech. "Back up, you big oaf."

Shane moved forward and snatched Mike's shirt at the shoulder, pulling him away from Gabe. "On your knees. Hands on your head."

Meanwhile Maon moved around the other side of the island, his weapon trained on Gabe, who fell to his knees without being told, slapping his hands onto his head.

Plasti-steel ties were locked in place, securing both men. A search found neither were carrying weapons.

His tone sarcastic, Shane said, "You can come the rest of the way out, Trey."

Trey stood to his feet and rubbed the top of his head. "I'm not good at taking orders."

"Uh-huh. It worked out this time, but it might not have gone so well. Anyone stupid enough to break the law is generally stupid enough to pull a gun on an armed marshal. We were lucky. These two were unarmed, so we'll never know how truly stupid they are."

Shane finished with an added measure of grim to his stern expression. "Next time do as I say. Don't stick your fucking head in the line of fire."

"Yes, sir." Trey gave Shane a chagrined look.

"Up on your feet, big fella," Maon said to Gabe, assisting the man to stand. "Into the other room."

Gabe swayed as he plodded past the door Maon had propped back open, whimpering under his breath.

A gun no longer pointed at him, Mike took the opposite tack from Gabe and unleashed a belligerent tirade at Shane.

"You're a traitor to your gender. Who do you think we're fighting for? Men like you. You fucking shitehawk."

"You're not fighting for me." Shane yanked the man to his feet with a tug on the restraints binding Mike's hands behind him. "Get moving."

"Bastards like you are so stupid you're happy to stay attached to your mam's teat, taking whatever handouts you're given. Marriage or the marshals service. Plain to see your choice."

"You have no idea," Shane responded, shoving Mike forward. "Now shut the fuck up."

Trey followed Shane and his prisoner into the living room, where Gabe was lying facedown in an open space on the floor. Maon stood near them, his finger to his ear, his gaze the far-off kind of someone using his internal comm.

"Go tell the others it's all clear," Shane said to Trey.

Patsy and Dan were sitting on Dan's bed, not a trace of space between them, tightly holding hands.

"You can come down."

To his left Adrianna lowered her weapon, her grim expression morphing to a cocky smile.

The evidence that Adrianna was prepared for the worst struck Trey two ways.

Good to know that Adrianna is sincere about Patsy's safety.

Bad to have a gun pointed at me.

It sent a creepy sensation through him, a chill, jittery feeling.

Downstairs Maon and Shane were leaning against the back side of the couch, discussing something quietly, ignoring the noise from the pair on the floor. Adrianna joined them.

Gabe was still whimpering, moaning pleas that he was sorry, punctuated by expletive-filled bursts from Mike to shut the fuck up.

Dan ran straight for the kitchen, Patsy close behind him.

The scene outside the bay window was pristine. Blankets of snow covered the blunt grays of the rugged crags that claimed the vista on this side of the lodge, softening their sharp angles. It was downright peaceful.

Holding in a long sigh, Trey settled on the couch to wait for whatever came next.

By the time a police transport shuttle arrived and packed the prisoners off, Trey was ready to see the others leave too. An atmosphere of gloom had fallen over the lodge that was entirely understandable, considering the revelations of the past twenty-four hours, but it wasn't welcome. Not to Trey.

He needed to be alone with Patsy. Needed to figure out what was next for them. Needed everyone to clear out.

Instead it appeared Shane was ready for a debriefing. He pulled the oversize armchair closer to the couch. Maon added two kitchen chairs to complete the circle.

"I've got iced teas for anyone who wants one," Patsy said as she entered the living room, followed by Dan. She placed the tray on the ottoman, which now served as a table in the center of the seating.

Shane settled himself in the armchair, still in command mode. "Thirsty? Hungry? Need to pee? Do it now. Then join the circle."

Dan peeled up the stairs, presumably to hit the bathroom.

The others sat. Adrianna next to Shane on a wooden chair. The other three on the couch, leaving the second kitchen chair for Dan when he returned.

"Dan will go to marshal headquarters with me," Shane said. "I've already chatted with the director earlier today. He wants to hear Dan's story himself before he makes any decisions, but I'm of the opinion we should keep the investigation of abuse in-house at the marshals."

"Patsy. Trey. You don't need to worry that this will be swept under the rug or that Dan will be handed back to his mother."

Dan slipped silently into the room, hesitating behind the couch. "Thank you. Should I leave?"

"No. Join us. This is important to you too."

Shane fell silent, letting his gaze rove over the others. "I believe we're all in agreement that what has been happening to Dan and others like him is appalling."

There were nods and words of assent.

The first swallow of iced tea did nothing to erase the bitter tang in Trey's mouth. Appalled didn't begin to describe his reaction to Dan's story.

Shane grimaced, looking as though he too wanted to spit something nasty. "It's the inevitable outcome of something that's been wrong on Tallav since it was founded. This experiment in matriarchy has gone on long enough to prove that, when one gender holds power over the other, the result is not the bucolic pastoral utopia that our first family founders expected."

"Exactly," Adrianna said. It was easy to see that the topic was something she and Shane had discussed in the past and agreed about completely. "The notion that women are nurturing and would always do what is best for men is as much a disaster of an idea as those who believe in men running things. We're people, male and female, but people. Failings apply equally to each of us."

Her fire was catching. "It's an experiment that needs to end," Trey said.

Maon leaned forward. "I propose a Committee of Correspondence."

"A what? A committee?" The are-you-kidding-me expression on Patsy's face was mirrored by Adrianna.

"What? Don't you remember your Earth history? The push for American independence started that way," Maon retorted.

The ladies were inching forward in their seats. Shane intervened. "He's right." Adrianna and Patsy turned on him. "Now. Now. Let me explain.

"We need to work together and to bring in others who can help. This is too big for us to take on by ourselves. But we'll need someone to make sure all the balls getting juggled stay up in the air. Suggestions?"

Dan spoke in a timid voice. "It should be a man."

The others looked at one another, Adrianna speaking for the consensus, "Agreed."

"I nominate Trey," Patsy said.

"Me? Don't be ridiculous."

"Ya've got the time. You're organized like no one else. And aren't ya the one who got all heated about men's rights when ya were talkin' to Dan?"

"You'd be perfect, Trey," Adrianna said.

The focus of everyone in the room drilled into Trey. "No. I wouldn't. I haven't gotten my own life straightened out. Besides, who the hell are we to decide who should lead a valid men's rights movement? Tallav already has men involved in advocating for men's equality. We're the newcomers."

Shane held up his hand. "He's right. I got way ahead of myself. But I've sat on my laurels for too long. Trey, Maon, Randolph and I have all managed to find accommodation with Tallav's political and social misandry and done nothing about changing it for others. No. I take that back. Randolph and Jen are in the final stages of opening a refuge for men who've been abandoned or neglected by their families."

How'd I miss that? More of Adrianna deciding what was best for me? Meddling with what she thought I should or shouldn't know? Trey glared at her, pressing his lips tight when she smoothed her expression into absolute innocence.

Unaware of the nonverbal exchange between Trey and Adrianna, Shane continued. "They have legal contacts that would be especially useful however we decide to move forward. Let's each spend time over the next week considering how we can individually and as a group take action.

"The matriarchists will flood the news with anti-male propaganda when the bomb plot is revealed. Nothing we can do about that but wait it out. I'll keep everyone up-to-date on the investigation into male abuse. Before that story breaks, we'll want to be prepared so we can seize the opportunity."

Maon took a glass of tea and raised it. "To the future. Men and women truly equal."

Patsy raised her glass. "To the future. Men and women truly equal."

The others joined the toast. "To the future."

Trey stood. "Now who's ready to leave? I'll help you find your coats."

The mood of the room brightened with knowing laughter.

TREY PULLED Patsy onto his lap, determined to finish the talk they'd started what seemed like a lifetime ago. Funny how two days could do that to a man. Interruptions were the hallmark of their relationship. First a sinkhole. Then Trey's own stupidity, causing the longest disruption. Then this minor —if you went by the time it entailed—distraction.

Maybe it was meant to be. Fate was taking them on a long, bumpy course. Why? To learn some lesson they were too dull to absorb the easy way?

It was true this last diversion had given Trey something bigger than himself to occupy him. But fuck fate anyway. Time for it to take its lessons and meddle with someone else's happiness.

"What's goin' on inside that head of yours?" Patsy massaged his temples, peering into his eyes. "Ya look like you're thinkin' deep."

"Hmmm." His smile was flat. "I was thinking fate needed to fuck off and leave us alone for the next decade or two."

"It's a good thing you're so far from Ireland. If the Morrigan heard ya talkin' so, she might deal harshly with ya."

He grunted, ruffling his fingers in Patsy's hair. "Then I'll try not to tempt her."

"Thank you, because I'd much rather have ya temptin' me." She stretched to bring her lips to his, flicking her tongue along the seam when they remained closed. "No fair holdin' back."

Hugging her tight, he kissed her forehead. "Later, *a leanbh*. It's time we settled our futures. Whether who we are will pull us apart or bind us together." He wrapped his palm around the back of her head, rubbing his other palm along her thigh. "I want to be together as much as you do, but I'm not sure how we're going to manage it. Even though you've left Bistro Coquin, you have a career, and I've already proven I'm not good at playing Patsy's love interest. I've got to have something to do of my own."

"I—"

"No. Hear me out. I would like to get involved in the men's movement, work with abused men, but that would require me to live on Tallav. I couldn't expect you to tag along behind me. You'd hate that as much as I would. I suppose we could buy a cottage in one of our friends' estate villages. I've got the credits, but you'd have to do the buying." He smirked and punched his fingers into his sternum. "Not allowed."

"Trey—"

"No. Let me finish." He covered her mouth with his forefinger. "I don't suppose…" He let his hand fall into his lap. "We could settle down. Have babies. Do the family thing."

"Are ya askin' me to marry ya?" Her gaze was full of more than that question.

"I don't know. Maybe." He scowled, his chest growing tight as he sensed he was bungling this. "I want to be with you, whatever we end up doing. And I don't know how to reconcile my needs with yours without compromising your hopes and dreams."

"Feckin' man, if you'll let me speak, I've a solution to offer ya."

The tension in his muscles relaxed a smidgeon. "A solution?"

"Before Dan and his jump from the fire to the fryin' pan interrupted us, I told ya that Adrianna, Jen, and Selina had created an opportunity for me. What I didn't get to say was that Randolph, Shane, and Maon came up with their own addendum that involves you."

He looked at her.

"You and BSDM."

"Explain."

"First me. The ladies and I are partners in a new venture. An Irish pub in Cahernamon. Your mom will be in charge of the kitchen. Your dad will manage the front of the house. There's an apartment above the pub where they'll live. And I get to oversee the whole mess."

Trey couldn't speak. His brain staggered and the words in his head went on vacation somewhere with warm, balmy beaches.

"Are ya all right?" She patted his cheek, which did nothing to wash away the dumbfounded astonishment that had fallen on him at the same moment his jaw had dropped.

"I'm… You…"

"I'm stayin' on Tallav."

He enveloped her in a bone-crushing hug. "That's…" Speech still deserted him, so he freed her to clasp her cheeks between his palms and put the words he couldn't say into a kiss. Not an erotic kiss. A celebration. A suddenly-everything-is-right-with-the-world kiss. It cleared the mental roadblock.

"That's... amazing. That's... incredible. That's... perfect."

Laughter spilled out of him, infecting Patsy until they were clinging to one another, tears streaming down their faces, rocking back and forth.

In the calm that followed while they caught their breath, Trey caressed Patsy's jawline and then pulled her in for another, more heated kiss.

He broke it, staring into eyes that had gone soft as a blue summer sky. "I thought all that about being a Tallavan resident was to come here and set things straight. I never imagined you'd want to make it permanent."

"There's more."

"I'm not sure I can take more."

"Daft man. Ya go from wantin' fate to stop dealin' ya trouble to actin' the sap when she showers ya with luck."

Trey took a deep breath and released it. "Tell me."

"It's somethin' that will allow you plenty of time to work with abused men at the refuge Randolph and Jen are opening if you choose. The boys have decided that Tallav, Cahernamon to be precise, needs a private BDSM dungeon. Startin' membership is we four couples, but more can join if they meet your requirements. You'll be totally in charge. Well, Selina expects ya to listen to her input on the Domme side of things. And you'll probably be handed wish lists from everyone, but you'll make all the final decisions. There's even an ideal building for sale near the pub."

Ideas he'd always wanted to try rushed through his mind. He fell backward against the couch and tipped his head to stare at the ceiling, his hands losing their grip on Patsy.

A shake to his shoulder brought him back to reality. "Where have ya gone? I've just told ya everything is goin' to work out perfectly. Plus I'm sittin' on your lap as available as a woman can be for celebrating, and you're not takin' advantage of it?"

Trey straightened and gripped her upper arms. "A new dungeon, one of my own making. My mind is blown with all the possibilities." Then a smile, devious and sexy as hell, crept onto his face. "So many ways to discipline a sassy submissive."

He altered his voice, sounding mystical and woo-woo. "I see the future fate has planned for you. The mist is parting. I see something. What could it be? It's like something I've never seen before. Something created just for you, *a leanbh*."

"Feckin' man, ya don't scare me."

"No?" He laughed, low and diabolical, waiting for the shiver that signaled Patsy was buying into his mind fuck. "But why wait? There are plenty of pervertibles I can use right here in this frozen wasteland. Maybe I should collect some snow."

"Don't ya dare."

He grabbed her and slung her over his shoulder as he rose from the couch, adopting her Irish accent. "Are ya tellin' your Dom what he can and cannot do now, *a leanbh*?" He swatted her on the bottom, chuckling at her yelp.

"I'm thinkin' we need to discuss my hard limits again."

"As I recall, sensation play up to and includin' ice was on your yes-please list." He felt damn near weightless, floating up the stairs to ravish his woman, his Patsy. He was in control again. It wouldn't last. He knew that. But a man didn't waste a perfect moment worrying about what came next.

"A girl can change her mind."

He gave her another swat, thrilled when she squirmed. "You'll love it."

EPILOGUE

Trey leaned back in his chair and took another pull from his beer. The pub, O'Shaughnessy's, was packed on its third Tuesday since opening. Smiling people stood three-deep at the bar, and every seat was filled, standing room only. The strains of contemporary Celtic fusion vied with the patrons to be heard.

His beer was dark and stout—not Guinness, but Patsy was working on getting the company to bring a microbrewery to Tallav. This was an excellent substitute. His dad had perfected his pull, reigning over the bar with an elan Trey hadn't known his father possessed.

The remains of dinner, braised lamb shanks and colcannon, prepared exclusively for them by Trey's mother, cluttered the table where he sat with his friends. The ladies had chosen to eat something lighter in the cramped but relative quiet of Patsy's office.

"I can't wait to see what you've done with the new dungeon," Maon shouted at Trey. "I haven't seen it since we first looked the building over together. It was a pit. And not in a good sense."

"Selina hasn't given you any hints about the piece of equipment she requested?" Trey asked.

Shane slapped his hand on Maon's shoulder. "She's been torturing him with one-word hints. Movable. Strong. Smooth. Accessible. Leather."

No one but the members of their table heard the groan that came from Maon when he dropped his chin to his chest and palmed the top of his head.

A wicked grin prefacing his words, Randolph said, "I helped her design it, so you know it will allow for ample manipulation of the submissive."

"Stop with the mind fucks. You're making my balls ache." Maon grabbed his crotch.

Amid the laughter that followed, Trey bent his head to Randolph. "How's Jen doing with the pregnancy? What is she, four months?"

"Yeah. Four." Randolph rubbed his mouth, a sheepish expression on his face. "She's been kicking up a fuss about me going too easy on her. Says I'm too damned tenderhearted." He shook his head. "I don't know. She's pregnant. Shouldn't I be going easy?"

"Everyone has their hard limits. I guess even sexual sadists have their fragile moments." Trey let a smirk ease onto his lips at the spark of *what the fuck* in Randolph's eyes.

Maon leaned forward to hear better. "Is he complaining about being a wuss again?" He wrapped his arm around Randolph's shoulders. "If you need someone to hold your hand, I'll be there for you. No worries."

"You're the one who should be worrying. I know what Selina intends to do to you." Randolph shrugged off Maon's arm.

Shane changed the subject. "The club's unofficial grand opening came just in time. Shit's officially about to hit the fan. Multiple locations. Dan really delivered."

"How's he holding up?" Trey asked.

"Good. Better than I expected. Did you know he wants to attend university off Tallav?"

Trey nodded. "Yeah. I've sat in on a couple of his counseling sessions at the refuge. Jen wants to establish a scholarship fund. The way she's pulled in donations for the refuge, it's practically a done deal, especially once Dan's story becomes public."

Pride shone in Randolph's eyes. "Turns out I married an organizing dynamo. But having Selina's mom and Shane's mom on the refuge's board of directors helps."

"Don't forget Evaline Braddock," Maon said. "Who would have

believed a couple of years ago that she'd become a stalwart supporter of legal reforms for abused men?"

Trey spotted Patsy, aiming a pointed look straight at him. He drank the last of his beer. "Time to go, gentlemen. The ladies are eager to begin."

They maneuvered their way through the crowd, picked up the women at Patsy's office, and, Trey in the lead, wound to the pub's back door.

Cahernamon's southern location meant the night was balmy, the opposite of the late winter that still had hold of Rathlin Island in the far north. The couples strolled along the street hand in hand.

The club, which Trey had yet to name, was housed in an unassuming, one-story, yellow faux-brick building. To say it was ugly would be an understatement. The land had been worth more than the structure itself because of the locale. Rehabbing had proved less expensive than starting from scratch. No one looking at it would guess it was a private BDSM club hiding in plain sight.

Trey keyed the entry lock and turned on the lights, revealing a sleek black reception desk. "Locker rooms are to the right. The dungeon is through there." He pointed to a pair of studded burgundy leather-clad doors.

Inside the dungeon Trey opened a panel that contained the interface for all the tech. A few taps later and a wall-sized vidscreen began playing erotic BDSM vids. The low thump of drums sounded over the sound system.

Muted lighting recessed along the floorboards and edges of the ceiling revealed the interior, but only to a degree. Much was hidden in shadows. Movable lighted plinths lit up intimate spaces where more light was desired. Armchairs, stools, and settees were sprinkled throughout, as were fully stocked cleaning stations.

"I can change the configuration of the play spaces and equipment available." Trey stood with his hands on his hips, gazing at the matte-black wooden flooring that covered the entire enormous room seamlessly. "I got the idea from Cosmic Cabaret's stage setup. But this required more thought. I didn't want anything hanging overhead except those who come to play. It's like one of those plasti kids' games where the tiles get moved around to create a picture or the proper number sequence. Except it's three-dimensional. What isn't being used is stored in the basement."

"This is amazing. I love the black and burgundy. Although"—Adrianna nudged Selina—"it may clash with your fire Domme red-orange gear."

"Time for some new leathers anyway. I'll incorporate burgundy," Selina said. She flicked a questioning eyebrow up at Trey. "I don't see something."

"We'll get to that." Trey rubbed his hands together. "First you'll notice above the space in the middle of the room, I've installed a bunch of chains, plates, and suspension hard points. They're raised or lowered by a handheld device. No zero-gravity gear. I know Shane likes to use it, but I've aimed to take us back to BDSM's roots. Per that, suspensions will be prohibited over two feet from the ground to the lowest body part. Rope, pulleys, carabiners, chain, rods, suspension plates. We're well stocked for safe suspensions."

Shane grunted his agreement. "Leave the showy stuff to the Whip Hand."

Nodding, Trey continued. "A well-trained rope master doesn't need his sub off the floor to create an effective scene—"

"Ya can't stop yourself from fallin' into instructor mode, can ya?" Patsy wrinkled her nose at Trey.

He turned and grinned, his smile part seductive and part intimidating, permeated by his obvious eagerness. "Shane and I intend to introduce you and Adrianna to the capabilities of the new suspension system tonight. Our plans can expand to include punishment."

"Mmm." Patsy rubbed herself against him like a cat demanding attention. "Promises. Promises."

Randolph, holding Jen around the waist, wandered to a station with what looked like a torture device from five centuries ago. "This is perfect." He ran a hand along the thinly padded black table and bent to pull out the footrest from the pale, mint-green, enameled metal pedestal.

"It's a gynecological exam table." Jen burrowed against Randolph, hugging him tight. "Thank you. This is going to be so much fun."

"There are costumes too," Trey said. "But before we head to the locker rooms to change as required for our scenes, I have Selina's surprise to reveal. If everyone would come stand over here by the entrance, please. I've maneuvered the plates before, but I still wouldn't consider myself an expert. This area of the floor is not part of the system."

They gathered where Trey had indicated, expectant expressions on their faces, especially Maon's. An empty section of flooring lowered and slid underneath the adjacent section. Another rose to take its place and locked itself with a clunk seamlessly into position.

Maon had been swapping bright-eyed glances with the others, but his gaze riveted on the odd wooden object that came into view. "What is it?"

"An articulated artist's model," Selena said, taking Maon's hand in hers to restrain him from moving forward to examine it. "You'll be familiar with it soon enough. It was designed specifically for you. To bend where you bend. Knees. Shoulders. Waist."

"Movable." Randolph dropped the single word into the conversation with a smugness that proved he too couldn't wait to see how Selina made use of the model.

"Padded for your comfort," Selina continued. "Leather."

"Yeah." Maon gave Selina a playful wink. "And the wood is smooth. It's strong enough to support me. Once I'm strapped on it, you'll have access to all of me."

His gaze once again pinned on the model, Maon whispered to himself, "Oh yeah."

"Yes." Selina scraped a nail along the five-o'clock scruff on Maon's jaw. "The ball joint that attaches the model to its pedestal will allow me to turn you upside down or fold you in half. Randolph and I decided hands and feet would get in the way should I decide to try a little bastinado on the bottoms of your feet, but we did have pegs attached for you to grab hold of when necessary." Her voice was a purr of seduction.

A shiver ran across Maon's shoulders.

The others watched, enjoying the interplay, as Selina brought Maon to his knees.

Literally.

He assumed the perfect submissive position without a care for his dress slacks. "Thank you, Lasair. You're so good to me."

Selina ruffled his hair, her long fingernails bright sparks of fiery orange amid his light brown locks. "You're welcome. It's time we changed. I want you naked, kneeling as beautifully as you are now beside the model in five minutes."

"Yes, Lasair." He rose and sauntered from the room, extrovert pride on full display.

Trey motioned to the dungeon entrance. "Shall we?"

The ladies made a beeline for the locker rooms, aware that play would begin when they met their partners once again in the dungeon.

RANDOLPH WATCHED AS Shane and Trey pulled out a cart preloaded with the supplies they would need. They had opted to work as a team and quickly stripped to don loincloths and metal bands around their upper arms, wrists, and heads. Barbarians had invaded the dungeon.

Fantasy was one aspect of BDSM play that Randolph enjoyed and added into his scenes regularly. Tonight he and Jen were going back in time too. He walked to the gynecological examination table that Trey had installed just for him, pulling a lab coat from a side drawer. He slung an antique stethoscope around his neck, ready for Jen's arrival.

To his right Shane and Trey lowered a heavy-duty ring and attached what looked like a trapeze for two topped by a triangle, spinning it to check that it rotated properly. The horizontal bars were rigid and so thin they had to be made of plasti-steel to be strong enough to support the weight that the connecting bar might feasibly hold. They tied four long ropes to a smaller ring inside the tip of the triangle.

Shane raised the contraption to waist height while Trey plopped bundles of varying lengths of pink rope and a set of suspension wrist cuffs on either side of the trapeze. Then they settled in to wait, standing, arms crossed over their bare chests, the epitome of tall, muscular ancient warriors. All they lacked were swords or battle axes.

Something he would never require. His weapon of choice was a bull-whip. He could engage it to defend himself, but he preferred to use it to mark his lovely wife and masochist's bottom. But she was pregnant, and he'd flinched from using his whip. The thought that he could miss and strike her someplace vulnerable while she carried their child was too painful.

Tonight would be Jen's first time to do a scene with others in the room. Until now he hadn't wanted to share any part of their BDSM relationship.

The Whip Hand wasn't intimate enough for his liking since he'd surrendered his heart to the love of his life.

This dungeon was exactly what was needed. By all of them. Not just him and Jen. Three longtime friends and their mates with the addition of Trey and Patsy. He'd become acquainted with the couple as his employees.

Together Patsy and Trey fit in well with the group as though they'd clicked into a slot designed for them. His band of male friends had grown into a foursome. A man could find no better.

His aroused cock jutting before him, Maon was first to return, sauntering as he had when leaving. Until Selina snapped her fingers. Then he sped up, sinuously sinking to the floor to sit on his heels, his knees spread, his erection on full display, and his hands clasped behind his back. Not once did he peek at Selina, or Lasair, her Domme name.

The entry of Jen with the other women diverted Randolph's attention. He had eyes only for her and the Mona Lisa smile that disguised the self-conscious anxiety roiling inside her. They'd discussed it. She'd agreed. Now the test came.

He alone knew the extent of her worries. It manifested in the reduced sway of her hips. In private she was no longer tightly controlled around him. But tonight that ass wasn't moving in the sexy twitch that was her nonverbal way of begging for his whip.

The demure old-fashioned dress she wore, covered in a tiny floral pattern she claimed was Laura Ashley, was perfect. She'd even added pink to her cheeks to create a blush.

An armchair stood near their ancient doctor's office. She settled in it, lacing her fingers in her lap. Already fully immersed in her role as nubile patient.

"Miss Meryon?"

She slid forward and gave a meek nod of her head.

"Come with me, please."

His hard length pressed against the closure of his slacks, a testament to the ability this woman had to flood his mind with erotic images—images of her, legs open before him, pussy shaven clean, and moist cleft awaiting his wicked gratification.

"Remove your clothing and climb onto the examination table."

"But"—she clutched a fist to her chest, drawing his gaze to the rise and fall of her breasts and the tight nipples that peaked the fabric of her modest dress—"don't I get a gown to wear?"

"No." He plunged his hand into his coat pocket to prevent himself from stroking her cheek. Turning her unease at participating in a scene in front of others into an element of the role she was playing was brilliant. "The condition I suspect you're suffering from requires you to be completely nude, every part of your body available for study and analysis."

The intensity of his gaze sent a shudder through her, causing the dress's fluttery sleeves to quiver. It never took long to get this reaction from her.

"Oh." She bit her lower lip, sending desire to sink his own teeth into its plump sweetness through him in a shudder of his own.

Yeah. They were perfectly matched. He dropped his chin to give her a stern look. "Now, please."

Her slate-gray eyes went wide as she hastily reached behind her neck and fumbled with the buttons that marked a line down her back. She chewed her lip again, teasing him, a smile edging its way onto her face before she purposefully pressed her lips together to fend it off. "I need some help, sir."

The high-waisted skirt ballooned out when she twirled to allow him access. He popped each button through the fabric in slow progression, avoiding touching her until the entire back was open, the sleeves threatening to slide from her shoulders. Then he trailed two fingers along her spine and slid his palm under the skirt to caress her bottom. She was naked beneath as he'd requested.

"Your spine is exactly as it should be. I don't think the problem lies with it. And your butt cheeks…" He squeezed. Hard. Eliciting a gasp that stoked his arousal. "Your butt cheeks are luscious."

He removed his hand from inside her dress and slipped the other in to take a tight hold of the side he'd neglected. His grip was again harsh and would leave lovely bruises on her skin.

The moans and near kitten-like purrs had already begun. He buried his face into the sleek black fall of her high ponytail, drawing into his nostrils the sugar-cookie sweetness that was pure Jen. His kinky vanilla goddess.

"They're like melons, firm and succulent. Will they turn watermelon red if they're spanked?"

Her response was husky, dripping with want. "You could find out."

"That would be delightful, but I must continue your examination." He abruptly withdrew from her to stand several steps away. "Off with your clothes and get on the exam table."

Instead of tormenting him by biting her lip, she jutted it in a pout she probably hoped was equally agitating.

It was.

She needed a thorough kissing, including bites of his own.

"Now." He barked the word at her.

She halted whatever she'd been doing to keep the dress from falling, allowing it to slide to the floor in a puddle of flower-sprigged innocence, and clambered onto the table knees first so her bottom was in the perfect position for spanking. She swayed a few times in encouragement, flipping over when her expectations were not met to perch at the end with her legs crossed and one foot swinging.

"Lie back."

She did, legs dangling off, deliberately causing delay, displaying her own little sadistic streak.

"Scoot up."

A slow squirm inched her up the leather padding, breasts tantalizing as they jiggled, her nipples tempting peaks when she at last settled. Hands clasped across an abdomen that had only recently grown rounded, she smiled tremulously at him, resuming her Miss Naive role again.

Gods, she's gorgeous. How would I survive without her?

The answer was plain. He wouldn't.

Oh, he might be physically alive, but none of the delight he took from mundane husband and wifeness would have been present.

He was a sexual sadist. At his age that wasn't going to change. Jen fulfilled that need in him too with a vitality that was rooted deep in a love of life that had somehow expanded to encompass him.

It was a miracle. A miracle that had multiplied into a child of their own. He would always treasure his niece. But a baby, forged from the elements of his and Jen's love, came close to bursting his chest with pride.

Nothing he'd done to this point in his existence was as significant.

In five months a child would suckle at those fine breasts. For now they were his exclusively. His fingers tingled as he reached out to cup her fullness, sucking the ruched tip between his lips. With each hard draw her nipple grew longer, distended. She arched upward, begging for more with insistent whimpers.

Pleasure ached through him, promoting an urgency to skip the planned scene and advance to the final act.

He bit, her squeal striking his groin and making his cock leap.

His laugh was cut off when she lifted herself to stuff his mouth full, so he nipped her again. This squeal ending in a protracted sigh.

No. Each step of the path he'd laid out would lead them to a mountaintop that haste couldn't reach.

He moved on to her second breast, reveling in the taste of her skin and the quivering of her muscles. She was a sumptuous feast spread before him, slathered in a condiment of breathy moans.

At length he pushed himself away from her, staring at marks that were already fading.

Ever since her pregnancy her breasts had been tender. He couldn't bring himself to take advantage of that lowered threshold to create the pain that had always made lust pulse through his veins. Screams of agony no longer gratified him, no matter how much she might beg for more.

He'd turned into the male version of Selina. Only so far and no farther. Minor pain. Sensation play. From the sounds behind him, she and Maon were enjoying her new piece of BDSM equipment.

Focus. He sucked Jen's nipple deep, pulling back until it popped from between his lips. Distended, it stood proud and inviting. He flicked it with his tongue.

"Your breasts are delightfully sensitive and delicious. If we have time during this appointment, I'll return to them. But now..." He straightened and moved his gaze to her face.

The redness of her lower lip had nothing to do with makeup. He rubbed a thumb over it, wrinkling his brow and giving a tut of disapproval. "You've been biting your lip."

He shook his finger at her. "You should never bite your own lips. That privilege should always be given to another. Let me show you."

A throb of desire pulsed behind his ribs the instant before he claimed her lips. The lushness of her mouth was drugging, so soft and responsive joined with his and parting in a wordless plea to be taken. Plunging his tongue inside, he savored her unique flavor, pinching her nipples as he did, swallowing her moans.

He licked across the curve of her lower lip, snagging it between his teeth and dragging it between them, and then he bit.

Her shriek fed his lust, an arrow of decadent bliss straight to his groin. Not the screaming agony of the past, but it would do. It would more than do.

That she didn't pull away but kept her mouth pressed close to his bolstered his vanity, increasing the ache in his chest. The devotion that saturated her gaze nourished his love for her, an ever-growing, irreplaceable wonder. At times like this Jen was all the food he needed.

"You see how much better it is to have someone else bite your lip?" He breathed the words against her mouth.

"I do. Thank you for your instruction, Doctor."

"My pleasure."

The fire in his crotch was flaming higher. He palmed his erection as he straightened, a light caress, a reward for his patience.

Smoothing his fingers down each of her arms and then her sides, he commented on his progress. "Muscle tone is excellent. Skin is taut." He pinched her waist. "But flexible."

Her nostrils flared with each deep breath she took, anticipation escalating to lust-filled expectation.

A groan slipped from her as he skimmed his hands along her hips to her knees, bypassing her pussy, which she'd elevated, seeking his attention.

"Your legs are in good working order. I don't believe the problem is to be found in them. Perhaps between them."

"I'm sure it must be." She came close to biting her lip but caught herself and drew her hand up to her mouth. A series of rapid blinks ended in a wide-eyed apologetic expression.

Images of all the things he'd love to do to her in this moment washed through his mind. None of them appropriate to the scene. Tossing her in the air, catching her, and twirling her definitely weren't. Laughing for the joy of her wasn't either. Sliding into the depths of her heat was, however, on the agenda.

He bent and pulled the metal stirrups into position at the end of the examination table, the chill from the cold surgical steel in his palm centering him.

"My dear, please place your feet here and here." He tapped each stirrup.

"Yes, sir."

An attempt to pin her knees together was unsuccessful. A gap of six inches remained.

He traced her inner thigh, her skin the perfect temperature between entrancing warmth and a minute trace of coolness that made his fingers glide across its silken surface.

"Relax and open wider."

Complying, she was unable to prevent the slight shudder that vibrated through her. She was as aroused as he, as ready for him to reach the center of her sexual pleasure as he. *Indeed. We are a matched set.*

He reached out and snagged the rolling stool that had stood neglected so far, settling on it between her raised legs. "Scoot your bottom to the edge of the table."

The aroma of her arousal wafted, filling the space between them. His mouth watered, forcing him to swallow hard.

He brushed the backs of his knuckles through her curls before pulling her labia apart and leaning forward, ostensibly to continue his examination. In reality he was breathing her scent in, enjoying the rhapsody of sparks that each lungful launched from his nipples to his groin.

He lifted his gaze, peering at her face above the crest of her breasts. "It's clear I've discovered the heart of your difficulty. I'll need a sample from your vagina for analysis."

"Yes, Doctor. Whatever is necessary. I'm relying on you to take care of me."

His gaze had dropped to the succulence of her pussy, but at her words he snatched a quick glance at her. Her expression wasn't that of the sweet miss of her performance, no matter her sugary tone of voice. Her head raised to watch him, she cocked an eyebrow at him when she caught his eye.

A great deal was said with that singular lift. She wanted him to get on with it. She wanted him to stop taking it easy on her. And above all, she not only wanted these things, she expected them or she'd switch roles with him, making him the masochist to her sadist.

The threat had been enunciated twice in the past. She wasn't kidding.

Fine.

He drew his tongue along the inside of her left thigh, reaching the spot where it curved in toward her pussy. The curls at her cleft tickled his ear.

He sucked a narrow strip of delicate skin between his teeth and bit.

"Shit. Shit. Shit."

She had a mark that would linger for a few days. Paper cuts and harsh nips hurt like hell, far above the degree of injury they caused.

He'd give her a few more.

This he could do.

He turned to the other thigh and gave her a matching bruise.

"Yitch! Do it again." Her fists were balled, thumping on the table.

A wicked chuckle spilled out of him. Fingers tingling, he clamped both hands to her leg and extended a series of bites from her knee to the first mark.

"More. More. More." Her voice was gravelly with demand.

"My pleasure." He took a swipe at her slit as he moved to her other side. There he added another stripe of fresh red bruises. He was forced to pin her leg to keep it still from the shaking of her body.

It would take little to bring her to orgasm now.

Pinching her labia, he jerked them apart and went straight for her clit. Stiff with excitement, it peeked from its hood.

He rolled it a few times with his tongue and then bit, not as roughly as he'd nipped her thighs, but enough to make her arch, smearing her juices all over his face as she came, every muscle in her body taut.

Guttural, unintelligible pronouncements flew from her mouth. He braced her hips and rode the release with her.

She melted into a boneless, magnificent jumble of satisfaction.

Fingers flying as though instruction from his brain were unnecessary, he unbuckled his belt and opened his slacks. The lack of underwear made the next step that much quicker.

He grabbed his thoroughly aroused cock, a pearl of precum at its tip, and guided it to her entrance, plunging into her until her inner walls cinched around him down to his balls.

His eyes rolled back in his head at the sensation of her tight channel pulsing, the remnants of her orgasm driving him closer to his own release.

A schwacking sound filled his ears. Was it the sound of his body slapping into Jen's or the smack of Trey and Shane's palms as they spanked their submissives? Or both?

He didn't bloody well care what it was. His rhythm increased, accompanying the crescendo that built at the base of his erection, swelling along it until he was as hard as synthsteel.

Beneath him, Jen tensed, a second release building inside her.

One thrust.

Two thrusts.

Biting his tongue, he restrained his climax.

And then she tipped over the edge.

Thunder crashed through him, rendering him deaf to all but his own heartbeat. His senses were dulled except for the pounding ecstasy that pulsed through him.

His balls drew up as he ejaculated deep into Jen, leaving her once again a boneless puddle. His own carnal gratification was so intense he nearly slid to the floor.

The stool was behind him. He managed to grab hold of it and slide it under his ass before he fell.

Head lying against her thigh, he waited for his breathing to slow and control over his limbs to return. He raised his palm with a weak effort and pressed it to her other thigh.

She's so damn…everything. Brainless. She'd rendered him brainless.

He chuckled, squeezing her leg.

"Did we die?" Her question was asked with notes of awe and humor.

"It would be my idea of heaven." He lifted his head to gaze along her torso, the curves of her body an interesting topography from this angle.

He stood. Pulled his slacks up and closed them. Removed the medical coat. Went to her and assisted her to remove her feet from the stirrups and rise.

Then he swept her into his arms and carried her to one of the sofas at the back of the dungeon, settling with her snuggled against him so that they could view the others' scenes.

After throwing a light blanket over them, he whispered against her ear,

"I love you." He tunneled his fingers under the nubby fabric until he found the swell of her belly. "Both of you."

MAON KEPT HIS gaze on Selina's face as she strapped him against the giant artist model she'd had created just for him. The wooden figure was spread flat so he could climb on and lie on his back. She started with the waist, chest, and thigh straps, leaving his hands free to wander when she came within reach. It was an indulgence she'd long allowed him during their scene time.

Her expression, what he could see of it beneath the red-orange feathered mask she wore when she took on the persona of the Domme Lasair, held elements of concentration, whimsy, and expectant desire.

Artistic genius dripped from her fingers. Drawing was central to her creativity as a fashion designer. She knew the human body's shape, the way it fitted together and moved. She knew his body in particular. Over the years of their marriage, she'd made an in-depth study of every inch of him.

He'd returned the favor.

Strapping him to a life-size artist model was a novel means of allowing her to embrace her kink fully. She liked to tease him. Call it sensation play or mild-mannered sadism; she wasn't as much about controlling him as she was controlling his pleasure and pain.

He heaved a lengthy sigh when she grasped his wrist and laid his arm out against the smooth wooden surface and buckled the straps around his upper arms, forearms, and wrist. The seductive smile she gave him perfectly matched the glints of coppery fire in her eyes.

Soon she had him secured. "Ready, sweet man? Let's see if I can pose you in some interesting positions."

"I'm all yours, Lasair."

"Mmmm." The ball joint at the top of the pedestal was well lubricated. Once the pin that kept it in place was removed, it rotated smoothly with minimal force. His feet didn't touch the ground when she moved him to a standing position. The leather bit against the skin of his torso, but his weight was spread across the entire system, so it wasn't more than a pinch of discomfort.

His cock took note and jumped. It wasn't tied down.

Whether the nip of the straps was an intentional feature of the model or not, it wasn't Lasair's focus. She was intent on moving the joints, shaping him into different poses. She adjusted his elbow. "There. You're a runner."

From his elevated height he could see Randolph and Jen playing doctor. *Maybe I can talk Lasair into trying that out some day.*

Shane and Trey were still working their way through their preparation. They didn't call it that. For them it was part of the fun. Not from Maon's perspective. *Pop me into wrist and ankle cuffs and have at me.*

Lasair stepped back to admire her work, drumming a finger against her lips, delectable lips that Maon would rather have kissing various needy parts of him. Apparently she'd forgotten about sex.

"Can you do the splits?"

"The what?"

"The splits."

Maon looked at her askance. "For fuck's sake."

Back in the day, he'd been extremely flexible. But he hadn't stretched those muscles to that extent for, good grief, over a decade, nearer to two. "I'm not sure if I can anymore."

"Let's try."

Damn her perky can-do attitude. He would be the one to end up with a groin strain. He frowned his disapproval at her.

She cozied up to him, placing her hands on his hips. "You have a problem?" Their height disparity was even greater with him off the floor. Her breath teased the hair on his abdomen, his erection tapping her chin.

Sooooo close.

The sigh that welled up inside him at his last thought would send the wrong signal, so he held it in. "Be careful, please."

"Of course." She nuzzled his stomach, reaching up to tweak his nipples. "Always. I have plans that must not be compromised."

The tension collecting in his core eased. Why at this point in their relationship he would grow uneasy was a mystery.

Am I turning into a wimp?

I'll think about that later.

"We'll start with your left leg." She straightened it and then rotated the hip joint to raise it behind his back, watching his face for any hint of discomfort, the tip of her tongue poking between her teeth.

Concentration, not seduction. But damn sexy.

"Now the other leg." She kept that knee bent, lining his thigh up in the form of a half-split.

So far, so good.

Slowly she pulled his foot up, trying to straighten that leg too. The muscles in his torso went rigid as the stretch grew uncomfortable. Sweat began inching down his temples. It would take force to go farther.

"Hmm." She moved his foot back so that his knee was at a ninety-degree angle again.

The sigh he released was slow, deliberately quiet. Pride wouldn't allow him to show overtly that she'd found a weakness in him. Even though it was obvious.

She patted his upper thigh. "Don't worry about it. We'll work on stretches at home. I could have a lot of fun with you posed in side splits." She leered at him and then consciously swept her tongue seductively over her parted lips.

"Think of the possibilities."

He could. And he was. And his cock approved, sending her a jerky wave as though saying, *Look at me. I'm right here. Ready, willing, and able.*

Ignoring pleas from Maon, verbal or not, came naturally to Lasair. Torment. Orgasm denial. Teasing. All came naturally to Lasair.

Of course that also meant she was fully focused on him, and that's exactly how he liked things. He was the center of her world as she was his.

Already growing adept at maneuvering the model's joints, she soon had him positioned on his back, head tilted so his mouth and chin were parallel to the floor, and his knees bent. Then she lowered the pedestal until the top of his head nudged her pussy.

His erection thumped twice against his abdomen as though applauding for what came next. Next on Lasair's menu: tender succulent female bits with a side order of climax cream. A treat that always made him as hard as granite. His mouth was watering.

She tapped his cheek. "Do a good job on this, or I'll add tongue exercises to the stretches."

"Tongue exercises. Is there such a thing?"

"I'll figure something out."

She widened her stance and slipped along his head, her cream smearing his forehead. The aroma was intoxicating, all woman, all Lasair, a combination of exotic spice and sex. A dart of his tongue brought him no nearer to tasting her.

He growled his frustration.

The husky laugh she employed at times like this sent a flush of heat down his neck and chest. He loved eating her pussy, especially when she had him pinned and rode his face. There was no escaping her fiery cleft, hot juice dripping onto his tongue and over his cheeks.

His hands were clenching and unclenching, keeping time to the throbbing beat of his heart.

The pause she took to swirl her entrance over the tip of his nose moved her into striking distance. He lashed out again. The taste of passion, her passion, was an unnecessary aphrodisiac. He wanted her with an ardency that couldn't be surpassed.

Now if she would just scoot closer. The delicious gift when it came brought a broad smile to his lips, totally at odds with the unrelenting need of the past instant to delve into her delights.

"Get to it." His cheek was no longer accessible, so she tapped his chin.

Having his mouth and nose buried between Lasair's thighs was a little like deepwater diving without air tanks. Breath control was everything. They had a signal, two fingers twirled in a circle, for when he needed to breathe. He tried never to use it.

He began by lapping indiscriminately, knowing she wouldn't put up with that for long, but he craved more than a sample of her luscious flavor, wanting his tongue coated.

Another tap to his chin commanded him to get on with things. A number of techniques were available to him, but one in particular sent her rocketing toward climax. He held it in reserve, asserting his own perverse streak. She didn't need to come too quickly.

"Maon." If the tap had been commanding, the tone of her voice was even more so.

A quick but deep breath was required, and then he stabbed upward as far as he could into her vagina and withdrew. As soon as he'd set a tempo, she pressed her pussy tighter against his face, rocking her hips in a slight back-and-forth rhythm.

Queening him was her favorite sex act, so the muscles he used were in great shape from all the practice. If she'd freed his hands and arms, he'd stroke her thighs or pluck her nipples or squeeze her bottom or...

A flick from her long-nailed fingers reminded him to stay focused. Time for clit swirls.

His intention was to give her the most enjoyment without touching her clit. Her objective was to twitch and squirm so that her clit caught his tongue. A game he called chase the tongue.

Whenever she succeeded, she won a tingle of sensual pleasure. His prize was her accompanying sharp hiss. It went straight to his cock in his own tingle of sensual pleasure.

Eventually tingles weren't enough.

"Maon, do it. Do that thing I love." Her voice sounded drugged.

The view above him was filled with a pair of succulent orbs, bouncing with every movement. From any angle the contours of her body devastated him, turning him into a petitioner lying prostrate before her, begging for her to notice him, take him in hand, and use him for her own gratification. But this sight had to be in the top three of his all-time favorites. It was intimate, seen only because her pussy was grinding against his mouth.

True. Before he'd met her there had been plenty of women who took advantage of his need for domination, but none that reached inside and squeezed his heart, creating an ache that never abated.

That she chose both to love and dominate him, to grant him his utmost desire, was the miracle of his life. That she gave him abundantly more than he'd ever sought was beyond a miracle. She was his lover, his wife, and the mother of his children. Had made him a father and a husband. Miracle of all miracles.

For these reasons and many more, he'd do anything for her, including that thing she loved.

From the first stroke the intensity of her response grew.

The muscles of her thighs tightened around his head. She became fiery sizzle and heat.

Moans swelled from deep inside her, each punctuated with the sibilant sound of a single word. "Yessss."

He fought to restrain the orgasm that prickled at the base of his spine. She hadn't given him permission to come, so it was out of the question. But the connection he felt to her as he brought her nearer and nearer to the pinnacle of release made his entire body shiver with a consuming need.

Then her fingers found the bottom of his shaft and pinched, blocking him from ejaculating. Somehow she always knew.

Two swipes of his tongue later and she was coming.

A flood of fresh cream covered his mouth. Lapping it up, he hummed his approval while above him, she remained tensely frozen, riding the crest until the last waves passed.

She released her grip on his cock, pulled off him to stand and slump over him, her pussy no doubt decorating his tousled hair with her juices. "That was…mmmm…that was lovely."

A sloppy grin on his face, Maon fervently agreed. "Better than lovely. Far better. Extraordinary. Mind shattering. The best ever."

Hand on his shoulder, she pushed herself to straighten. "It's always the best ever according to you."

"And I'm always right."

Her lips lifted in a private smile, followed by a low, husky chuckle. "You deserve a reward."

"Yes, please." His erection was an ache that needed soothed.

A sinful twinkle lit her eyes as she brushed her finger over his mouth. "I thought about making your body arch so that your cock stuck straight up in the air, and I could bring you off that way."

"I think I could tolerate that."

Another chuckle. "I'm sure you could. But I'm not sure I can get your erection to stay put in that position. So I'm going to ask Shane or Trey their advice before I try it."

Thoughts of spurting straight into the air while her hands pumped him sent a shock wave to his groin. "It would be like a volcano erupting. I bet I could shoot three feet. Easy."

She laughed out loud. "You are still the cocky sub I first met."

"Why change perfection?" He flashed the half grin he'd been using from the beginning to charm her.

The only acknowledgment he received was the uh-huh look she sent him as she changed the subject. "I could also use Randolph's green goo on you again. What do you think?"

Oh gods. The green goo. "Didn't that nearly kill me?"

She lowered her head to whisper in his ear. "It didn't. If you'll remember, you only thought you were dying from the extreme pleasure. *Le petite mort.*"

The gentle kiss she placed on his lips silenced any response he might have made.

"Enough talk. I want you in me." Briskly efficient, she maneuvered the model until he was sitting leaned back with his knees bent to form a backrest once she straddled him. She dropped the pedestal farther and then climbed aboard.

Thighs that had bookended his face now brushed his hips. Breasts, dark nipples jutting toward him, were within reach. But hands pinioned, he couldn't touch or pull her forward to taste.

"May I touch you, please?" He used his gaze to drill her with his longing. "Please."

Without words, she released the straps that restrained his arms.

His fingertips explored soft curves, skimming up her sides, across her shoulders, and up her neck. They edged along her jawline to her ears, tracing the shell before plucking her lobes.

Lasair always wore her long sable hair in a ponytail. She didn't stop him when he pulled the stretch band and freed the silken flow, easing his fingers through it to cup her head between his palms.

"May I kiss you?"

Impossible unless she lowered her face to his. His heartbeat kicked up a notch when she did, her lips taking possession of his, her tongue licking the remains of her own arousal and then delving inside his mouth.

He met her with equal ardor, her piquancy making him reel. Hot fire licked nerve endings already fraught with unabated yearning.

The lavish heat of her moist slit skimmed along his hardened length.

Not enough. He gripped her by the hips, catching himself before he lifted and wrested control from her.

Not happening.

His impulse must have registered with her because she pulled away, firmly grasped his cock, and positioned it, his tip teasing her entrance.

Could she move any slower?

"Please, Lasair. I need to be in you."

"I know, sweet man."

Then she sank onto him in a glide that drove his sanity to the stretching point.

Finally fully encased in her snug sheath, time stood still for Maon. She remained motionless, fiercely provoking him to react first.

The glint of flames in her eyes was his cue. She expected him to allow her to control his pleasure.

An ache flared in his chest. An electric charge zipped through him, inciting a shudder he refused to permit by tightening his core. Once he let his body take over, he was lost.

A groan sliced through him when at last she circled her hips, pulled up, and descended onto him again.

His eyelids slammed shut.

His breathing grew faster.

Sweat slicked the rigid muscles of his abdomen.

She rode him, quickening her pace until the spiral toward climax was near its pinnacle. There was nothing but the glorious sensation of a hot, fierce woman claiming him.

His balls drew up.

He resisted. She should come again before he did.

A sharp tweak of his nipples, complete with the pain from her fingernails, was his downfall.

Orgasm rolled through him, his nerve endings exploding like a string of firecrackers as his cock fired off multiple rounds of cum deep inside the seductress astride him.

Sated, she fell against him, snuggling. He wrapped his arms around her, united with her by more than mere sex, floating in a cocoon of peace and contentment.

SHANE MOVED HIS gaze over the room. The idea that Trey ought to establish a BDSM dungeon on Tallav had been his originally. But Randolph and Maon had taken it up wholeheartedly.

Somehow over the years, they had all ended up settling on their birth planet. As a young adult, he would never have believed that would happen.

They were now old, committed, if not married men. With kids. All but Trey, and he was doomed to fatherhood if the way their females put their heads together was any indication.

Doomed. He chuckled inside, remembering Maon and Selina's wedding over a decade ago. Randolph had agreed with Shane that they weren't and never would be candidates for marriage, let alone parenthood. And then Shane had met Adrianna. And Randolph had met Jen. And now calm, composed Trey was tightly ensnared by a lively redhead.

The ladies entered the dungeon with the *click, click* of Selina's thigh-high boots and Patsy and Adrianna's sky-high fuck-me heels. Jen was the sole female to go barefoot.

Jen and Selina broke off to move to their respective mates while Adrianna and Patsy walked to the center of the room where he and Trey awaited, Adrianna moderating her strides to accommodate Patsy. Tall, lithe, a long dark-brown braid trailing down her spine, Adrianna was the opposite of the red-headed pixie at her side, but the pair were becoming close friends. As were he and Trey.

Bonding during the months Trey had spent recovering at Shane's mother's estate, he and Trey had deepened their friendship, to the point they could discern the other's preferences as though they were born twins. They looked nothing alike.

Trey was brown-skinned. Shane was white.

Trey shaved his head. Shane tended toward shaggy.

Trey was born into the serving class. Shane was born into wealth.

Combined, they represented much of the Tallavan male population.

The attributes they held in common linked them in what Adrianna called a mind meld.

They were neither one talkative by nature.

They both preferred to be organized, to make plans rather than jump straight in and damn the consequences.

They were both Doms and rope masters, virtuosos in different but complementary styles of tying knots.

Grunts, nods, gestures, and facial expressions blended into a nonverbal language that they spoke to each other fluently.

The ladies' faces as they approached were full of appreciation. Patsy had suggested the costumes as a passing remark, but Trey had latched on to the idea, reminding Shane about it later.

So here they were, dressed like barbarian warriors in loincloths, bare skin oiled so every muscle showed to best effect, gazes riveted on the women who flowed to their knees and locked their hands behind them, legs spread and eyes lowered.

They'd chosen matching harem outfits. Patsy in light blue. Adrianna in the sage green that reminded him of the dress he'd had made for her on Runner's Hub. She still had it in her closet and pulled it out when they had the estate to themselves, showing up in his study to sit at his feet.

Nice thing about loincloths, they didn't bind when his erection burgeoned.

Trey had laid the ropes they would use into separate piles. Shane had met Trey's suggestion that they use hot pink with a nod and a laugh, acknowledging what popped into both their minds, the bright pink of a well-spanked bottom.

He offered two fingers to Adrianna. "Rise and follow."

Her grasp was cool to the touch. She'd learned at the Opio Institute to restrain her physical, mental, and emotional responses. This made her as close to the ideal submissive as possible, at least for him. From the conversation going on behind him between Trey and Patsy, Adrianna wasn't Trey's perfect sub.

All to the good. Adrianna was his even though at one time Trey had been her mentor.

Nothing was more delectable than Adrianna in sheer clothing. Her breasts, nipples darker since having the baby, were larger than when they'd first met. She was no longer nursing, but they hadn't returned to their former size. She'd punched him when he'd remarked that he loved them no matter how big or small they were, freeing him to admit, he liked them bigger. But not with fabric between him and them.

"I love the look, but this is coming off." He yanked the bodice apart. It gave as he'd expected it would. The costumes had been designed to be ripped off.

Her nipples, already perky, tightened further. He scooped both breasts and weighed them in his palms before stooping to suck a luscious bud into his mouth. The moan that followed might have been hers or his. Probably they both had responded audibly.

He moved to the second, giving it several long intense pulls. That moan was definitely Adrianna's. It struck a bass note that rumbled in his balls. He straightened and gave her a quick, hard kiss.

The harem pants had slits from waistband to hem down each leg. They came off next with a jerk at either side of her hips. They puddled on the floor around her ankles. He bent and snapped the hem apart on each ankle. He pulled the pants from under her and threw them out of the way.

Every inch of her smooth, agile body was now exposed to him, including the dark vee between her legs. Before the night was over, he would be balls-deep inside her. His cock jerked, making the fact that he'd tented his loincloth even more evident.

I must look ridiculous.

"Master?"

"Yes."

"You've never looked sexier than right this instant."

He grunted. Her empathic skills were hard at work.

"I'd have jumped you already if I weren't such a good girl." She eased into a flawless standing submissive position, intended to divert his attention back to her physique and away from her interruption.

"Uh-huh," he responded with a rumbling, predatory growl. "Give me your hands."

Time to get moving. It seems she needs the spanking I've planned. She's reading me too damn well.

The suspension cuffs were easy to buckle to each of her wrists. Padded black leather, he'd had them made to her size and his specifications, including a bar for her to grasp. He'd had a set made for Patsy too.

They could tie cuffs from rope, but this wasn't a demo. It was for fun. Wrists were nice, but there were other parts of Adrianna's body that he preferred to bind. Besides, rope cuffs had a shorter time limit.

Whatever he did, Adrianna was perfectly patient, lithe limbs properly positioned, outwardly calm.

He lifted her chin to gaze into green eyes gone dark. Her composure never reached them when they played. He'd forbidden her to cut off her empathic senses when they were together. Knowing she could perceive his emotions ramped up the experience of dominating her. His arousal strengthened hers. His lust brought out her darker, kinkier side.

Eventually she would express her responses to him openly, but not until he had earned it. If his own level of desire were any sign, it wouldn't take long. A drop of precum oozed from the tip of his penis, leaving a damp spot on his loincloth. No, it wouldn't take long.

The plan he and Trey had crafted required a harness with d-rings tied to opposite sides of the back below the waist. But a utilitarian harness wasn't ever on Shane's agenda, not when it could also be a beautiful corset.

He'd spent many hours designing a corset that would allow him to suspend a body elegantly, comfortably, and safely while exposing Adrianna's bottom. Over the years he'd refined his design, adding or deleting decorative features.

Trey had showed him how to add a butt flap, but tonight he'd gone without. It would only get in the way, but the idea held promise for the future.

He started at Adrianna's shoulders, positioning the rope, sliding it over her skin, and pulling it from behind to overlap and knot in front. The feathery kisses he planted from time to time elicited tiny shivers from her.

Each length was placed exactly, creating equidistant parallel lines and picture-perfect diamonds or squares. Each knot was tied precisely. The overall effect was an artistic masterpiece. Nothing else was worthy of the flawless woman he adorned.

Lemonade and sunshine filled his nostrils as he worked around her, the bright citrus scent especially intoxicating when he nuzzled her temple.

Touches and nips continued as he constructed the lower half of her corset, swiping along her cleft when he threaded his rope between her legs. He brought his fingers to his mouth, sucking clean her desire. The second time he lifted and wordlessly demanded she lick her essence. The flick of her tongue sent a sweet zap to his balls.

Before he had the corset completed, they were both breathing deeper, expectation heavy between them.

Trey finished tying Patsy's corset ahead of Shane and was taking the extra moments to kiss her.

"Those two could heat a dungeon all by themselves," Shane whispered in Adrianna's ear.

She hummed her agreement, swallowing the sound as he meshed his mouth with hers, slipping his tongue between her lips to savor her erotic tang.

A throat cleared, breaking through his intoxication.

"If you can pull yourself away, maybe we can get these ladies up in the air."

Shane looked up to find Trey repressing a laugh, and flashed a you'll-get-yours smile at the master. Then he returned to kissing Adrianna. Not long. But enough for Trey to chuckle out loud.

He finished the kiss with a peck and then pulled Adrianna toward the waist-high bar. Trey did the same with Patsy, positioning her on the opposite side of the bar from Adrianna.

The setup had been Shane's idea, but Trey had insisted it not be elaborate. The bar, although it resembled a trapeze, didn't swing. The swivel shackle to which they attached it was held in place by four chains that kept it motionless, or nearly so. It was designed to spin.

Once Patsy's cuffs had been secured to the bar, Shane added Adrianna's, overlapping her inside arm with Patsy's. This put the womens' faces closer to each other and allowed them to watch what the other couple was doing.

Shane used the process to palm each of Adrianna's breasts and squeeze her ass. *Nothing softer than Dria.*

He moved behind her and rubbed his groin against her, letting her feel how hard she made him. "You'll be getting this"—he nudged his cock more firmly against her back— "thrust to your core. Eventually. First I believe this beautiful bum of yours needs seeing to."

The sound she made was part hum and part moan. She knew where this was going. Spanking was, after all, one of his favorite activities. He'd spanked her in so many locations and in so many ways, he didn't think he could list them all. Her rear end brightened to a glorious red was guaranteed to turn him synthsteel rigid.

Tonight he and Trey would use their bare hands instead of paddles, floggers, or other tools. Doing so fit with the design of the suspension.

Shane grabbed the remote and lowered the bar. "Bend at the waist and not at the knees," he commanded.

Placing his palm over the crack of Adrianna's bottom as she scooted backward wasn't necessary. She let him know she appreciated the attention with a squeak each time his fingers patted her pussy.

A tap on the remote froze the bar in position. Both ladies stood bent at right angles, their arms extended in line from hips to shoulders to wrists, noses pointing to the ground.

He smacked Adrianna's bum and then went to assist Trey in looping the four ropes they'd added to the ring above the trapeze earlier through the d-rings on the backs of their corsets.

Shane snatched hold of the two ropes attached to Adrianna. The tension increased, and her backside slowly rose into the air, her feet hanging. He reached to lock the pulleys and tie off both ropes.

Patsy was dangling on the other side of the bar, her bottom at the same height as Adrianna's, which put her feet in their shiny shoes farther off the floor. Straps kept the heels in place. No plain pumps for rope bunnies.

The last step was a quick one. Using the remote to raise the rig so that both women were high enough that he and Trey could plant kisses on their subs exposed ass cheeks.

Now the fun begins.

The order of business was spank, feast, fuck.

Shane gave Adrianna's right cheek a pop that set the trapeze spinning. "Count, Adrianna."

"One."

He was doing the right side; Trey was assigned the left side. Patsy swung around, and he smacked her, going easy until he established her comfort level. By the handprint Trey had created, he could hit harder.

The pattern, previously decided with Trey, was six swats, stop to play, six more swats, more play. Repeat until they were satisfied.

Rotating would make the ladies dizzy. A bonus as far as Shane was concerned.

Adrianna called out *two, three, four, five,* her ass getting the start of a glow while Patsy's was a brighter pinkish red.

"This is a lot like that game I remember playing as a child. The one with the ball tied to the top of a pole with a rope," Trey said as he gave slap number six to Adrianna, sending her spinning toward Shane.

Shane grabbed her by the hips, stopping her in front of him. "Yeah. Tetherball. Boys didn't play that when I was a kid." He smirked at Trey.

The remark Patsy made was low enough that Shane didn't pick it up. A stifled snort proclaimed that Adrianna had, and that it amused her.

His hands holding Patsy in place, Trey draped his torso over her back and spoke quietly to her. She raised her head, fixing her gaze straight on Shane. "Master Shane, I'm sorry for makin' smart remarks about your childhood balls."

Trey lifted his gaze to the ceiling and sighed. Adrianna snorted again. Patsy looked smug before lowering her head. Even with an apology, Shane knew he hadn't come out on top in that exchange. And he still didn't know what she'd said.

"I'll allow you to deal with your submissive, Master Trey. I admit, she's beyond me."

A slight smile lit Trey's face. "She's nearly beyond me. *A leanbh*, you've earned some orgasm denial."

"Ya know ya were plannin' that anyway, tormentin' man."

Shane ignored the pair, sensing the back and forth could go on longer than he had patience for. Especially with Adrianna available at tongue level.

He spread her ass cheeks and buried his face, sucking on her labia and then licking her in long strokes from her clit to her vagina. Her taste was like no other woman's. It was addictive. A spark of citrus and musky female. The more he worked her bud, the more sweet nectar she gushed. Breathy moans punctuated each brush of his tongue.

Trey was tracking the intervals. His call to return to spanking came all too soon for Shane yet just in time for Adrianna, who was trembling with the need to come.

Shane grazed his teeth across the brightest red area of her bottom. "Did you enjoy that?"

"Yes, Sir. Thank you, Sir. More please?"

"Oh, you'll be getting more. Lots more, eager girl."

The rhythm of play with Adrianna settled over him like rain that starts out with a gentle patter of sprinkles and grows until it inundates, soaking through him, saturating the scene with domination and control. Every smack of his palm against her rosy-red bum and every needy cry that burst from her lips while he prevented her from falling over the precipice into release drenched him in powerful satisfaction.

And an even more powerful craving to thrust his hungry cock deep inside her.

"Shall we give these women what they want?" Trey asked from the other side of the rig.

A glance and a grunt communicated Shane's desire to consummate the scene too.

Putting thought into action, he lowered the trapeze so that Adrianna's backside was in line with his groin. He removed the rope that held his loin-cloth in place and dropped the costume to the ground.

He was past ready to shove his erection balls-deep into her swollen channel. Each stroke of his tongue and rub of his fingers had primed her inner walls to clasp him in a taut embrace.

He took hold of her hip with one hand, wrapped her long, dark braid around his other, and plunged into her, growling a two-word command.

"Don't come."

Compliance was a nonissue. Adrianna always obeyed him in bed and in the dungeon. A well-trained submissive was a work of art. And she was his.

Her responses were no longer muted. She gave full throat to her carnal pleasure as he brought his thrust and release to a crescendo. He pounded into her, knowing that she could take it. And that she loved it.

Her cry of, "Sir, Sir, Sir," flung him over the edge. The frenzy of their mating ignited an orgasmic flash point that shot through him with unstoppable flames.

The climax shattered him, rendering him too weak to move, let alone relinquish his grip on her body or her hair. He felt a vibration where his fist touched her back. She was humming. How she avoided coming when she was so attuned to his emotions amazed him.

He shook his hand free of her braid and then caressed her thigh. "*A mhuirnín*, you are so fucking amazing. I'll never get enough of you."

"Mmm. Thank you, Sir. Me too." She hung limply in his ropes, awaiting his decision on where to go next with the scene. Aware of what was coming, she didn't push him to get there any faster than he chose.

He made short work of removing the lines that bound her to the rig, keeping an arm around her waist to support her, otherwise she would have slumped to the floor.

One sofa stood empty. The others had claimed or were settling into their own. He went directly to the open one.

Rather than covering them with the blanket laid across the sofa's back, he settled sideways with her high on his lap, plunging his fingers into her pussy and rubbing her clit with his thumb.

By adjusting their positions, he could…

Yes. He sucked her nipple between his teeth.

In seconds she was arching into the attention he was giving her erogenous zones, shuddering against the arm that held her firmly next to him.

The cry that escaped her lips when her climax hit was earthy in its ecstasy.

If his fingers had been his cock, she'd have milked him a second time.

They all watched, except for Maon, who was as usual blissed-out. Displaying Adrianna like this, flaunting his absolute sexual control over her was almost as good as the orgasm he'd just had. Almost. Not quite.

The initiation of Trey's dungeon was a complete success. He grabbed the blanket and pulled it over Adrianna, sliding her down so her head lay against his chest, enjoying the warm, mushy feeling that filled his heart. After care had its benefits too.

PATSY PEERED AROUND the cracked open door of the dungeon, waiting on Jen and Adrianna to exit the locker room. Arms crossed over his chest, Trey stood next to Shane, watching Selina in her Lasair persona finish strapping Maon to the man-sized artist's model she'd had built.

Jealousy flared inside Patsy. Selina in full Lasair regalia was an exotic firebird that even with fiery red hair, Patsy couldn't hope to match. Black leather miniskirt, red-orange brocade corset, midnight thigh-high boots and long fingerless gloves, and a multicolored flaming feathered mask.

Yeah, the woman knows how to dress to her own benefit. But ya can't be seriously thinkin' she's a threat to ya? Patsy squelched the nasty emotion.

Further consideration of Selina with Maon brought an appreciative smile to Patsy's mouth. The Tallavan marshal was taking advantage of his hands remaining free to caress his wife, heaving a lengthy sigh when she claimed his arm to bind to the model's wooden replica. Boy did Patsy understand what induced that sigh.

But she wasn't peeking out the dungeon door to check out the action between Selina and Maon. No, tonight was all for Trey. This would be her only opportunity to watch him without him knowing he was being observed.

His resting thug face was nowhere in sight. A wicked grin played around his lips. He nudged Shane with his elbow and tipped his head in Maon's direction. Both men laughed one of those mouth-closed, almost-a-grunt laughs that made the muscles of their chests bulge.

The pair were nude but for a loincloth each, every inch of taut skin oiled to highlight their solid brawn. *Yum.*

Trey wasn't as tall or as broad as Shane, but every bit of his body was in perfect proportion. It wasn't likely that she'd be allowed to run her hands through the tight black curls that poked their way above his low-slung loincloth. Or lick the hard nub of his dusky brown nipples.

He had told her to be herself and not worry about what the others might think. She was the submissive he wanted. Needed. And especially not to compare herself to professionally trained Adrianna, whose person-ality differed completely from Patsy's.

Fine. But there was a matter of the respect she owed Trey as her master. She intended to be on her best behavior.

Over her shoulder she heard the ladies chatting as they came through the locker room door and walked in a cluster toward Patsy.

The assembled women all wore costumes, although none as vibrant as Selina's.

Adrianna, in a sage-green harem outfit that matched Patsy's except for color, was a fascinating cross between elegant and wanton. Jen was the only one among them that appeared virtuous in the demure, high-waisted floral dress she'd had donned. She'd told them that Rand called her his sugar cookie, and damned if she didn't fit that name to a T right now.

Patsy giggled at the way they had clustered outside the entrance, costumed like players in a cabaret show.

"What's funny?" Adrianna asked, dropping her gaze to scrutinize herself.

"My roots are showin'. That's all." Patsy grinned to herself. "Sorry. Inside joke. I'll explain sometime. But not now."

She turned and slapped open both swinging doors and swayed into the dungeon.

I need to slow down, or I'll fall off these dang shoes. Remember Adrianna's lessons on the correct way for a submissive to walk. Keeping her gaze riveted on the floor like a good sub wasn't the problem. She'd loved how her long dancer's legs were enhanced by the 4-inch copper-colored heels she was wearing, but she hadn't fully adjusted to the added height. It was imperative to keep track of her feet.

By taking her time, she managed to sashay toward Trey. She peeked at him from under her lashes the last few yards. He didn't pay attention to Adrianna gliding at Patsy's side; his gaze was fixed on Patsy. Her pussy dampened as he took in the tempting view of her cleavage through the pale blue gauzy fabric of her harem blouse.

His lips pursed slightly and released. *Yep, he loves the outfit.*

If he likes the costume, this next bit is goin' to knock his socks off. She repressed a giggle, but it fought its way to the surface, turning into a delicate snort. *He isn't wearin' socks. Hold back the daft, idjit.*

She and Adrianna reached their men and went to their knees in one fluid motion, assuming a submissive pose, hands behind their backs, breasts lifted, and gaze on the ground.

Shane had Adrianna stand at once, moving to the pile of rope set aside for their use, but Trey didn't say a word and appeared not to move from the restricted perspective Patsy had of his naked feet and ankles.

Sweet mother Mary, even his feet are sexy.

This pose, its pure, perfect submission, was Patsy's gift to Trey. She was often recalcitrant and sassy, but beneath the sound and fury, she understood and respected him.

Tonight his lifelong dream to own his own BDSM club, run by his own rules, was reality. Officially she owned it. He couldn't because of Tallavan matriarchal law. But it was his. She'd never lay claim to it.

Patsy offered him a visual demonstration that here, in this club, she recognized him as master, king of this domain.

"You are exquisite, *a leanbh.*"

The reverence in his voice was lovely.

Really.

But he needed to get over it.

Soon.

Whatever the black flooring was made from, it was damnably hard on the knees.

A quiver began in her hips and thighs.

"You may stand."

Her attempt to rise went haywire at once. She toppled sideways, the shoes refusing to stay where she put them. Trey caught her, righting and steadying her until she had her balance.

She pressed her lips tight, her cheeks flaming hot, and glued her gaze to the floor.

"I didn't know ya were goin' to keep me on my knees that long. And I've never worn four-inch heels in my life. They're a death trap." She kept her voice subdued, hoping the others would be too preoccupied with their own play to notice her outburst.

Resisting the finger Trey placed beneath her chin to lift her gaze to his was impossible. He maintained steady pressure until she relented.

His eyes had darkened, impassioned from their usual dark brown to black, but the gold flecks around the edges of his irises remained. An erotic glitter that amplified her craving to be consumed by this man's voracious appetite.

"Sir." The title wasn't an afterthought added by habit after ranting during play. It had been the only possible response to the strength and control that oozed out of the man before her.

Trey didn't take it that way.

He laughed out loud as though joy were bubbling over in his soul.

One corner of her mouth lifted, and she poked out the tip of her tongue.

That's all it took. He clasped her in arms corded with muscle, lifting her against his chest, claiming her lips and tangling his tongue with hers in an ardent kiss that sizzled through her, firing a yearning to be one with him, to take him deep into her body to attain the release that had already established an eager thumping pulse.

She wrapped her legs around his torso, digging the spiky heels into him, giving him a taste of her own intentions to drive him to fervid arousal.

Light-headed, she wobbled when he placed her carefully on the ground. He moved to her side while still holding on to her. "Bend at the waist."

Her knees sagged as she complied.

"No, keep your knees straight."

What the…?

The pop he gave to her rear would have sent her tumbling if he hadn't kept a solid grip on her shoulder. It arrowed a spike of pleasure to her clit.

Her bottom wiggled almost of its own accord. Out of habit in hopes he'd send another zap to that sweet spot between her thighs.

Instead he squatted to brush a palm down the back of one of her legs and then the other.

"I love looking at you through these, but I'm done looking."

A gasp shot from her when he snapped the waistband with a yank to the back, parting it on either side of her waist. The hems at the ankles alone remained holding the pants on her body.

She steadied herself, palm flat on his shoulder, just in time. The front and back sections were puddled on the floor around her feet. He bundled them in either hand and jerked, snapping both ankle hems at once.

Her voice tart, she couldn't suppress an observation. "It's a good thing that was meant to be ripped apart, or that might have hurt."

"Shane already did it to Adrianna's costume."

"I see. And here I was thinkin' ya only had eyes for me."

"Situational awareness. Part of being a proper dungeon monitor. Now hush." Trey smacked her bottom and stood. He collected one of the cuffs Shane had had made for Patsy from atop a hot pink pile of rope.

"Stand." He drew his fingers along one arm from her shoulder to her wrist. "So smooth… except for the goose bumps."

Feckin' man. "Ya make it hard to keep still." She wriggled, keeping her feet planted.

He slipped the cuff on, fastening it before doing the same to her other arm.

"Ya make it hard." He scooped her breasts in his hands, kneading them beneath the barely-there fabric, and then bent to tongue each nipple, leaving a spot of damp.

Whatever remark she'd been about to make was drowned by a moan that originated deep inside her. It flew from her along with whatever she'd been thinking.

Fortunately instead of rending her top with hard yanks as he had the pants, he broke the threads holding the garment together with his fingers. Otherwise she might have peeled out of her skin and hit the ceiling.

The top's pieces had scarcely reached the ground before his mouth claimed the tight bud he had freed.

Anything and everything he did to her breasts wound her higher, building a voracious lust for him that was like multiple pachinko balls falling and rebounding, striking erotic nerve endings but never making it to the cup with the big payout.

She bit back a long tirade when he pulled away, settling for a simple, "Feckin' man."

Trey had explained his theory of rope bondage to her. He aimed for elegant solutions where less was more while still maintaining a high level of safety. Years of teaching had made him deft at knot tying.

The color of the ropes had to have been his idea. He hadn't said what hot pink stood for, but if she could guess, it was for the bright pink color he intended to apply to her ass.

He efficiently looped and knotted. None of the kissing and caressing that Shane was doing as he tied Adrianna in a much fancier corset.

Patsy preferred Trey's way.

The feckin' man spends more than enough time rilin' up my body and denyin' me release. Extra stimulation while trussin' me up? No thank ya.

Behind her, metal chinked on metal. The sound was familiar to her now after the many sessions they'd spent together at the Whip Hand. He had squatted and was adding rings to the corset. From their placement she figured she'd be hanging from her pelvis. But why the suspension cuffs on her wrists then?

He gripped her hips and rose behind her, bring his body flush against her back. The warmth that radiated from him was welcome, especially since goose bumps had sprung up again.

Powerful arms swallowed her in a bear hug. His head bent, and he nuzzled behind her ear. "I love you, *a leanbh*. Enjoy. Tonight is all for you."

A bubble of pleasure popped inside her chest. He would say that. But then she'd been thinking the same thing about him.

Trey generally used words for instruction, but she loved it best when he communicated his commands with physical touch. *Push. Pull. Lift.* A finger down her spine to remind her to stand straight.

He clasped her shoulders and turned her to face him. Palming the back of her head, he threaded his fingers into her hair and massaged her scalp. His mouth closed over hers, kissing her with a fervor that made her insides melt and her girlie bits excitedly perk up.

Tingles and goose bumps. The man brought them as surely as thunder-heads brought lightning.

Giving as good as she got, she drowned in the taste of man passion, dark and rich. There must have been pauses for breath, but they were negligible moments, swiftly lost in the intensity of the kiss.

His hands stroked. His fingers teased. He lavished the kissing and caressing he'd forgone while tying her corset.

It took a moment for her to realize he wasn't fully focused on ravishing her when his lips stilled. Her legs were too wobbly in her sky-high shoes to make stamping her foot a safe idea. She loosed a petulant groan at him that had no impact whatsoever.

He propped his chin on the crown of her head and cleared his throat. And then a second time, louder and with more authority.

"If you can pull yourself away, maybe we can get these ladies up in the air." The rumble of his words reverberated through her.

One of those male bonding moments was taking place above her. Silent except for Trey chuckling out loud.

Denial that she was his was impossible. Not while this massive man engulfed her, his heartbeat thudding through her and his strength binding her to him.

Not that she would ever deny it. It was equally impossible to deny that she had him wrapped and bound securely in her love. Which made them both masters of bondage.

Trey pointed at the trapeze and pushed her on the bottom toward it. She didn't sigh at the loss of his warm body snugged tight to hers. *Time for Trey to have his fun.*

She grinned to herself. *And then I'll be on his lap, enfolded in his arms again. Choose Trey first* worked as promised in the dungeon, and so far it was working in their everyday lives.

She swayed her hips to entice him and was rewarded with a caress and squeeze before he brought her wrists to the rod and attached her cuffs to it.

The next thing she knew, her backside was being hauled into the air, her feet dangling, her nether parts exposed for all to see. Adjusting to having her pussy on display had taken a while. Trey had had to do a lot of encouraging until it had grown easier. Even now her chest tightened and a brief urge to run overtook her.

She turned her head and stretched her neck to get a look at Adrianna, who was trussed and receiving the same attention from Shane. The placid expression on the woman's face was a tad annoying, igniting another spark of jealousy that Patsy snuffed immediately.

If Trey had wanted Adrianna, he could have had her a long time ago. But he'd passed even back then when he'd believed he wanted calm and composed. He'd finally discovered he wanted the opposite of placid. Her. Patsy O'Shaughnessy.

The game the men had devised became clear when they'd finished positioning her and Adrianna. Spanking was on the agenda. Adrianna had said it would be because Shane loved to make her bottom glow.

The whole rotating trapeze had been the innovation. Each spin brought her in line to receive a swat from Shane or Trey. Shane's first spank was lighter than Trey's. Any thought that he'd be going easy on her was dispelled by his second.

The best part of spanking wasn't the brief bite of pain or the growing burn in each cheek. The best part was the tingle in her clit from the vibration of the impact. Well, that and the muzzy dopiness that Trey called sub space.

The zip of each tingle would normally have her lifting her rear for the next smack, but in this rig she could do nothing but hang and twirl.

Shane ordered Adrianna to count each time he clapped his hand to her bottom. She'd reached five when Trey said to Shane, "This is a lot like that game I remember playing as a kid. The one with the ball tied to the top of a pole with a rope."

Slap six from Shane sent Patsy spinning toward Trey, who brought her to a stop by grasping her hips.

"Yeah. Tetherball. Boys didn't play that when I was a kid."

Patsy lifted her head to see Shane smirking at Trey.

Murmuring so Shane wouldn't hear, she made her own impertinent observation. "When he was a kid, he probably spent his days playin' with his own balls."

The remark didn't escape Adrianna, nor the emotional sting that went with it. She stifled a snort.

It was disconcerting to know that Adrianna could sense the emotions of the people around her. Patsy supposed it might be more of a burden than a gift, knowing when someone inwardly envied you or even hated you without showing it outwardly.

Thoughts of Adrianna's empathic abilities were erased when Trey slid a hand along her spine and brought his head next to hers, his lips nudging her ear.

His voice was low yet pointed. "*A leanbh*, I allow you to use that sassy tongue of yours on me, but you will not use it to say offensive things to any other Doms. Do you understand?"

She winced, wishing her resolve to show Trey the utmost respect tonight hadn't snapped so easily.

"No matter how funny."

Now she was confused. Did he mind or didn't he?

"Sorry, Sir?"

"Don't apologize to me. He's the one you offended, although I'm not sure he heard what you said."

Was that amusement in his tone?

No sense ditherin'. In for a penny, in for a pound.

She lifted her head and caught Shane's gaze on her. "Master Shane, I'm sorry for makin' smart remarks about your childhood balls."

Beside her Trey audibly sighed. Adrianna snorted again.

The smug expression she couldn't keep from her face gave away that her words were at best a slanted apology.

Shane's response sailed over her now lowered head to Trey. "I'll let you deal with your submissive, Master Trey. I admit, she's beyond me."

She puffed up in triumph.

Trey had moved behind her again. He pinched her where her ass cheek met her upper thigh. "She's nearly beyond me. *A leanbh*, you've earned some orgasm denial."

"Ya know ya were plannin' that anyway, tormentin' man."

He pinched her again, but then his fingers brushed across her slit. "Shane's got his tongue buried in Adrianna. But naughty girls like you will have to make do without. Behave if you want more."

Damnation, did he really think denyin' her his tongue when he had magic fingers was a punishment? Feckin' idjit.

"Oh."

"Does that feel good?"

"Ya know it does. Sir."

His teeth grazed her right buttock, his fingers never stopping, swirling and dipping.

If he kept it up, she'd easily come in the next minute.

She tried for the millionth... er... thousandth time to move her bottom so his fingers hit her clit just right.

"Time."

He withdrew his fingers.

Crap.

More expletives flared in her mind over the course of what seemed infinite alternating periods of spanking and pussy play. The frustration of endless orgasm denial had her snapping a mounting number of those curses out loud. Counterproductive, but she couldn't help it.

Opposite her on the trapeze bar, Adrianna was making mewling sounds and breathing as heavily as Patsy.

"Feckin' man, Sir. Can ya not tell my head's about to explode?"

Trey responded, his tone deadpan. "That would be messy."

"Ya haven't seen messy. Yet. Sir."

He swatted her ass.

Feckin' man.

"Shall we give these women what they want?"

Shane grunted, latching on to Adrianna and putting the thought straight into action. An *oh* of satisfaction flew from Adrianna, becoming a rhythmic response to every stab of Shane's cock.

"I'll have what she's havin', Sir."

"My pleasure, *a leanbh.*"

Trey's long, nimble fingers grasped her hips.

The rig lowered.

She waited.

Where's his—

The rest of the world, the others in the dungeon, faded to nothing. An astonishing sexual wave inundated her, surging as his cock speared into her and retreating as he pulled out. It reformed with each thrust, growing into a monster that shook her depths.

"Now, *a leanbh*. Come now."

She flung herself to the crest and rode its peak until release buried her beneath its ferocious intensity.

Inside her Trey reached his own culmination in a gusher of warm cum that added to the heaping dose of pleasure. The effect she had on him was giddying.

Before her breathing returned to normal, Trey had her off the trapeze and snuggled against his bare body under a blanket, reclining on one of the deep burgundy sofas he'd had delivered just the day before.

If only she could rinse and repeat the last few hours. But memories of this beyond brilliant day would have to suffice. That and the many wonderful new memories they would make.

TREY TRACED A circle on Patsy's thigh beneath the blanket he'd thrown over them. His tigress was now in kitten mode. Humming with satisfaction, if not actually purring.

The others had claimed the couches Trey had positioned in a semicircle along the back wall.

Jen had slipped on her old-fashioned dress. She and Randolph were seated sideways on the couch, her between his legs. He'd removed the doctor's coat, looking as sophisticated and elegantly turned out as always, his slacks closed and his shirt tucked in.

The difference that was obvious to anyone who had known the man prior to Jen appearing in his life was in the relaxed set of his shoulders and the contentment of his expression. When Trey had first met Randolph back in his Opio Institute days, his friend had had an edge to him that women perceived as wickedly sexy. Trey had recognized it for what it was— hidden rage, long tamped down. It was gone, and although he was still a sexual sadist, he'd transformed into a family man and soon-to-be father.

Patsy stroked a finger on Trey's cheek to gain his attention.

"Yes, *a leanbh*?" He brought the finger to his lips and brushed it with a kiss.

"Shane never let Adrianna come."

Trey loved that Patsy was still observing and questioning the BDSM lifestyle. "He's a more traditional Dom. In complete control. He saved her release for after care."

Patsy shifted to bring the couple in view. "Oh. I see."

Shane pulled Adrianna high on his lap, her breast in his mouth, his fingers between her open thighs. His other arm firmly held her in place, so that her writhing didn't send her sliding to the floor. She arched her back, body trembling, and cried out as her orgasm hit.

Every gaze in the room, except for Maon's, was riveted on Shane and Adrianna. Even Jen, who'd been uncertain about playing in public, wasn't able to keep from watching the erotic scene.

Still in a serene fog, Maon lay with his head in Selina's lap, gazing up at her with a blissful half smile while she curled and uncurled a lock of his hair around her finger. The mask she'd worn as Lasair was gone, so the pleased expression she wore was visible. She caught Trey's eye and dipped her head to him, acknowledging her approval of the night and the dungeon.

Pleasure ballooned in Trey's chest. He returned Selina's nod and squeezed Patsy, bringing his cheek to rest against her copper-red hair.

"Tonight has been perfect," he whispered for her ears alone. "This is what I've dreamed of creating. A community of people who take the BDSM lifestyle seriously. A respectful space that allows all members to reach their potential, to express their sexuality openly."

"Ya've made a fine start."

"It'll take work once I open registration for membership. And lots to do before that can happen. Finding the right employees will be the hardest task."

Patsy rubbed his abdomen. "It'll all come round. Ya've got what it takes. And ya've got me to help. Plus, workin' for yourself, ya've got the best boss in town." She laughed up at him and stretched to plant a kiss on his smiling lips.

"Dreams do come true, *a leanbh*." To prove his words, he covered her mouth with his and gave her another taste of what she called his masterful masterin'.

Discover more of Cailin's sci-fi romance on her website at
https://cailinbriste.com
Subscribe to her newsletters for monthly updates on her releases, sales, and events.
https://cailinbriste.com/cailins-newsletter-sign-up/

Read on for an excerpt from *It Takes a Cat Burglar* from the A Thief in Love Suspense Romance series.

IT TAKES A CAT BURGLAR EXCERPT

Darcelle's reflection stared back at her from the solid mirror that covered the side of the Jepsen Building where she hung, suspended twelve hundred feet above the city sidewalk. Anger and determination filled the charcoal-gray eyes of her mirror image. Even as an infant, the darkness integral to her nature must have peered out of round, solemn baby eyes that weren't the expected dark brown of her mother and father or the amber of her twin sister. No, she'd been born with eyes best described as a grayish mist. With each passing year, they'd grown darker. Someday they might rival the night sky that tonight was a wash of black pushed back by the ineffectual streetlights below and the pale serenity of a waning moon. The skull cap she wore covered the braids she'd used to tame her masses of kinky cinnamon curls.

No breeze stirred the night air, for which she was thankful. The micro-cable anchored to the sidewalk didn't allow for much sway as the winch above pulled her higher. The noise of traffic wafted up like a soundtrack to another reality.

She swung a leg over the ledge surrounding the roof of the building. Sunrise was less than an hour away, but for now, the wealthy residents of the Jepsen slept below her, convinced that the security they spent thousands of credits on created an impenetrable barrier around them. She smirked, satisfied she was about to prove them wrong. The latest anti-skimmer technology may prevent aircars from landing, but it didn't keep out birds or, as in her case, people who avoided the domed security field by slipping under it at the edge of the building's roof.

Security plans always had holes. Her day job at the *Art et Antiquités Institut de la Sécurité* was to close those she discovered in her client's protection profiles, or at least render them too small to be exploited. Your average cat burglar couldn't accomplish what she was attempting. The mirrored facade of the building resisted any attachments, so any of the standard slick surface anchors were worthless, as were the nonslip soles of her shoes. It was worse than trying to climb on ice.

Over the last year Darcelle had honed her skills to surpass those of the typical thief. The instructions she received before each job had included training exercises and detailed steps for committing each robbery. It was as though she was being mentored by a master thief, a man she'd never seen much less met or spoken with. Notes were his sole means of communication, written in a flowing script that was both masculine and artistic.

This was the most difficult assignment she'd received. She couldn't land on the top of the building, she couldn't climb the side, and attempting to penetrate through an entrance was equally impossible. Not a problem.

The surface of the roof was covered in fine-grain sand. She dropped from the ledge, squatting to avoid skidding and falling on her ass. The bands of her harness burned as though they were embedded in her skin. She snapped the releases and pulled the harness off, rubbing between her legs and over her lower butt cheeks. The painful part of this operation was over. She let the harness fall next to the winch. When the break-in was discovered, they'd find the hoist chem-sealed to the ledge of the Jepsen's roof. Let the security guards figure that out. It hadn't taken her long the previous night to use a gravity drone to slip it under the security field and drop it onto the ledge. The breakable containers filled with chems on the winch's underside had smashed, allowing the contents to mix and bond the winch to the stone, and the hoist had been ready to use.

She turned, squinting across the roof at an aircar circling in the distance. *Time to get indoors.* The heat tap was to her left and, next to it, the entrance to the main utility conduit. The cap had a standard entry lock, but the keypad was on the inside. Tough luck if the cover shut and you got stuck up here, unless you had the gadget she had tucked in her pocket. In less than thirty seconds it ran through a gazillion keystroke variations, and the cap popped open. She swung inside, bracing her feet on a rung of the synthsteel ladder that scaled the conduit from top to bottom. The cover thunked when she pulled it closed. Her destination wasn't far.

She stopped her descent and clamped one hand tightly on the textured metal of the ladder. With the other hand she pulled the hood of her used hazard suit over her face and sealed it. Ugh! Nothing smelled like the stale odor of air inhaled through secondhand hazard suit filters, but it was better than breathing in the poisonous air she'd be entering.

No one was supposed to be home in the penthouse. Sand nits had invaded the CEO of Trans Vargas Shipping's lofty domain. Once established, the only way to get rid of the bugs was fumigation. Who would have thought the anonymous floral bouquet sent to the man's wife would be infested with nasty critters? Threat assessment of deliveries didn't include scanning for the hundreds of tiny little eggs waiting to hatch and release a horde of pernicious pests. After all, the flowers were organic, and they weren't meant to be eaten. Thoughts of sand nits made her back itch, right in the center along her bra strap where she'd once been bitten by the nasty buggers.

Gah! Not real!

She wrenched her mind back and climbed through the hatch into the dark utility room. "Lights." Her voice was muffled by her hood and the sound-dampening walls. Across the narrow room crowded with the mech required to create modern luxury, a door led out to the main apartment. She'd taken a set of the original Jepsen Building plans from the *Bureau de la Conformité de la Construction*. Over the last week she'd memorized the route she would follow and alternates. She'd learned the hard way to do just-in-case planning when her third venture outside the law had taken a turn for the worse.

The utility room was in the staff area of the suite off a short hall that led to a swinging door. It was the dividing line between the haves from the have-nots. She hadn't grown up on the haves' side of such doors, but once her sister made tubs of money, she'd learned her way around the other side. She loped to the door, cracked it open, and scanned the serving foyer. The safe she planned to crack was in the study. That room had two entrances, one from the main hall that connected the bedrooms and another that opened from inside the master bedroom. She'd chosen the second route even though it was longer. Retrieving the item in the safe was only part of the reason for breaking and entering this luxurious home. Her primary purpose was to find what the mastermind behind her crimes had promised to leave her.

His instructions detailed the location and description of a valuable piece of art or an antiquity she was to reacquire and return to the person or institution designated. All of them had been stolen. This was her twenty-ninth burglary. Once the artifact was restored to its legitimate owner, a clue to the mystery that dominated her existence was delivered. Who was sending the notes? Why had he chosen her? She never discovered how the messages and the clues ended up where she could find them. Sometimes they were in the desk drawer in her office at work. One she found stuck to the mirror in her bathroom. Whoever was sending them was an expert cat burglar. He'd made it evident he had free run of her personal and business space. She'd nicknamed him Matou, tomcat, for obvious reasons.

Tonight's initial task, scaling the Jepsen Building, was the toughest task she'd so far encountered. Opening the safe would be easy. She could crack any safe made. You might as well gift wrap your valuables if you relied on a safe to keep burglars from walking off with them. This time her instructions had included no how-tos, just where and when. And sniggering information about sand nits. Figuring out how to get into the penthouse suite was up to her. He'd increased the difficulty.

He'd also told her this was her final exam. Whatever that meant. And after she recovered the artifact, she would find a reward waiting where the master laid his head at night. Okay. Look on the pillows of the bed in the master bedroom.

Now the end was in sight, through the entrance to the penthouse master bedroom that stood before her.

She swung the door open soundlessly. The bed was against the far wall. It had been stripped of bedding and covered with a large gray sheet. A single pillow lay at the head, a bright yellow piece of paper visible on it. The ancient Viking knife in the safe was supposed to be her priority, but she'd check the pillow first. Matou wouldn't know she'd switched things up.

She strode to the bed, her pulse pounding in her ears.

Four words. That's all that was written on the paper in the same ornate handwriting used on every preceding communication.

Congratulations. I'm behind you.

She froze.

How could she have missed it? The same dark, prickling tension that had inched along her spine every time she'd sensed Matou observing her in the past was now knitting her muscles and bones together, turning her to stone. It was him. He'd never let her see or hear him, but her body reacted when he was near, as though when he gazed at her, a furnace ignited inside her. It was damn spooky.

She jumped when his fingers closed on her shoulder.

"Don't turn."

Like a low, throbbing bass note, his voice resonated through her to the ends of her fingers. *Hell.* She couldn't move, much less turn. He trailed his hand along her collarbone. Despite the thick layer of duracloth between her and his fingertips, Darcelle was certain warmth penetrated the fabric.

His sudden yank startled her. Shock pulsed through her. He was undoing the seal on the hood of her skin suit.

"No!" She batted at him, twisting to escape his grasp. He clamped her in a bruising hold, immobilizing her.

"I said don't turn. Stop struggling."

Rapid inhalations of the sour combination of aged body odor and fear inside her skin suit made her nasal passages burn. She continued to writhe, fighting to free herself. *He's going to kill me!*

"Fuck it. Stop. The air is pure. Look."

Several moments passed before she registered the sun-darkened arm and hand waving in front of her. Long elegant fingers twiddled. Her breathing hitched. No gloves. He wasn't wearing a skin suit. She stilled, allowing him to remove her hood.

"Do exactly as I say, and all will be well."

With gentler hands he turned her toward him. She gasped. He was gorgeous. Only a master sculptor could have formed a face of such perfect symmetry. The masculinity of his high cheekbones, angled jaw, and straight brows was softened by his exquisite lips. Heat flushed through her body.

From beneath black locks slanting over his forehead, pale green eyes stared at her. Was he waiting for a response?

"Ummm."

A smile flashed across his lips. "Are you ready to trust me?"

Darcelle pursed her lips. "I'll try."

He grunted. "Good enough. We are alike, minou, my kitten. Our trust must be earned."

In the silence that fell, Darcelle waited, her legs growing restless. An instant before she burst into anxious questions, he spoke.

"This skin suit is repulsive. Clothes have been laid out for you in the master bathroom. I assume you know where that is located?"

She nodded her head, trying to keep her respiration steady even though her chest was tight. This calm, gorgeous man, her cat burglar, her Matou, had her flustered and, beyond all belief, compliant.

"Change and meet me in the study."

"Yes, Mat—"

Her confusion must have shone on her face, because he filled in the missing designation. "Sir. Call me sir." He quirked an eyebrow at her.

Darcelle dropped her gaze to the floor. "Yes, sir."

"Go on."

She heard a smile in his voice. When she looked up, his lips were twitched in a half grin. She returned his expression before skittering off toward the bathroom. *Gods, he's so damn hot!*

Purchase It Takes a Cat Burglar #1
https://books2read.com/cat-burglar

ALSO BY CAILIN

A Thief in Love Suspense Romance

It Takes a Cat Burglar

How to Steal the Pharaoh's Jewels

A Touch of Greed

Book #4 Coming Soon

Sons of Tallav

Shane: Marshal of Tallav

Maon: Marshal of Tallav

Rand: Son of Tallav

Trey: Son of Tallav

Other Books

An Earthbound Christmas

ABOUT CAILIN BRISTE

Cailin Briste is a USA Today Bestselling author who writes erotic science fiction suspense and erotic fantasy suspense romance. She invites readers to step outside of their every-day lives and enter the sensual worlds she creates far in the future.

Cailin spends her days writing, reading, and creating jewelry. She lives with her husband in an RV named Floyd that's pulled by a '97 Freightliner truck named Fiona.

www.ingramcontent.com/pod-product-compliance
Lightning Source LLC
Chambersburg PA
CBHW052047240626
47153CB00006B/2248